IMPROPER
SEDUCTION

Improper Seduction

Mary Wine

BRAVA

KENSINGTON PUBLISHING CORP.
www.kensingtonbooks.com

BRAVA BOOKS are published by

Kensington Publishing Corp.
119 West 40th Street
New York, NY 10018

All Kensington titles, imprints, and distributed lines are available at special quantity discounts for bulk purchases for sales promotion, premiums, fund-raising, educational, or institutional use.

Special book excerpts or customized printings can also be created to fit specific needs. For details, write or phone the office of the Kensington Special Sales Manager: Kensington Publishing Corp., 119 West 40th Street, New York, NY 10018, Attn: Special Sales Department. Phone: 1-800-221-2647.

Brava and the B logo Reg. U.S. Pat. & TM Off.

ISBN-13: 978-0-7582-4205-1
ISBN-10: 0-7582-4205-0

First Kensington Trade Paperback Printing: January 2011

10 9 8 7 6 5 4 3 2 1

Printed in the United States of America

Chapter One

H er mother was nervous.

Bridget Newbury considered her mother with curiosity. Lady Connolly was normally the perfect model of poise.

"Good morrow, Mother."

Jane turned in a flurry of wool skirts. She was wearing one of her very modest Sabbath dresses. There was no lace upon it, the only trim formed by contrasting persimmon wool cut into thin strips and used to border the brown wool that made up the garment. She even wore an over-partlet that covered every inch of her chest, all the way to her neck.

"Good, you are here."

"I came straight after receiving your summons, Mother."

Jane smiled. A gentle curving of her lips that was genuine. She held out her hands, and Bridget moved forward to clasp them. Even through their gloves, the embrace of fingers and palms was warm.

"Of course you did. You have ever been an obedient child. God blessed me with your sweet heart." Her mother's smile faded. The hands grasping Bridget's tightened momentarily before releasing their hold. Jane clasped her fingers together in a practiced pose, one she used as mistress of the house.

With the maids always observing them, appearances were important. Bridget held her chin steady and waited for her mother to speak.

"I have word from your father."

Her mother's voice hardened. Bridget knew the tone. It was one that often showed itself when letters from her father arrived. Lord Connolly resided at the court of Henry the Eighth. Her sire often sent home detailed instructions on how the family was to conduct themselves. In the quickly changing climate of the aging king's court, her mother was always sure to instill a deep respect for each sentence her husband penned. It was the wisest course of action given the king's history of beheading those nobles who displeased him.

"A marriage has been arranged for you."

Bridget was startled. "Do you mean that Sir Curan has returned from France?"

Her mother's face drew into an expression that Bridget knew too well. It was the look her mother always wore when circumstances were not to her liking but unavoidable.

"Your father has negotiated a new arrangement for you with Lord Oswald. The wedding is to be celebrated within a fortnight."

Her mother's voice was full of impending duty. It lacked joy and even mild liking. Bridget felt dread chill her heart.

"I gave my word to Sir Curan." She had sworn to wait for him. "With Father's blessing I swore, Mother."

Her mother nodded and fingered her skirt. Bridget understood the nervousness now. Yet she might wish that she was still ignorant. Curan Ramsden was not a man you broke promises to. He was one of England's border lords. Unlike many who swarmed around the aged King Henry Tudor, Curan was a man of action. He'd earned his spurs of knighthood on the field in France alongside the king on one of Henry's campaigns to regain soil in Europe.

"You were young and obedient to your father."

"It was only three years ago."

Her mother's fingers gripped her skirt. "Yes. However things change quickly these days. You shall wed Lord Oswald. We are to leave for London three days hence. Lord Oswald is one of the king's advisors and resides at Whitehall Palace."

"Lord Oswald." Bridget searched her memory. Her father went to great lengths to keep her away from court. Maidens did not maintain their virtue very long once in attendance. At twenty-two years of age she was in awe of her sire for being able to keep her in the country. Having her betrothed to Sir Curan Ramsden had kept the gossips from her.

"His daughter passed a night here a few years ago."

Bridget felt her face drain of color. The lady in question was older than her mother. She tried to cover her dislike. It was unseemly. Many a nobleman's daughter found herself married to a man well past her in age. Even Queen Catherine Parr was many years Henry Tudor's junior.

"He is widowed?"

Her mother's lips pressed into a hard line. "No. Lord Oswald has divorced his newest wife for failing to conceive. The poor girl has been sent back to her father."

Bridget lost a bit more of her color. She pressed her lips together tightly, resisting the urge to make some sound of protest. Her mother's face was just as stark. When their father sent a letter, it was to be obeyed. There was no questioning the wishes of the lord of the house. According to the will of the king, her sire was master of the family. Especially over the female members. To argue was to question her place and offer greedy men the opportunity to name her a heretic so that her father's lands might be forfeit. There were plenty of men who would make use of any reason to depose another noble peer, even if it was so low as to use the women in the family to accomplish that goal. Now that all the monasteries were claimed and their land and riches divided, the hungry looked to new sources to gain quick wealth.

Marriage was one of the favorite methods for amassing funds. Divorce was more common than anyone dared say. Many young wives suffered the same fate as Catherine of Aragon; Henry the Eighth's first wife was shuffled off into the country to live out the remainder of her days in near poverty once her child-bearing days came to an end. Things had only become worse since that time. Now new brides were often discarded only months after their wedding nights and sent home without their dowries for failing to conceive quickly. Such was a grim fate. Years could go by before lawyers agreed on what parts of their wedding agreement might be recovered. The discarded bride could not remarry until such was done. Even after legal negotiations were finished, not many men wanted a girl who had failed in her primary duty as wife.

Jane clasped her hands together. She was still agitated, and her leather gloves made a smacking sound when they met.

"We must do all in our power to ensure that your union is a solid one."

The look in her mother's eyes was one Bridget had not seen before—a sort of determination that almost looked desperate. Jane looked at Bridget in a way she had never done previously. It was an assessment from one woman to another. Her mother settled on some firm decision.

"Come with me, Daughter. I have someone for you to meet."

* * *

Bridget stared at the woman her mother took her to. Hidden behind the thick oak door of her mother's solar was someone she had never thought to actually converse with.

"This is Marie. She is a courtesan. We shall refrain from mentioning her family name. The staff does not know she is here. That is best for us all."

"I've heard of such women before."

Jane looked displeased. Bridget merely stared back at her mother.

"What is the point in behaving as though I have not heard of courtesans when you have brought me to meet one?"

Courtesans were women who captivated men. They were not common prostitutes. Most of them serviced only one rich client at a time. Such women were well educated, schooled in dance, and versed in several languages. More than one nobleman's illegitimate daughter was a member of their ranks. Most important, they were demure and silent, keeping their exploits hidden behind closed doors. Men flocked to them, often waiting for long periods before being able to sponsor one of the elite women and thereby gain her personal attention.

Her mother sighed. "I suppose you are being more practical than I." She drew a deep breath and gestured at Marie. "In light of the perilous times, I have purchased some of Marie's time in order to have you instructed. She has graciously agreed that you should not remain ignorant."

"In what subject?" The question slipped out because Bridget was too busy looking at Marie. Yes, she had heard of courtesans, but the reality was far more intriguing than the whispers. The woman was gowned in wool as fine as Bridget and her mother wore. The courtesan's gloves were leather and lacked no tailoring detail. Her face was smooth and lightly accented with powder. Her lips were stained the color of ruby, and not some garish shade of red that was too bright. Marie looked for all the world as if she might be a woman of noble birth on her way to court. The only difference was the lack of jewelry. She wore no pearls or gems. Such things were only for the blue-blooded nobility. But Jane's tone also reminded Bridget that Marie did not have to answer her summons like a servant. The courtesan was there of her own free will.

"The subject of seduction."

Bridget turned a curious look on her mother. "You have already taught me what to expect in my marriage bed." Jane had seen to that task the night that she and Curan had knelt in the family chapel to swear to one another. She was practically a wife after such; the only detail lacking was a bedding. Curan had said that he would not claim her until his last duty to the king was served. It was not an uncommon arrangement. Negotiations for a wedding between noble families often took many years, often difficult to time exactly. A "pledge to marry" ceremony often took place when the families reached agreement but the knight still owed service. Moreover, such a ceremony was expected to be honored by both families, drawing its strength from the codes of chivalry. But it was a truth that legally her father could wed her to another. She had simply never considered that her sire might break with the knightly code of conduct.

"What you have not been taught is how to please a man." Bridget's mother flushed slightly, but she didn't appear uncomfortable. The stain on her cheeks was paired with a flicker of enjoyment in her eyes. "Since the men of this country have become so greedy, taking numerous wives whenever the whim consumes them, I believe it is time we women employ a few tactics of our own to ensure our futures."

Jane looked at Marie. "I will trust you to teach my daughter everything she needs to know about stealing a man's wits in bed. I shall be in the outer chamber making sure you are not disturbed."

Or discovered. Bridget added the little comment inside her head. Her mother cast a look at her before leaving the room. Bridget returned her attention to Marie, curious to discover just what seduction entailed. Certainly she had heard the word, but in truth she knew little of the details.

A slow smile curved Marie's lips as Bridget watched. Something very intriguing swept over the courtesan; a confidence seemed to radiate from her.

"We shall begin with how to disrobe." Marie strode into the center of the chamber. Her eyes took on a slightly slanted appearance. "Men can be slaves to their lust. They are greedy like children looking for sweets. Learn to control that appetite and you shall master the man."

She turned in a graceful flare of skirts. "Always make him watch you. Do not give in to his demands to rush. Once he is spent between your thighs, your power over him recedes."

Marie paused with her back to Bridget. She peeked over her shoulder in a gesture that was both teasing and naughty. Her eyes were half closed, the lashes veiling her deepest thoughts. Bridget heard the popping sounds of the hooks opening on the front of Marie's bodice. That sound sent a little heat racing into Bridget's cheeks. Hearing it, yet being prevented from seeing the opening of the garment, sent her mind racing with ideas. Marie laughed. Low and sultry, the sound floated over her shoulder.

"You understand, don't you, Bridget? The idea of what I am doing is more powerful than the act itself. Tease him with it. Make him wait for you to reveal yourself to his eyes."

Marie rolled her shoulders, and her dress slid over them. It was a slow motion. The dark wool slipping inch by inch to reveal the creamy fabric of her chemise.

"Disrobing in front of the fire is pleasing. The flames illuminate your body beneath the fabric of your undergarments. It tantalizes men."

Marie turned and stepped out of her dress in a smooth and graceful motion. Her chemise was held against her body by a set of stays that did not match the somber color of her dress. Peacock-blue silk shimmered in the afternoon light. Such a rich fabric spoke of a lover who did indeed keep her very well.

"Now you try."

Bridget felt her throat constrict. "Me? Do you mean to say that you want me to disrobe?"

Marie walked across the solar on little steps that looked lazy. She was completely at ease in her lack of clothing, almost content.

"I'm pleased to hear you say it plainly. At least we shall not have the chore of washing puritan teaching out of you."

"Puritan habits are wise considering how Queens Catherine Howard and Anne Boleyn both met their ends."

Marie lifted a hand and began slowly pulling her glove off, one fingertip at a time. "To court a crown is a dangerous game. Resist the urge to be too greedy when it comes to the power men like to believe should be theirs. Politics has always been deadly. With greater gain always comes higher risk. Remember to stroke the ego of the man who thinks he owns you."

"Thinks he owns me?" According to the law, a husband did own his spouse. Even if Bridget wished it otherwise. Why did her gender make her less in the eyes of the world? She was every bit as keen witted as any of her brothers.

Marie pulled the glove free. Her hand was clean and smooth. She trailed her fingertips up her own neck before answering. In spite of the fact that she was another woman, Bridget found herself watching that touch. A faint tingle crossed her own neck in response.

"If you are wise, you will never forget that your heart is yours alone. It can be the greatest gift, but never can it be commanded." Marie aimed a firm look at her. "You cannot entrance a man unless you are comfortable with your own body. Turn and disrobe."

Bridget found that her hands shook. She fumbled the hooks that normally she opened with ease. A shaky breath rattled past her teeth as she tried to force herself to relax. It was only another woman, after all. What shame was there in showing her body to someone who had one exactly the same?

Her hands still trembled. But she finished and rolled her shoulders to send her dress down her arms. A least that worked well. Her dress slumped to the floor in a pile.

"Tomorrow I shall have you watch me while I entertain a man."

"What?" Bridget's arms crossed over her body in defense. Marie had no pity for her, though. She reached across the space between them and flicked Bridget's quivering chin back up with one firm finger.

"You heard me correctly. I will arrange a place for you to view me giving pleasure to a man. You must gain confidence or you shall be doomed to be taken on your back like countless other brides. With nothing to do but endure being used to relieve your groom's lust."

"You mean there are other . . . positions?" It was a bold question, one she normally wouldn't have voiced. Maybe sin was intoxicating such as they said in church. Now that she was on the path, each step was easier to take. She craved knowing more.

"Oh, yes. There are many positions for a man and woman to

make love in and several other things that will keep your husband eager to join you after sunset."

Enjoyment flickered in Marie's eyes again. Bridget smiled without thinking. She wanted to know whatever it was that made Marie look that way. It was some secret that promised to bring pleasure when she at last discovered what it was.

"First we shall refine your entrance and disrobing. You must grasp your partner's attention the moment you enter the room."

Marie proved a tough taskmaster. Bridget redressed and unhooked her bodice countless more times.

"Better. Now we must proceed, for our time is limited. Once your dress is removed, take your shoes off, and always wear lace stockings. Change into them before supper."

"They are so expensive." Or time consuming to produce. The only two pairs Bridget owned were ones she had made under the watchful eye of the estate tailor. She had labored until her shoulders ached to knit them.

"But they draw a man's eyes to your legs." Marie sat down. But she didn't use one of the chairs the solar offered. Instead she lowered her body onto a padded footstool. She parted her knees so that the point of her corset dipped down to cover her mons. With one hand on top of either thigh she slowly drew her chemise up to display her lace-stocking-clad legs.

"I see what you mean." It was captivating. Naughty. But ever so clever. The subtle demonstration played on the submissive role that a wife was expected to embody while wielding a measure of control that Bridget had never considered she might. The last traces of her childhood felt as if they were evaporating, and she was happy to allow it. Here was the thing that she had felt the need to discover ever since accepting that she would wed Curan. Deep inside her, she had felt a surprising rush of heat, unsure what its purpose was.

"Good. Now you try it."

* * *

Sleep eluded Bridget that night. She heard the fire crackling beyond the bed curtains, but her mind was still engrossed with her lessons. She was caught between the things she had practiced and the unknown lessons that were to come. How was it possible to spend so many years being tutored only to discover an entire subject untouched? Since she had been allowed out of the nursery, she had been groomed to be a well-educated companion and an expert accountant for her husband's holdings. At the center of it all had always been her marriage. It was what a nobleman's daughter did—wed well and manage her husband's estate.

And produce heirs.

That was the part in which she found her education lacking. Her cheeks heated in spite of the night's chill. Well, in all truth it wasn't nearly so lacking now. Yet she was not arrogant enough to believe that learning how to disrobe with some skill was all there was to enticing a man. If that were so, no man would be paying for peacock-blue silk corsets for a courtesan.

She knew it was more. It had surrounded Marie like a mist. Some would label such a thing witchcraft. The king had accused Anne Boleyn of using unnatural skills to enchant him away from his wife. But was that the same thing she had witnessed in Marie today? That subtle motion of her body and the slanting of her eyes. Was it a ploy of the devil or merely a clever use of what God had given her?

She liked the latter idea. There was no mistake about it. Bridget felt her lips curve up with enjoyment. She had never been very fond of the lectures given in church to wives. Strict instructions drilled into her every morning on the merits of obedience and submissive traits.

Why? Did not boldness breed strength? Whoever heard of

choosing a docile mare to be covered by the strongest stallion? No. Never. When her father was home, he would go out and watch the mares to see which ones had fire in them. Only the ones that displayed courage and life would be allowed to breed with his prize stallions. The same held true across the estate, from prize-hunting hounds to the falcons. Strength was sought, not meekness.

Maybe that was the difference between men and women. The solid truth was that the two genders were very contrary to one other.

Curan's face rose to the front of Bridget's thoughts. It wasn't the first time he'd invaded her bed. There was something about his features she liked to dwell on. He was a hard man with a body thick with muscle. Such was to be expected since he still rode alongside the Earl of Pemshire and then with the king. That was no place for soft courtiers. Each man was expected to wield his sword with a skilled hand and a strong arm. To do any less was a sure way to end up dead . . . Curan did not disappoint.

She suspected it was the reason her father had contracted with him. The border lords were men who took estates along Scotland's border. It was an uncertain place. Many of England's nobles had failed to keep their land secure against the clans that lay on the other side of that border. Curan was earning his land and title by holding an estate for England. When he had ridden into sight for their swearing ceremony, she had shivered. Every man following him was hardened, all in firm command of their warhorses.

She had felt that strength in the light touch of his fingers against her skin, a faint brushing of his fingertips across her cheek as he cupped her face for a kiss. She had trembled and studied his face in an attempt to discover if he was moved by her. Curan never complimented her hair or her eyes. Others had. Her hair was the lightest brown that turned copper in the sunlight, but he didn't seem interested in it. He made no comment on her smooth, freckle-free complexion, either. The only thing that drew his dark eyes to her with interest had been the way she stared straight into his eyes as he bent to kiss her. She saw clearly a flicker of admiration before his lips made contact with hers, the hand on her cheek tightening ever so slightly while his mouth pressed against hers. Time had frozen—as still as the lake did in winter. She had been suspended in that moment, with his body looming over hers and his lips impossibly hot against her own. Even now she recalled it vividly.

Maybe too much so.

For certain she felt lust for him. Hidden behind her bed curtains, Bridget refused to be dishonest with herself. Out among the staff, tending to her father's estate, was another matter. There were appearances to maintain. Here, she felt the heat over her cheekbones and the way it spread down her throat and across her chest. Wearing only a chemise beneath the bedcovers, she was aware of her nipples drawing into hard pebbles as though she were cold. Yet she knew that was not the cause. A flush of warmth spread along her skin, not startling any longer because she had become accustomed to it. Whenever she allowed her thoughts to dwell on Curan, her body responded.

For certain, it was a pity that she was not to wed him.

Marie kept her word.

Jane was not as composed when facing the prospect of leaving Bridget in the company of the woman when her intention was to take her away. Her mother stared at the courtesan, but Marie returned the look without wavering.

"There are things that words simply do not convey. Men

take advantage of that in maidens. I only agreed to these lessons because I thought you wanted your daughter to avoid being led to her marriage like a blind child, as you most likely were."

Jane scoffed. "That is a fact."

Resentment edged Jane's words. A little crack in the polished exterior she normally presented. But there was also a shimmer of victory in her eyes. The look she aimed at Bridget was full of achievement.

"Do not judge me too harshly, Bridget, but I would see you standing on firm feet when you meet this man who discards young wives. I cannot stop this marriage, but I can make sure you are not helpless. Learn to arouse your husband, and you shall conceive."

Jane watched them as they walked down the steps to where two horses were held ready.

"You are very fortunate to have a mother who is so cunning," Marie said.

"Cunning?"

Marie arched one slim eyebrow. "Oh, yes, Bridget. Your mother is cunning. I suspect your father has promised your groom a sheltered, country-raised virgin."

"Will these lessons displease my husband?"

"Not if you are wise enough to give him the innocent looks he expects. It really is no deception; you are a maiden." Marie offered her a smile. "Listen to me and you shall never regret losing your innocence."

She kicked her horse, and the two rode away from the house. The countryside was still bright this morning, and their horses covered the distance quickly. Yet not so fast that Bridget didn't have time to think herself almost to death. Anticipation held her in an iron grip, the idea of what was to come both teasing and tormenting her. Marie led her toward a smaller house that Bridget had seen before. Her father owned it, but no one had lived in it for some time. The dwelling was kept in good repair and cleaned in case someone important might come to visit. Marie lifted one gloved hand to her lips. The woman dismounted and tied her horse up a good hundred yards from the house.

"My client is inside. You will watch us but remain perfectly silent."

Bridget bit her lip to avoid having her jaw drop once more. She was shocked, but she was also insanely curious about what exactly coupling looked like. From her mother's description, the act was difficult to picture. Marie gripped Bridget's hand and pulled her toward the house. They did not approach the main doorway but went toward the kitchen entrance. Marie led her up the back stairs and into the small doorway that was intended for a manservant. The opening led to a tiny room that was big enough only for a narrow bed on one side and a single chair and space for clothing on the other. A noble would expect his manservant to be able to hear him at any time. Such rooms were discreetly built alongside the master. There was no door but a carved wooden screen that formed a sight block, which was intended for the master, not the servant.

"Stay here and be silent."

Marie entered the room next door and looked it over. Nothing escaped her notice, and she walked over to the bed to inspect it as well. The covers were turned down and violets sprinkled across the sheets.

She reached up and gave the cord that was attached to a bell in the kitchen a pull.

She unhooked her dress and stepped out of it. She moved faster today, but her actions still had a grace to them that was slightly hypnotic.

"I was getting tired of waiting." A man entered the room, his expression surly, but that changed when he looked at Marie.

"Some things are worth waiting just a little bit for, Tomas." Marie made it her business to learn the man's name before-hand.

Marie arched that eyebrow once again. She fingered the tie that held her stays closed. Her cleavage swelled just above it, and when she pulled on the ties, it tightened the stays just a small amount, making her breasts plump up even more. Who-ever her client was, he appreciated her efforts. His attention was drawn to her breasts, and his lips took on a slight curve.

"I hope so, this was a long ride."

He was a large man with wide shoulders and long legs. There was nothing boyish about him, even if his face was shaved smooth. He reached up and unbuttoned his doublet with steady fingers and shrugged free of the open garment a moment later to face Marie in his shirt and britches.

"I can see you are anticipating something that would make your long ride worth it." She moved toward him and reached up to cup his face. Bridget leaned closer to the screen and watched the courtesan boldly kiss her partner. He kissed her back, a long moment of their mouths slipping and sliding against one another. Marie broke away from the kiss and rubbed her hands down the man's chest and farther until she rubbed over the bulge that was pushing his britches out.

"Ah, I seem to have discovered your motivation for seeking me out."

Marie backed away from him, gaining a frown, but she lifted her hands to the tie of her corset and regained his full atten-tion. She pulled the tie and the knot popped. The weight of her breasts immediately pulled the loosened lace through the eyelets.

"Now that is a fine sight." His voice was turning raspy, and

Marie trailed one fingertip over her own breast. His eyes followed her motions.

Bridget felt her throat constrict again. Never had she thought to watch such a thing. She forced herself to swallow. It wasn't as if the man was going to touch her. Her virginity must remain intact. She took a deep breath; she wasn't a child any longer and could not afford to be shocked by something she would be expected to do within a fortnight. Far better to know what to expect.

"Confidence is the key to enchanting a man . . ."

Marie's words suddenly became more than another lesson. True understanding dawned on Bridget. It was something that only the look in Tomas's eyes could have taught her. He watched Marie with absolute devotion as she shrugged out of her corset and set it aside.

"Well done. I never thought I'd enjoying watching a woman undress so much."

Marie turned, and her chemise flared out as she moved. She moved toward her partner and began to untie the laces at the collar of his shirt.

"Tossing skirts is only part of the fun." She drew his shirt free and ran her hands along his bare skin.

Marie fingered the hem of her chemise. Tomas's attention focused on her action. Bridget stared at his face, studying the way he watched the other woman. Something flickered in his eyes, and his lips parted slightly when Marie began to pull the ivory fabric up. She bared her thighs and showed a pair of pink garters holding up the tops of her knit stockings.

Hearing about it had not truly driven home what Marie meant by "enchant." Bridget understood now. It was in the way Tomas watched her bare her body and the confidence with which the courtesan performed the act, truly showing that she had the upper hand. Yet there was a coldness to it—a callousness that sent a tiny shaft of disappointment through her. Perhaps it was due to her night dwellings on Curan, but Bridget looked at the couple in front of her and noticed how little affection there was. Even horses played more before mating.

She could not expect anything else from Lord Oswald. Must not, for her own sake.

Bridget banished her thoughts of Curan. That was in the past now, although her conscience tormented her over the vow she was expected to break. Yet in order to keep it, she would have to disobey her father's will that she wed at his newest command. Being a daughter was difficult at times.

"You're a good sight in nothing but skin."

Marie stood in only her stockings and shoes. Her breasts hung free, the coral nipples flat.

"You think so?"

Her tone was sultry, and she smoothed her hands up her body until she cupped her own breasts. Slipping her fingers all the way around each globe, she smiled while touching herself.

"I came to touch, not watch."

Tomas didn't wait for anything else. He moved forward and took over the duty of cupping Marie's breasts. His eyes were focused on her flesh, his hands cupping each globe gently. He brushed his fingers over the nipples, and they beaded into hard points. A moment later he leaned down and sucked one of them into his mouth.

Bridget gasped and pressed one hand over her mouth to remain silent.

The sight of them sent a little ripple of pleasure down her back. It should have repulsed her to witness two people engaged in such actions, but Bridget admitted it did not. She craved an understanding of intimate matters that went beyond lying on her back and being taken. The idea of having her thighs spread and her body penetrated sounded so cold. But the thought of having Curan kiss her nipples was quite exciting.

Lord Oswald. She would have to begin thinking of him in relation to her lessons.

Enjoyment sparkled in Marie's eyes. Bridget felt her cheeks burning with a blush, but she was far more intrigued by the moment to care about what was proper.

Tomas pulled his lips away from Marie's nipple. "I want to feel how talented your lips are."

There was arrogance in his tone and a smirk on his lips. With another quick motion of his fingers he unlaced his pants. Bridget felt her cheeks burn hotter as he bared his male flesh.

Her breath froze in her throat, but she truly did not notice. Everything was suspended while her gaze studied the one thing she had heard about yet never seen. It was not so different from a stallion's penis. Long and thick. It stood up through the opening in his pants. The head had a ridge of flesh circling it and a slit directly on top. It appeared hard and firm.

"You will not be disappointed." Maire's voice was sultry but brimming with confidence.

"I'll be the judge of that."

He sat down and leaned against the padded back of a chair. The position allowed his cock to stand straight up.

"Come over here and show me the French fashion. That's why I agreed to your price. I ain't ever paid for a fuck before, but I want to be Frenched. I hear the king gets it every day."

"His majesty does indeed enjoy having a pair of lips suckling his cock."

Marie took command of Tomas with one delicate stroke of her fingers. So gently she stroked that hard pole from base to slit. Tomas shuddered, his face drawing into a harsh mask. Yet when Bridget took a longer moment to study Tomas's face she noticed more. A deep enjoyment of what Marie was doing was etched into his features. Bridget felt her cheeks flame, but she didn't take her attention off the lesson in front of her.

Marie traced his cock with gentle fingers for long moments. She did not rush nor did she hesitate. Sure and steady, her hand stroked and finally closed all the way around that cock. Bridget could hear Tomas breathing roughly. He was leaning farther back against the chair, his hands gripping the arms. Marie was truly in control. It wasn't so complete that the man couldn't rise and escape her touch. It was more a matter of him choosing to remain right where the courtesan might continue to touch him.

Marie shifted her attention to Bridget. A bright look from beneath hooded eyes. There was a wealth of knowledge in that look. Bridget stared at the confidence Marie displayed and felt envy burn inside her. She was jealous of the poise and knowledge, but more important, Bridget envied Marie's lack of fear. There wasn't a single trace in her eyes. Coupling did not concern her, not at all. In fact, the courtesan looked as though she was anticipating something enjoyable.

Bridget lifted her chin. She banished the quiver inside her that was causing her face to burn with a blush.

Marie sank to her knees in a graceful motion. She maintained her grasp on Tomas's cock, slipping her closed hands down to the middle of it. Leaning forward, she opened her mouth and licked the head of his cock.

The blush returned to Bridget's face. Nonetheless her eyes stayed focused on the tip of Marie's tongue. She circled the crown in a slow lap before teasing the small slit that topped his length.

She looked back at the hard flesh in her hands. Leaning

down over him, she opened her mouth and demonstrated exactly what the man had meant by Frenching. The sight was as shocking as it was fascinating. Marie took the entire head of his cock inside her mouth. Her lips closed around it while her hand began working up and down on the portion that did not fit into her mouth.

Tomas drew in a hard breath and reached for her head, his hands threading into her hair. His hips actually began to move, thrusting in quick little motions. The action drove his cock deeper into Marie's mouth, but she didn't resist. She maintained her position, moving her head up and down in unison with his thrusting. A soft growl filled the chamber and then several more. Tomas's hands gripped her head tighter, and his thrusting became faster. It looked as if something was building in him, something he was struggling to maintain control over. His breathing was rapid and harsh now, hunger drawing his face tight.

Marie suddenly pulled her mouth away from his cock. He snarled at her, his face becoming a mask of rage.

"Bitch."

He growled the single word at her, but she didn't take it as an insult. Instead a look of sultry confidence covered her face. She pumped her hand up and down on the length of his cock, and he suddenly stiffened. A sharp cry came from his lips while his cock erupted with a squirt of fluid. Marie kept her hand moving, drawing several more streams from him. Her client gasped and shuddered, his face a mask of strain, but he collapsed back into the chair with a satisfied smile.

"Holy Christ, the king is one lucky man."

His words were labored as though he'd been running. Marie reached behind him and plucked a small linen from the table. She cleaned away the fluid before licking the underside of his cock once more.

He groaned but smiled brighter, like a child who was going to get a second treat from the cook. Greed shimmered in his eyes, and his cock remained rigid as Marie licked and teased it.

"I always send my customers away satisfied. Very satisfied."

She rose to her feet and lifted one foot up, then placed her knee on the chair next to his left hip. His attention was instantly snared by the opening of her thighs.

Marie lifted both of her eyebrows in a sultry motion while she reached out and stroked Tomas's cock once again.

"Stop teasing me." His voice was strained, but the courtesan took it as a compliment, her lips rising into a smile full of achievement.

"You enjoy the teasing as much as the riding. Possibly more."

Tomas chuckled, but it wasn't a happy sound; it was deep and full of male enjoyment. "I do indeed. But I'm ready for some fucking from you, woman."

He seemed to have no difficulty with speaking bluntly, but Marie didn't appear shocked. Raising her other knee up, she grasped Tomas's shoulders and crawled up onto his lap. His hands landed on her hips and reached around to grip both sides of her bottom. She was poised above his rigid cock for a moment before lowering her body down onto it. There was a soft sound of wet flesh against flesh before she took the entire length inside herself.

A soft gasp passed her lips. A little sound of pleasure that lent evidence to the fact that she did indeed enjoy what she was doing.

"Fuck me." Tomas sounded impatient.

He didn't wait for his words to gain action, either; he lifted Marie up off his cock but not all the way. He released her before the head was free and let her body weight push her back down to the base. He groaned, and she did, too. Her hands gripped his shoulders, and she began to lift herself up exactly as he had. They moved in unison. When Marie lowered her body, Tomas thrust up toward her. Their breathing became harsh, their movements harder and faster. The chamber was filled with their harsh breathing and cries of delight. The chair shook under their combined efforts. Tomas gripped her bottom, his fingers white. A moment later he snarled and surged up toward her, straining against her body as a growl of satisfaction ripped from his lips. Marie was not outdone. She ground herself down against his cock, her hips straining and moving in quick little motions. Her entire body shuddered when she cried out. It was a sound of extreme pleasure that bounced around the walls of the chamber. Marie collapsed against her companion, his arms closing around her and his hands gently stroking her bottom in the first sign of tenderness he had shown her. They remained still for a long moment, their breathing slowing.

Marie drew a stiff breath and lifted her head.

"You were worth the price. I'll be back." The man smiled and patted Marie on the bottom.

"I am glad to hear you say so."

She sounded tired and distracted as though forming her thoughts into words was an effort she would rather not make. Both appeared satisfied in some manner. Bridget bit her lower lip, actually jealous for some reason. It felt as though she had missed out on some treat. Disappointment gnawed at her insides.

The man stiffened before setting Marie aside and reaching for his pants. He was gone quickly and without any further conversation. Marie walked toward the window and watched to make sure he had left the house.

"You may come out now."

Bridget felt awkward emerging from behind the screen, which was foolish considering that Marie knew full well that she had been there the entire time.

"You must take your husband's seed inside your belly and keep it. If he has you ride him like I just did, roll onto your back once he is spent."

Marie began dressing, but she paused and cast a look toward Bridget that was full of frustration. "Men are greedy creatures, the ones at court more so than any you have met. That is why I showed you the art of Frenching on Tomas. It is almost assured that any man in a position of power at court will expect such service. Be the one to give it to your husband; that will keep him from wondering and thinking of divorce. It is unfair the way men expect so much of women, but you must make the best of it. Make sure he sinks his member into you before his seed erupts." She shuddered but drew herself up.

"I will return tomorrow for your final lesson."

Chapter Two

What more is there? Bridget turned the question over and over inside her head. The lack of attention saw her scrambling, when the sun began setting, to finish the tasks left unfinished.

She stared at the three trunks sitting in her bedchamber. Her belly was knotted with anticipation. For years the topic of marriage had been a common one. She realized it had taken on a surreal significance—something much talked about but not truly a reality. Tension had drawn her tight for the two days Sir Curan had slept under their roof three years prior, but it had left when she stood on the front steps and watched him lead his lines of retainers away.

Taken to the altar and yet not a true bride. The circumstances had placed her in a unique position. No reason existed any longer to strive to learn court manners and dances. Or to maintain a constant written correspondence with those at court to learn of the recent happenings. She did not have to worry about being sent to court. Her attentions had turned to running the estate.

Yet now she packed for a journey to court.

Her mother was frantically attempting to gain knowledge of what was happening at court from her neighbors. Which left

Bridget with the chore of packing her belongings. The chamber became bare as she and two maids took down the tapestries she had woven to impress Sir Curan when she arrived as his wife.

Now they would go to Lord Oswald.

Her best dresses were rolled and placed in the trunks. She packed all of her wool ones, too, because she had no hint as to what her true destination might be. Would she be expected to attend court or to remain in Lord Oswald's town home in the hopes that she might conceive quickly? There were many who believed a new bride should be kept from distractions until she performed her primary duty.

All that much better to keep you from finding a lover among the court gentlemen.

Heat colored her cheeks, but she could not keep her memory from offering up the vision of Marie wrapping her lips around the head of that cock. Tomas had enjoyed it. She'd witnessed the pleasure rippling over his face.

Did men ever do anything that made a woman feel that good?

She wondered and was suddenly grateful Marie had promised to return. There were questions she wanted to ask. Of course the courtesan might not answer her. After all, she was the student. Her duty was to listen, not annoy her tutor by chattering.

The trunks were packed, and Bridget found the sight of them depressing. Her chamber was so cold now, it felt as if a death had passed in the house. She made the sign of the cross over herself before realizing what she was doing.

Well, in truth it was a form of death. The ending of her life with her mother. The remaining hours she had under her roof seemed more precious than gold. Once she left she would be expected to remain strong in the face of all things she encountered. No one would give her comfort, save the church. Yet that was her place, her duty, and she was no coward.

"Let us take these trunks downstairs." She wanted to be finished the soonest so that she might sit with her mother and enjoy her company.

"Yes, mistress."

The maids lowered themselves before hurrying out of the chamber to seek out the boys who worked in the lower kitchens. Before long she heard their booted steps on the stairs. With a quick pull on their caps, they lifted the trunks and carried them from the room. Bridget followed them, the chill chasing her. She doubted she would sleep at all, finding it best not to retire until her eyelids were drooping with fatigue.

She followed the trunks and watched them being set in the receiving hall. Their estate was not overly grand, but it was newer than those of many of their surrounding neighbors. Each spring, new construction added to the main house. The receiving hall was new and set with glass windows. Even covered with shutters, the night chill crept in. The last of the day's light illuminated the open doorway. The kitchen staff placed the trunks in a neat row near the door. The trunks appeared small next to the uncertain future looming large outside.

A steady beating began in the distance, rumbling along the ground first. Bridget felt it as much with her feet as she heard with her ears. There was no mistaking such a thing—the sound of many horses. The noise grew louder and was joined by the household retainers running along the edge of the house. But there were few armed men here in the country. Her father expected his position at court to protect his holdings. Besides, any nobleman who kept too many retainers fell under suspicion if they were not engaged in the king's business.

Bridget reached for the door. If they came at sunset, they

had been on the road all day. Pulling it open, she stared out into the scarlet horizon. The estate sat on the high ground of her father's land. Streaming up from the main road were columns of mounted men, their shoulders and thighs covered in armor. The slap of hundreds of small plates of metal against metal added to the sound of their arrival.

But the leader of the horde drew her attention. His lower face was covered by a scarf, the fabric tied around his neck to keep the dust from the road out of his mouth and nose. Every man behind him wore the same. Chain-mail hoods flattened their hair, the low edges hiding their eyebrows. It was a frightening sight—men ready for war and riding in perfect harmony with their mounts.

The leader held up a gloved hand, halting the men who followed him. They pulled up on their reins with powerful motions of their hands, their thighs gripping the saddles. The leader's hard gaze swept the front of the house completely, his keen stare missing not a single soul. His dark eyes returned to hers. A shiver shot down her back. Her breath froze in her chest, and she was sure her heart almost paused.

Curan.

She knew his eyes, but the man of her dreams paled compared to what sat facing her. This man was far more imposing than she recalled. Maybe it was due to the fact that they had only met under very controlled circumstances. Standing on the ground and tipping her head up to look at him, the man appeared impossibly large. Some sort of blending of legend and flesh that she had trouble believing was real. He reached up and pulled the scarf away from his face to reveal a hard jaw that was dark with a hint of whiskers, telling her that he had been in the saddle for many hours without stopping to attend to his vanity. Yet his eyes were keen and sharp and staring directly into her own.

"Mistress Newbury, I greet you."

His voice dispelled any further ideas of him being unreal. That deep tone burst into her head and jerked her into a shaky breath. His dark eyes cut into hers with an intensity that sent fire down her back.

"Sweet Christ . . ."

Her mother's voice was startling. Bridget turned to look at her mother and then wished that she had not. Jane's eyes were wide and filled with a fear Bridget had never seen before. Not even when they had received word that the plague was on the move again two summers past.

"Take yourself upstairs, Bridget."

Her mother didn't wait for her to comply. She reached for her arm and pulled her toward the open doors. "This moment." Her mother's voice rose with her distress.

"Delay that."

Curan's voice rang out loud and clear, the men behind him angling their heads to get a clear look at what was happening. His horse tossed its head in the wake of its master's order, almost as if the huge war stallion was agreeing with the man who sat astride him. A sure pull on the reins stilled the animal before Curan swung a leg over its hindquarters and dismounted.

"Go." Jane gave her another push and stepped in front of her.

"I said delay that command, Lady Connolly." Several other men dismounted and fell into step with their lord. Curan closed the distance between them very quickly. But Bridget didn't truly have a choice. A half turn of her head showed her several knights behind her. Curan was a man of action. He'd sent part of his force over the ridge to surround them.

"I have come to collect my bride. It is time she stands and meets me as she will be expected to do once we are settled on my lands."

Jane drew in a stiff breath. "I am pleased to see you have fared well since our last meeting."

It was a polite statement, devoid of true emotion.

"As I am delighted to see you both in good health."

Those dark eyes cut to hers again. This time he was close enough for Bridget to see something flickering in them. Men were still riding up to the house, their numbers continuing to grow until there must be three hundred of them. Wagons and carts made up a large portion of the back of the ranks. There were even cannons being pulled by thick-legged oxen. This was the entirety of Sir Curan's force. It was more than impressive, the sheer numbers of them filling the green in front of their estate home. Men dismounted and went toward the wagons to begin pulling tents from them. There were orders being issued by the lower-ranking officers while Sir Curan and his higher staff remained near her.

Suspicion clouded his eyes. Her mother drew another stiff breath.

"You are, of course, most welcome to pass the night."

"You are too kind, lady." Curan's tone was anything but pleased. He looked at her mother and back to Bridget.

"Yet, on the morrow you will have to seek my husband at court."

A frown appeared on Curan's face. The man had never smiled, his lips an unemotional line. Now they turned down and he hooked his hands into his wide sword belt.

"My negotiations with your husband were completed three years past."

"Yet—"

"Yet what, lady?" Curan took a step forward. Jane stumbled back into Bridget, drawing a sound of disgust from him. His frown deepened, but he retreated a step to allow her mother space.

"Explain your timidity, lady. What causes you fright? I have come to claim my bride as agreed upon. You have had plenty of time to become accustomed to the idea."

Her mother didn't seem to have the courage to tell him. Bridget discovered that she couldn't tolerate waiting any longer. She stepped up beside her mother.

"My father sent for me three days past. He has ordered me to court and marriage with another."

Those dark eyes returned to her. A hint of approval lasted only a moment before his temper flared bright.

"We have already been blessed by your husband." His face reflected his anger, and he reached for her. Jane stepped between them.

"As I said, Sir Curan, you shall have to take issue with my husband."

He stopped his hand in mid-air. He took his eyes off her mother for a brief moment. A quick flick of his hand, and her mother gasped when she was moved to the side by one of the men behind her. It was the boldest of actions, but one that Bridget decided suited him. This man would be polite only so long as he was gaining what he desired.

"I am ennobled, lady, and here to claim the bride sworn to me by law and church. Do not place yourself between what is mine and me again. Or I shall have you removed, permanently."

His men shifted, and Bridget moved in front of her mother.

"If you do consider yourself my husband, you should have more respect for your mother by marriage." Bridget wasn't sure where the urge to argue with him came from, only that she could not resist it.

An incredulous look appeared on Curan's face. Obviously the man was not accustomed to being questioned.

He bit back his first response, his gaze raking her from head to foot. "If she wishes to be respected in that manner, she will have to dispense with this notion that you are going to London and not my holdings, Bridget."

He spoke her Christian name very purposely, as if a public declaration of ownership. One that blew more air on the flames of her temper. Her first name was an intimate thing. Meant to be used by her parents, her immediate church clergy, and a husband behind the closed door of their chamber. Even her brothers did not use it unless they were in private.

"We are bound to respect the wishes of my father. That is not disrespectful."

"And what of the vows you took on your knees beside me, madam? Where is the respect for the promises you made to me?" He stepped closer, seeming to grow larger, but she did not care. Her chin lifted to keep their gazes locked.

"What man would have a wife who disobeyed her father before she was wed?"

That flicker of approval entered his eyes once more. His frown smoothed out as something that might almost be considered a hint of a grin appeared on his face.

"Not I. You are correct to think such." His voice was rich with warning now.

"Then you will understand my mother's request that you take your argument to my father in London. It is the only honorable thing we might say unto you. To obey you means to disobey my father, something you agree would displease you. So there is nothing to do except advise you to ride for London."

So simple and yet so devastating to what she truly wanted. Bridget bit her own lip to keep her lament private. She was disappointed, very much so. Perhaps too much so.

One dark eyebrow lifted. His chain-mail hood still covered his hair, but that single brow lifted mockingly.

"I understand how you might think that is the way things

should be. However, our union was blessed by an archbishop. It is sealed. There is no point in further discussion. You are my bride, and I am here to celebrate our wedding." His lips became a small smile. "Bridget."

He raised a hand, and his men swept inside the house. She and her mother went because the alternative was to be run into by the larger men. They worked together, leaving neither she nor her mother any space to dart around them. Of course that was no true option, not with his men making camp on the lawn. Smoke was rising above campfires now, confirming that they intended to remain through the night.

Bridget stepped into the entry hall and turned her gaze back to Curan. For all her dreaming of him, the man was a stranger, a hardened knight who did not resemble the fables written in her books.

And he considered her his. Heat touched her cheeks as she considered how close she might be to discovering what it felt like to do all the things Marie had shown her. Of course she did not think this man would need very much enticement to enter her bed.

Yet I wonder if he would still enjoy being Frenched . . .

She shook her head. Such ideas were misplaced under the circumstances. Wedding against her father's wishes would spell disaster. There were not even convents in England any longer for her to be banished to once her sire hunted her down.

"You need to see reason, Sir Curan." Bridget tried to moderate her voice. It proved a difficult task with her temper so hot. She was not normally given to such high emotions but could not seem to cool the flames.

"Save your pleading, madam."

His voice was stone hard, his attention on the three trunks waiting by the door. He looked up at her mother first.

"Be very sure that I shall have correspondence with your husband upon this betrayal of my trust."

Jane straightened her back. "These are uncertain times, Sir Curan. It may be that my husband was ordered to arrange a new match by the king himself."

Two of the knights behind Curan seemed to consider that amusing. Their lips twitched up, and one even cleared his throat to avoid laughing out loud.

"In that case, you shall be relieved to know that I came from Henry's side just two days past with his expressed good wishes on my union." He shifted his attention to her for a moment. "And it is Lord Ryppon now. A barony bestowed on me for service well tendered."

"Congratulations, my Lord Ryppon." He watched her intently, but she did not shift from her position. "It is unfortunate you were unable to meet with my father while in London. Surely that would have been most fortuitous."

He stepped toward her. One hand rose into the air. There was a scuff of booted feet against the stone floor and a soft exclamation from her mother. But Curan's men swept her from the room in a smooth motion in response to their leader's command. For the first time she felt icy anxiety grip her. Bridget refused to label it fear. She would not cower.

He took a quick look over his shoulder to ensure that they were alone.

"Your father managed to be sealed behind closed doors each time I attempted to converse with him."

"He is very busy with serving the king."

"Or Chancellor Wriothesley." Suspicion edged his tone. His dark eyes cut into hers. He took another step toward her. It brought him within arm's length. For some reason she was keenly aware of how simple it might be for him to touch her.

Lift that large hand and stroke the fingers across her cheek as he had in the past. It seemed so very long ago right then.

"What I wish to know, madam, is what means these trunks?"

His question sliced through her distracted thoughts. She stepped away from him, drawing a disapproving look from him.

"As I told you, my father bid me to travel to London."

"And you planned to do so in spite of your vows to me?"

He pressed his lips into a hard line. His face darkened with judgment before she had a chance to answer. His hand did reach out between them but only to point one finger at her.

"We are bound by the blessing of the church, and I shall have my wife."

"But my father—"

"Pressed his signet ring to the parchment in front of my own eyes and that of an archbishop, too." His fingers curled into a fist. "Go to your chamber, Bridget. We shall ride for the border at dawn. I suggest you rest while the sun is down, for the day will be long. Go now, I needs have words with your mother."

"My mother is a good wife; you should not be angry with her."

His expression became even more disapproving. She could see his temper flickering in his eyes now. A muscle twitched on the side of his jaw, betraying how greatly she vexed him.

"And I am a knight. Your concern insults my honor. I will have words with your mother, nothing else." He drew in a deep breath and snapped his fingers. She heard the solid step of boots on the floor in response. She shivered, not having considered that he might set his men to guarding her.

His eyebrow dipped in response. A tiny response of concern that did not last long. Yet he reached out and gently stroked her face. His touch burned, the heat shooting down her body so quickly she felt light-headed. She stiffened and stepped away without thinking. There was no consideration, only response.

"I will forgive you the slight to my good nature for the sake of how strange we are to each other. We will celebrate our union at Amber Hill."

He didn't wait for a response. His fingers gestured to whomever he'd summoned. The knight moved instantly, closing the space between them until he was close enough to reach for her. He didn't, though. The man inclined his head with respect and gestured to the doorway that led to the stairs. A look into Curan's eyes showed her a man with no mercy. Only solid determination stared back at her.

She would not disgrace herself by being dragged away by his men. Besides, she felt more like demanding that he see her dilemma. She lifted her chin and left. The knight followed her silently all the way to her chamber, yet the man did not leave. He joined another who stood outside her chamber door. She closed the door, but a quick look out the small hatch that allowed her to see anyone who wanted entry showed her the pair of knights keeping guard over her.

That dread returned, clasping its icy fingers around her neck. Never once had she been imprisoned. Nor had her honor been questioned. A person was nothing without their word. Especially a woman. She walked in a wide circle, her thoughts churning. Never before had she questioned her father's honor, yet there was no way to avoid it, considering the circumstances. She had taken vows. How then did she go to London? Even at her sire's command?

The world was a far kinder place for men. Curan did not have as much to lose as she. Her father controlled whom that dowry was paid to. If she married against her father's wishes, her dowry might be withheld, or end in the wrong hands, thereby leaving Curan the legal right to divorce her and send her back to her father without her virtue. It might take years in court to sort the matter. For all Curan's insistence, men often changed their minds when there was money to be considered. He might take her virtue and turn her out when the dowry was denied him. He would be free to contract another wife.

She would be soiled and labeled a disobedient daughter. No one would shed any tears of pity for her. It would be quite the opposite. Mothers would point out her flaws as lessons for their own daughters. Her own mother might refuse to shelter her for disobeying her father's command on whom to marry. She might end in the street. It was a mess, to be sure. In decades past, many who found themselves in such a quandary had fled to convents. The church welcomed them because the clergy was wise and patient. Restitution was always made by the court to a religious order, even if it took twenty years. Being a nun was preferable to whoring on the dockside to keep yourself from starvation.

But you want to lie with him . . .

Her thoughts might be wicked, yet she could not deny the truth of them. She did want to be Curan's wife. Even more so now than when she had met him for their vows. His touch made her quiver, not a fearful sort of thing but one that shook her all the way to her toes. She could feel it traveling over her skin, chasing the chill away. Little bumps rose up on top of her arms and legs. Her breasts tingled before the nipples drew into pebbles.

Was that arousal?

Marie's words came to mind. Was this the thing that would make it easier to endure penetration? Her cheeks flamed brighter.

You do not wish mere comfort, you want the same pleasure you witnessed.

Indeed she did, but at what cost? She needed to focus on the future that would come after she had yielded her innocence. Of course, she might conceive, making it very difficult to discard her, but not impossible.

She was still pacing and stopped when a trickle of sweat ran down the side of her face. Her skin was unusually sensitive. She realized how grimy she felt, the day of packing having left its mark.

Turning around, she went to the only things she had left in the room. A clean chemise and surcoat. After picking them up, she turned toward the door. The knights were still there, and they frowned when she opened the door.

"I am going below to bathe."

One of them snapped his mouth shut quickly and considered her words. Bridget did not linger in the doorway. Striding forward, she descended the stairs but heard their boots hitting the floor behind her. Each footfall felt as if it pierced her. It was an effort not to wince. Only prisoners were guarded, and this lack of trust grated against her pride.

She moved faster, seeking out the privacy of the bathing room. It was next to the kitchens to make it easier to have warm water placed into the tubs. Theirs was a simple life with no time for hauling water to the upper floor. Such would be a selfish act. Her mother had raised her to be a good steward of the estate, thinking of the overall well-being of everyone instead of her own comforts.

The kitchens were built along the back of the house, a separate building to reduce the risk of fire. But wooden troughs were built between the walls of the kitchen and the bathroom. A pull on the bell cord and water could be dumped into one of the troughs in the kitchen, which would spill into one of the large tubs kept in the bathing room. There were three tubs and two others used for laundry. Bridget could feel the heat ten paces before entering the doorway. A splash made her stop. There was no way to keep her eyes from falling on the very bare shoulders of the man in one of those tubs. They were wide and covered in thick muscle.

"Who has come to help me?"

Curan sounded amused, and he turned with a grin on his lips. Surprise flickered in his eyes. His attention shifted to the two knights behind her and then onto the clothing draped over her arm. His lips twitched, and something flickered in his eyes that reminded her very much of Tomas when he looked at Marie.

"So you've come to help me as a wife should? How delightful. My back welcomes your sweet hands."

Chapter Three

She didn't have to remain.

Oh, yes you do, or he will call you coward, and it shall be the truth.

Bathing a guest was a time-honored trait of hospitality. Bridget was surprised her mother wasn't in the room. She worried her lower lip. Considering how unhappy Curan was with her mother's insistence that he return to London, maybe it was no surprise that he was bathing alone. Women might be legally chattel, but annoying the lady of the house was not a wise choice unless you enjoyed being overlooked by the staff.

"Unless you are too timid, Bridget."

Challenge coated his words along with an arrogance that sent her temper back into flames.

"That is not a word I have heard used to describe me before."

He turned his head and eyed her. The scrutiny needled her. Walking over to one of the clothing racks in the room, she laid her things on it. Set near the fire, the rack would allow the garments to be warmed while she bathed. A pair of britches was already there, along with a creamy shirt. Her gaze lingered on the male clothing for a moment.

"Good. I've little tolerance for timidity."

"Is that another warning I should heed?"

Pausing to roll up her sleeves, Bridget kept her eyes on the fabric. She refused to worry if the man's ego was bruised by her question. He was the one tossing out barbed comments, after all. She refused to buckle in the face of a few harsh words. A desire to show that to him refused to allow her to maintain a demure silence.

"It is not."

There was a hint of remorse in his tone. But when she raised her eyes she found him watching her. Heat teased her cheeks almost instantly. Her poise deserted her for a moment, her eyelashes fluttering and breaking their connection. She detested the way she responded to him. Forcing herself to look straight at him, she refused to appear submissive. Let the man see that she was not some marzipan bride who would be easily molded to suit his ego, so perfectly molded into the ideal of beauty but with no strength.

This defiant gaze allowed her to view him completely. He had dark hair that was shiny from the water and curling gently across his forehead. There was nothing boyish about him. Not a hint of weakness anywhere on him. His shoulders were cut with thick muscles. Beginning at his wrists, his forearms were corded. That same condition continued up his arms, where his biceps rose into thick display. His chest was wide and had a sprinkling of dark hair across its expanse. She moved her gaze over his square-cut jaw to discover his eyes glittering.

More heat surfaced in her face. She glided toward him, reaching for the soap neatly laid out next to the tub. Bathing guests was a tradition because keeping fleas out of the house was a Herculean task that fell to the women. It was easier to control the pestilence by seeing to the scrubbing of all their guests.

She had assisted her mother many times, but today she paused before beginning the task in front of her. Touching

Curan, even the idea of it, still caused a quaking inside her. Sending her hand along his shoulder, she hoped that the first contact might banish the anticipation, but it did not. Instead, she had to tighten her fingers on the soap to maintain her grasp on the slippery bar. A faint hint of rosemary arose from it. He leaned forward to allow her to wash more of his back.

Marie's lessons suddenly surfaced above the strange quivering inside her, capturing most of her attention. The courtesan had never rushed. Drawing a deep breath, Bridget slowed her own motions, taking more time to smooth the soap across his shoulder blades. She made several lazy passes, making sure to work up a good lather before setting the bar aside and taking up a cloth. Even through the fabric, she felt the heat of his body. Her fingertips suddenly became more sensitive. They wanted to discover what he felt like when there was nothing between them at all.

Soon enough . . .

It was stunning how quickly her body responded to that idea. A flush of heat poured over her. No hint of night chill was left anywhere on her body. She was warm from head to toe, even longing to remove her outer dress.

"I enjoy your hands on me, Bridget."

She fumbled the cloth, tightening her fingers to keep it in her grasp. A tiny gasp crossed her lips, and she looked at him to judge if he had heard it. There was no way to tell from the back of him. He stretched his hands out to the foot of the tub so that she might reach all the way down to his lower back.

"I believe I shall take to bathing twice a day."

His words were arrogant, but her temper did not flare up. Instead her attention was captured by the hint of huskiness in his tone. She had heard it in Tomas's voice, too. That bit of knowledge filled her with confidence. It was an odd feeling that combined with the quiver that touching him produced.

She leaned over to work the cloth down his spine, and her senses filled with the scent of his skin.

It was dark and very male. What surprised her was the way she enjoyed it. Her nipples hardened even further. They ached behind her stays. Only this time she knew exactly what the little points craved.

The touch of his lips against them.

She trembled and hurried through the last few motions of washing his back. Becoming prey to lust would not assist her. She longed to have that last lesson with Marie. Maybe the courtesan would have given her instructions that would have enabled her to control her responses.

But that was not to be. So she reached for a small jug and pushed it beneath the surface of the water to fill it. Curan made a soft sound of enjoyment when she poured it over his back to rinse the soap away.

"Now my hair."

He remained in place, with his head bent over the water.

You have washed many a head of hair, you ninny . . .

Not on a man she longed to touch, however. After pouring more water over his head, she set the jug aside. Her heart seemed to be working faster than it should be. Her breaths came in short gasps, too. Anticipation twisted in her belly so tight, she felt as if it would snap her in two.

"Come, Bridget, I believe you said you were not timid."

His tone was still husky, but the mocking amusement mixed with it did stoke her temper. The flames burned away enough of her unsteadiness to allow her command of her hands.

"I did not realize you were in a hurry, my lord. Forgive me for taking up so much of your time." Her voice was perfectly mild and polite. A true credit to every tutor her parents had paid to instruct her. She might have been talking about the laundry for all the emotion in her tone. If he wanted to treat her like a toy, she would give him the personality of a wooden top.

His face turned in an instant, his dark eyes stabbing into hers. He captured her hands that were reaching for his hair. His fingers curled easily all the way around her wrists to clamp them in a grip that felt like steel. Hunger danced in his eyes. And he tensed, as though he were going to rise. Her breath caught in her throat while she waited to see what he would do.

"I suppose toying with you means that I deserve the same in return."

"I do not know what you mean."

His lips pressed into a hard line while he considered her.

"Maybe not. Then again, maybe you are an accomplished female when it comes to twisting men."

She dropped the soap. It sent water splashing up into his face. He shut his eyes quickly to avoid having the strong lye soap burn them. Any other time she would have been mortified to cause such concern to a guest. Yet for the moment, she was quite pleased.

"I have done no practicing on any men. I have never even bathed one before without my mother present, sir. You are the one who bid me enter else wear the title of timid."

He released her wrists and drew his forearm across his face. But when he opened his eyes they glittered with amusement. A soft male chuckle filled the chamber.

"I suppose I have been in the company of men too long and forgotten that women do not enjoy being teased. Still, I find your tenacity enjoyable."

"You were being insulting, my lord."

He laughed at her words. This time it was a full sound of amusement. One hand disappeared into the water and retrieved the bar of soap.

"Possibly. Maybe I was merely admitting that having your hands on me twists my emotions."

She almost dropped the soap again. Something crossed his face that fascinated her, something hard and hungry. The quiver inside her responded to it and increased tenfold.

He looked down again, but the hands that rested on the edge of the tub were gripping it. She stared at the white knuckles for a moment before drawing a deep breath. So strange. Yet so intoxicating. Reaching over the edge of the tub, she began washing his hair. It was silky-soft and thick. She had to work the soap into a lather and curl her hands to find his scalp. When she poured water over his head to rinse it, he shook like a large hunting hound. He scraped a hand down his face and opened his eyes before she had time to reach for a dry cloth for him.

His face reflected his dislike of being blind. That made sense. A man such as he most likely did not allow his guard down very often. He took the cloth from her hands anyway and dried his face with it. But when he pulled it away from his face, his lips were sitting in a mocking grin.

A second later he stood up. Water ran down his body, glistening in the firelight and turning him crimson. She couldn't keep her gaze from tracing his long legs or from looking at his cock. It stood tall and proud, thicker than Tomas's and longer, too.

"Aren't you going to wash the rest of me, Bridget?"

He was toying with her again. She raised her eyes to his, determination making her bold.

"It is a truth that I have never washed the front of a male guest. My mother would never allow such. Yet who am I to argue with a baron?"

She picked up the cloth and swiped the soap across it with a quick stroke. His forehead furrowed when she extended her hand toward him. But she did not aim for his cock. Marie's slow motions sprang to mind. She slid the cloth over his thigh, making sure to wash all of it from his hip to his knee. His leg was just as hard as his back, her fingertips communicating how solid he was. Even with her eyelids lowered and her gaze focused on his thigh she caught glimpses of his cock. She simply could not prevent herself from stealing quick looks at his manhood. The thing seemed to swell and grow larger while she worked.

Dunking the cloth in the water, she then applied more soap to it before washing his opposite leg. She refused to look up to see what he thought of her actions. There was the chance that he might consider her glance a plea for reprieve. Her pride forbade her to do anything that might be interpreted in such a way.

Washing his other thigh seemed to take only half the time. She was too aware of what stood between them. That hard flesh was the only thing left to wash. Maintaining her grip on the cloth, she slid it along his inner thigh. Higher and higher until she cupped the twin sacs hanging below his staff. He shuddered. Just a tiny amount, but she saw his powerful legs move. It restored her confidence. She gently rubbed those sacs before gliding the washcloth along the length of his erect flesh.

"You have made your point, Bridget."

He sat down too quickly. Water sloshed over the edges of the tub. She sprang away, but was too slow; water soaked into her skirts. She landed on her bottom in a pile of wool while the water made it all the way to her legs.

But the scowl on his face made it worth getting wet. He glared at her, his fingers rubbing against one another.

"I don't know what point you mean. Unless it is that I am bendable to your will."

Pushing her feet beneath her, she rose. Her wet skirt stuck to her legs and pulled down on her waist. It made the fabric too long in front, so she grasped a handful of fabric and pulled it up.

"I would not say bendable. 'Tis more like you are challenged by my demands."

She looked down to avoid his seeing how much pleasure his words gave her. He sounded too pleased by far. Like a boy who had discovered a new game where he could be the victor. Yet she was pleased. There was no denying that she enjoyed knowing that he did not find her meek. If that was a sin, she was guilty.

"Since you have aided me so sweetly, I believe I shall return the favor."

Her head jerked up to meet his eyes. "What do you mean?" She sounded too breathless. Swallowing hard, she tried to force her nervousness down where it would not be so noticeable.

He pointed at the drying rack. "You came to bathe. A rather good idea since we are to take to the road on the morrow." His lips resumed that mocking grin she detested. "I will remain and wash your back."

"That is not the custom."

His grin faded. "Neither is departing for London to wed another when you have already had the blessing of the church given to you to wed with me."

"You may say that as often as you like, and still I will not change my response to you, Lord Ryppon. I am not ashamed of being obedient to my father's will. He is the one who commanded me to kneel beside you."

His face was set into a disapproving mask, but it suddenly broke when he chuckled. "I am pleasantly surprised by how much courage you have, Bridget."

It was a compliment. She turned and busied herself with taking the used washcloth to the basket for soiled linens. She heard the water swish behind her and his wet feet connecting with the floor. He must have tugged the little cork stopper from the bottom of the tub, because the sound of rushing water filled the chamber. Gravity took the water away from the tub through a hole in the stone floor that led to a carefully maintained gutter beneath the house. Such a design allowed for bathing year-round and was a sign of the more modern construction of the estate. The bathing chamber had only been added a few years ago after her father had seen one at the palace. He'd had to bribe the royal guards to get a look at the king's newest comfort, but he'd declared it well worth every bit of silver to not suffer stinking during the winter.

She felt a prickle along her nape and looked up to discover Curan within arm's reach. He moved quickly for so large a man, a length of toweling wrapped around his waist now, but the fabric was wet and lying over the hard shape of his erection.

"I am grateful that you respected your father's wishes to wed me."

"We are not completely wed."

He reached past her and picked up his britches. "Then why did you just stroke my cock?"

He whispered the words, but that did not lessen their impact.

"You should not say such things."

His hand reached out and captured her upper arm. A moment later she was pressed against him with a hard arm securing her around her waist.

"I enjoyed it."

Three words had never sounded so enticing before.

She was captivated by the sound of his voice and the flicker of hunger in his eyes. The hands that she'd laid on his chest to push him back flattened. Her fingers spread wide in enjoyment. His skin was warm and his flesh firm beneath her hands. It was a delight for the senses. Pleasure began seeping past her temper. The sweet sensation produced by their skin meeting swiftly became more important than whatever had upset her.

"And now I wish to see you enjoy my touch."

He angled his head and pressed a soft kiss against her mouth. She sprang away from it, using her hands to push him back, a soft growl her response. A moment later the arm around her waist slipped right up her back, pulling her toward him again. His other arm encircled her waist, and her hands became trapped between them.

"Accept my kiss, Bridget. It is my right to taste you."

It was a command, one given in a husky tone. He didn't wait for her to agree, his lips pressing against hers in a hard kiss that demanded compliance. But it was not unpleasant. Her lips tingled and her belly tightened. He slipped his lips across hers, teasing the tender skin with his own. Pleasure rippled through her when he took instant advantage of her open mouth, the tip of his tongue sweeping along her lower lip before venturing inside her mouth. A soft sound issued from her, but she wasn't sure if it was distress or delight. She shivered in his embrace, her body twisting as she became overwhelmed by too much sensation. His tongue boldly penetrated her mouth, stabbing deep inside to stroke her own. The feeling was too much to understand. She struggled to pull her lips away from his only to hear her own breath gasping when she succeeded. Her hands strained to push him away. Her strength was nothing compared to his. One of his hands cupped her nape and turned her to face him.

"Look at me."

She couldn't seem to resist. Even as her body burned with a multitude of impulses, she was eager to look into his eyes. Drawn there for some reason. The hold on her neck became tender, his fingers stroking the soft skin beneath her braid.

She was not frightened. Bridget ordered herself to meet his gaze. His dark eyes were full of hunger. She understood what he craved. Beneath the layers of her clothing, her passage was heating and yearning for exactly the same thing. She felt empty. Never had she noticed her passage so aching to be filled. She craved the same penetration she had witnessed Marie receiving. Call her wanton, yet she was honest enough to admit her hunger.

"I will not take you here, beneath your father's roof." Pride edged his words. "We will consummate our vows at Amber Hill. That is more fitting."

A muscle jerked on the side of his jaw. His attention dropped to her mouth for a long moment, and his arms tightened around her. But he suddenly released her and turned his back on her. The toweling dropped, and Bridget turned to avoid looking at his naked body again. The sight was too much to resist. She forgot every reason not to touch him when her sight was filled with his bare form. Never had she considered that she would find a male body so pleasing. Curan's body drew her attention to each hard ridge of muscle and then onto the rigid cock standing proudly between his thighs. Obviously she was too weak to resist temptation.

She heard him dressing, the sounds of fabric being drawn over his body a relief, but it also drew a lament from her.

He turned with his shirt still untied.

"Finish dressing me, Bridget."

Confusion drew her lips into a frown. He reached out and lifted her chin.

"I enjoyed your hands on me when you did it of your own free will. I would have such again."

"As you will."

It was an unpolished response. But her mind was crowded with too many sensations and the impulses they drew from her. She could not seem to sort it all into any manner of logical understanding. But her hands lifted and smoothed his collar into place before tying the ribbons to close it. Part of her raged against the action. But she finished and took up the ribbons that would close the cuff of his shirt. Her fingertips lay against his inner wrist for a moment, and then the contact was severed when she pulled the laces. She bit into her lower lip. Concentration seemed to elude her when he was near—quite bothersome, but exciting, too. In truth, she longed to be out of his sight for a few moments to compose herself.

But he wanted to wash her back.

She continued to worry her lower lip. There was no way to leave without turning coward. Maybe she should. He liked her courage. If she showed him weakness, the man might very well turn his back on her.

Every fiber of her person rebelled against that thought. Whether it was because her pride refused or her body, she didn't know.

But she stood back and reached for one of the pins holding her braids to her head and tugged it free. He watched her. Her stomach tightened with nervousness. But Marie's lessons surfaced above the tension. Taking a few steps away from him, she peeked over her shoulder and drew another pin. His face became hard and unreadable, but his gaze followed her hand with absolute devotion. A few more pins and her braids loosened before falling down her back. She placed the pins aside before turning and slowly untying one of the ribbons that kept her hair braid from unlacing.

Heat filled her once more. She could feel his eyes on her, watching her every motion. This knowledge bred another form of excitement in her, a new understanding of her own attractiveness. She had never been vain, but this was different, having nothing to do with the dress she wore and everything to do with how she looked without fashion's creations. Her fingers began to tremble, making it harder to untie the second ribbon. But she finished loosening her hair, and a shaky breath rattled her when she finished. She had to force herself to look at him. But once she did, she was hypnotized by his dark eyes. Hunger blazed there, a deep appreciation that was very male and very intimate.

He moved forward, reaching out to finger a lock of her hair. For such a simple touch, her body responded violently. She shuddered and drew a rough breath. Her hair slipped over his fingers, and his eyes narrowed.

"I regret that I am going to fail to repay the kind service you did for me, Bridget." He pulled his gaze from where her hair was draped over his fingers to look at her face. What blazed in his eyes unsettled her. He had appeared so strong and disciplined. At that moment, though, something wild lurked in his eyes. "But I must confess that I doubt my own ability to keep my word on not taking you beneath this roof if I remain."

He lifted a handful of hair to his face and drew in a deep breath. His eyes closed and his face became a mask of enjoyment. It was mesmerizing. Bridget stared at it and still found it difficult to believe that she might inspire such a look, especially on such a man. Perhaps a boy might appear so enthralled but not a mature knight such as Curan. Her hair looked delicate against his fingers. Her head did not reach to his chin, and she felt small next to him.

"Until later, Bridget. No one will disturb you."

He turned and left with that final warning spoken. Her arms came up to hug her body as all of the heat he'd inspired left her. Her body became chilled, and the need pooling in her belly made it ache.

It was by far the most confusing thing.

Curan didn't sleep very much. His discipline failed him. After only a few hours of rest his mind became too crowded with thoughts to sleep. He knew better, had served too many days on hostile soil to not take sleep when he might.

His bride was a distraction.

Of course that was not something to be lamented. Most men battled to find enough interest in their negotiated wives to beget their heirs. His cock throbbed softly with unsatisfied hunger. It would seem that he would not have to suffer that difficulty.

Bridget's mother descended the stairs at the first sign of light on the horizon. Lady Connolly clearly was not content with his intention to claim her daughter. The woman strode straight up to him without flinching. It was clear where Bridget learned her courage from.

Jane did not lower her eyes.

"You should understand that these times call for adjustments."

"What I understand, madam, are things that you do not know of." Her demeanor softened, allowing Curan to moderate his tone. "Your husband is a compatriot of Chancellor Wriothesley."

"I am aware of that."

"Are you likewise aware of the fact that Lord Oswald is another compatriot of the chancellor?"

Jane clasped her hands tightly together. "Your tone implies that you are angry with my husband's choices."

"I am certainly not happy to discover my bride being read-
ied to travel to another man's bed."

"My daughter was heading to the marriage her father
arranged for her. Not to be anyone's mistress."

Curan drew himself up in the face of her outrage. He did
not suffer such a tone from many men and even fewer
women. Yet the woman was insulted on behalf of her daughter, and that was a just cause. He had spent his entire adult life
serving honor. A mother was right to defend her daughter's
name.

"I should have said marriage."

Jane looked ready to argue further, but she paused and bit
back her reply.

"The king sent me here to claim my bride. With full knowledge that I plan to take her to my border holding and settle
into family life."

Jane's face became one of confusion. "Yet my husband
writes of a very different course for Bridget. I cannot ignore
his summons."

Curan drew in a stiff breath. "Court is a place full of men
trying to achieve their own goals." He paused for a long moment, clearly weighing his next words. "The chancellor is rumored to be seeking evidence against Queen Catherine Parr."

"*What?* That is madness. I hear nothing but good tidings
concerning our queen. She is a devoted wife." Jane's eyes
went large.

"Yet she would not be the first queen brought low by men
seeking to install some other in her place."

Jane's face drained of color. "You should not say such
things. I shall not have such things spoken of beneath my roof,
be you noble or common."

"A wise rule to keep."

She shot him a hard look. "I do not understand what you

are hinting at, Lord Ryppon. It still remains that I was doing only as instructed by my husband. You should understand that being dutiful is not something that may be questioned."

"I do." He stepped closer but took a look abou᠁ ᠁ see if there was anyone listening. "Yet I believe that your ᠁᠁and is placing his name on a very risky gamble. If the chancellor is working to bring down the queen, be very sure that blood will flow."

She nodded and began to make the sign of the cross over herself. Curan captured her wrist, stopping her.

"Careful, lady. There are men with me who have family related to these men of whom we speak. You are not the only one who will have your loyalties tested by this scheme. Do not give them hints as to what we discuss."

She clasped her hands together once more. "Of course. You are correct. Yet I still do not understand what you want here."

"I came for Bridget. She is my bride, and I plan to protect what is mine, even if her father is intent on placing her in the center of this plot." He lowered his tone. "I will not allow anyone to do that."

The woman didn't argue further. She considered him with eyes that were full of distrust. Curan understood that. Chancellor Wriothesley and his compatriots were plotting a very dangerous thing. Personally, he felt they were fools. The king was dying even if no one dared say it. Soon England would have a boy on its throne, and the man favored to become regent was in love with Catherine Parr. Any man who plotted against her risked a great deal more than his own life. His family and estates might become forfeit. The chancellor knew that and was trying to tie as many men to the scheme as possible. Lord Oswald would be bought with Bridget. The man was old noble blood with many connections, his only weakness a liking for young girls in his bed.

He had made a mistake in casting his eye on what Curan believed was his. The Earl of Pemshire had repaid him well in making him wise of the plot. He would allow no man to take Bridget from him. Only duty had done that so far.

Yet his time was done, at least in France. Henry Tudor had made his last campaign. The next few years would be unsettled times for England. Holding his border lands against Scottish invasion was his new duty.

"I would bid farewell to my daughter."

Jane's voice was smooth now. She offered him a curtsy before leaving the room. Curan watched her go. Suspicion ate at him. He allowed it to burn in his gut for a time. He was still alive due to heeding his instincts. But even if he did not trust the lady, he could not decide what she might do that would cause him worry. He had the church's blessing and Bridget's father's seal on the parchment agreeing to his marriage. Jane was one woman against his entire army. Instructing her daughter to hate him was the worst she might do.

But the kiss he'd shared with Bridget was all he needed to dispel any worry about that. His bride was not cold toward him. His cock stirred behind his britches. He was likewise anything but unmoved by her. If he had kissed her that way three years ago, he would have found a way to consummate their union sooner.

He walked to the doorway and looked at the pink fingers of dawn cutting through the night. Soon enough he would have her. The trunks drew his attention. They intensified his need to take to the road and gain the high ground before those plotting men in London knew what he was about.

Her sweet kiss only made him more anxious. But it was something he allowed himself to enjoy. Once they departed he would have to focus on the protection of his men and bride. Nothing was certain in these days. He planned to keep his mind on the matter of making it home, not on what delights awaited him once he arrived with his bride.

For the next few minutes while he watched the horizon surrender to the sun, however, he indulged himself in allowing his thoughts to dwell on the moment when Bridget would surrender to him.

Chapter Four

Curan was a confident commander.

Bridget watched him from her second-floor room. Dawn was turning the sky pink. Even before what she would call daylight, his men were rising. The few tents they had erected were being disassembled in the meager light.

A knock at her door startled her. Whoever it was did not wait for her to respond, either. The door was pulled open by one of the knights standing outside. A little sigh of relief passed her lips when she saw her mother standing there.

"Good. You are awake." Jane entered the room and turned to make sure the door closed completely behind her.

"I did not sleep long."

Her mother came closer and took her by the hand. She led her to the far side of the chamber in front of the window.

"There is nothing I can do to stop Lord Ryppon from taking you." Her mother scanned the men below. "In truth, I am not sure I should."

"What do you mean?"

Her mother was pale. There was fear in her eyes Bridget could not recall seeing before, except for the brief time her brother had been ill and the physician suspected smallpox.

"Lord Ryppon claims there is a plot to gather evidence against the queen and that your father is helping those who would see her brought low."

Bridget felt her own face drain of color. Her mother's hands tightened around hers. Men made decisions that too often had terrible effects on the women in their families. If her father or brother became entangled in a scheme against the queen, the entire family would be stained. Their lands possibly forfeit. She and her mother would become beggars at the tables of their relatives.

"Lord Ryppon claims that the king is dying."

That at least made sense. No one dared say Henry Tudor was dying. There were men who would try to gain the king's favor by delivering anyone foolish enough to say such a thing out loud as a possible treason plotter.

That did not keep many from thinking that the king's days were drawing to an end. Times were turbulent indeed. Henry's only son was a boy too young to rule. That fact would plunge England into dark days filled with regents and noble families struggling for power. Marriage was a common way of uniting those powerful names, yet if the king discovered the vultures gathering to feast on what he left behind, Bridget doubted there would be any mercy in him. No man liked to admit his own mortality, and Henry Tudor would be no different.

"I cannot go to London."

It didn't matter if it was a disobedience against her father. Bridget felt her stomach clench at the mere idea of riding into the swirling plots circling the king. Only a fool sought such a fate, or a woman who was greedy for power. She had lived this long without it. Marie's words rose from her memory.

Bridget stared at her mother. "I will not go there, Mother." Her voice was edged with respect but full of determination.

"I do not believe that Lord Ryppon intends to allow you a choice on where you go, Bridget."

That brought her a measure of relief. Her mother read it off her face.

"That does not mean you should celebrate your marriage, Bridget."

Frustration filled her. "What is it you suggest I do, Mother? He has every right and an army to enforce his will."

Her mother nodded. "I know. Yet I fear for you if you go to his bed. Your father has powerful friends. To lie with Lord Ryppon is an insult to Lord Oswald now that your father has given the man his word on a match between you."

"Mother—"

"Forgive me, Bridget; I know I am making no sense." Jane cast a look behind her to ensure they were still alone. "You should allow Lord Ryppon to take you north."

Excitement flickered in her belly. Bridget looked down to conceal the unexpected response from her mother. But Jane cupped her chin and lifted it.

"Your cousin Alice is married to a Scot. Their land borders Lord Ryppon's."

"Of course, that is why father arranged this match."

Her mother sighed. "Well, one of the reasons, Daughter. There are others, but it appears that your father feels those reasons have diminished compared to the gains he might secure with Lord Oswald."

"You want me to seek Alice for sanctuary?" The idea sounded absurd but she could think of nothing else her mother might be suggesting. Yet she had not seen Alice since they were children, and Scotland was not a place for an English noblewoman to venture into without a great deal of thought. As well as prayer.

Jane's face lit with satisfaction. "Yes." She pressed a small bag into Bridget's hands. It was heavy with coin. "Use this gold to bribe Lord Ryppon's men once you are on his land. Go by night, and your cousin will give you shelter. I will write to her today so that she expects you. Make sure you only bribe someone without a sword. If a man carries a sword with Sir Curan, I doubt his loyalty is for sale."

Bridget looked at the small purse; it reminded her of a serpent because it would indeed give her the means to escape Curan. The memory of his kiss rose thick and hot from her mind.

A heavy knock made them both jump. It was loud enough to echo off the far wall of the chamber. Only a man's fist made such volume of noise.

"Well now. Up with you, Bridget." Her mother offered her a smile that she knew was false. It was the expression she used when hiding her true feelings behind a lady's manners. Bridget responded with a similar one. Genuine approval brightened her mother's eyes. Bridget savored the moment and tried not to think that it might be the last time she saw such.

"Lord Ryppon has called for you, Lady Bridget."

The knights who had been guarding her door stepped into the chamber. Distaste for invading her personal room flickered in their eyes, but they did not retreat. Instead they halted a few paces into the room, leaving a space between them for her to pass.

"I will get your surcoat." Jane turned to retrieve the garment from where Bridget had laid it across the foot of her bed. Tears stung Bridget's eyes, and she turned to hide her moment of weakness from Curan's men.

Grabbing her gloves, she pushed her right hand into one while blinking away her melancholy. When she finished, her composure was firm once more. Her mother held out the surcoat and helped ease the heavy wool garment up onto her shoulders.

"Remember what I have told you, Bridget, and all will be well."

To the knights, her mother's words were innocent. Both of them stood unalarmed and relieved to see her making ready to depart.

"I shall, Mother."

Jane cupped her cheeks. "And do not forget your lessons."

Bridget felt her cheeks color, but her confidence swelled, too. A naughty little smile replaced the polished proper one. Her mother returned it.

"I shall, Mother. Indeed, I shall."

The man was insufferable.

Bridget stared at the inside of the wagon cover and allowed her lips to curl into a snarl.

A wagon. The man had her loaded and transferred like a sack of grain. It was an insult. There were horses aplenty, and yet she sat on the floor of a wagon bed. A bit of guilt pricked her. In truth, someone had gone to trouble on her behalf. A thick wool blanket was folded and placed beneath her. Two large bedding rolls were pushed against the sides to form a corner that was soft. They kept her from knocking her elbows against the hard sides while she was jostled about.

The cover was stretched over a rounded frame of poles. No one could see in unless she opened the corner near her. The sound of horses and men filled her ears. Bridget could hear the plates that made up their armor hitting against each other with every step of their mounts, swords clanging against belts, and the creak of the wagons. Even if she weren't alone, the noise level was too high to compete with. There was little to do. She left the cover in place for the first hour, not trusting her discipline to witness the last sight of her home. It was better not to dwell.

Yet that left her battling with her temper. She adored riding, the wind chilling her cheeks and the feel of the powerful animal beneath her. Sitting in a wagon was dull and turning her stomach queasy. Even when she looked out, she could not see forward. A cloth sat near her with bread and cheese. It was good fare for traveling, but her belly protested. She sipped at the wine, but even that brought another threatening heave from her stomach.

Well, she did not need very much strength under the circumstances. A few missed meals would not be so difficult to bear. Once she reached Amber Hill that would change. She would need all her strength and more to cross the border into Scotland.

Should she?

The question occupied her thoughts for hours. The times were so perilous. A woman was nothing without her family. Wedding against her father's wishes would not be wise. Such disobedience might even have an effect on her mother. After all, it was her mother's duty to raise the children to respect the master of the house.

Bridget felt her throat tighten. Indeed, she could see that Curan would not be a man who would shoulder anything that was not to his liking, either.

She sighed and flipped the wagon cover up to look out. The line of wagons appeared endless, as did the number of men. Her mind had been set on the realities of becoming a wife, but she had never expected to feel so out of place when she departed with her groom. The movement of the wagon cover drew instant attention. These men were fresh from hostile soil, and they looked at her the moment her face was in sight. Their attention left her just as quickly, clearly making it known that they considered her their master's possession, his personal property.

Was it respect? She honestly doubted. Still, the manner in which they looked away suggested that they were granting her an honor by not imposing on her modesty. That was chivalrous, something spoken of in legends.

Curan didn't call a halt until the sun was almost gone. Light was meager, and his men hurried to build fires. Bridget gratefully scooted toward the end of the wagon. Her dress and surcoat bunched up beneath her, making it a frustrating journey.

But the need for a bit of privacy was far too pressing. She made it to the end and gratefully let her feet dangle over the edge. After the entire day her muscles were sore and reluctant to work. The moment she stood up, pain shot up her legs. She forced herself forward a few steps, searching the hordes of men clustered around her.

They did their best to ignore her, which suited her needs. Grasping a handful of her heavy surcoat, she climbed the steep incline away from the road. Amazement rippled through her mind when no one shouted at her.

Gaining relief from both her body's needs had never pleased her so much, but once she finished she noticed that she was also free of the constant presence of being watched. Her shoulders were tense, muscles aching. With no one about, she lifted her arms and made wide circles with them to ease the strain. A little sound of delight passed her lips.

"My apologies for not allowing you a break to stretch."

She jumped and spun around too quickly. Her surcoat and dress kept going even though she tried to stand facing her company. The motion of the fabric pulled her out of her steps. She stumbled twice before catching herself. Heat stung her cheeks as she looked straight at the amusement decorating Curan's lips. Lifting her chin, she offered him a smooth expression.

"I assure you I am fit and able to endure, sir."

The grin melted off his lips. Still a good ten feet down the embankment, Curan had one hand resting on the pommel of his sword. His fingers were curled around it, not draped in some casual display. His gaze cut away from her to sweep the area behind her briefly.

"You shall not endure long without eating, Bridget. Did you decide not to partake of what was given to you because I neglected to allow you some privacy to attend to your body's needs?"

"No." She answered too quickly.

One dark eyebrow rose. He took several steps toward her, his longer legs covering far more distance than her small steps did. Strange how she was aware of that. Her eyes were drawn to the way his body moved, powerful, almost mesmerizing.

He stopped a single pace from her. "The fare was not to your liking?"

"It was very well." To say otherwise would be childish.

"Then explain why you did not eat."

The man was clearly accustomed to being in command. He wasn't asking; it was a command and one she was expected to quickly obey. Her eyes narrowed with annoyance.

"I should think that you would not care for a wife who complains." Gripping the front of her surcoat, she took a step away from him and back toward the men she could hear just beyond the trees that shielded them.

Curan caught her upper arm. It was quick and the grip solid. A gasp escaped her before she mustered the discipline to contain her reactions. The ease he felt in touching her was unsettling. Years had passed since even her mother had been so quick to reach for her. Odd that she had not noticed the lack of human contact until Curan placed his hand on her. A tiny flicker of pleasure filled his eyes.

"What I prefer is a wife who answers me plainly when I ask her a question, Bridget."

He was using her name on purpose, as a sort of demonstration of his claim on her. Determination flickered in his eyes, and her chin rose in response.

"Are you so set against our union that you intend to try to force me into returning you home out of pity because you will not eat? It takes a long time to weaken from hunger, lady. Longer than you think."

"I thought no such thing."

The grip on her arm tightened. "I am glad to hear you say so." He held her steady and closed the remaining distance between them. With him so close, she had to tilt her head back to maintain contact with his eyes. What she witnessed in their dark centers sent a ripple of awareness down her body. Determination, hard and unwavering, stared back at her.

She pulled against his hold. It was an impulse—her body simply tried to escape without any thought. The attempt was a waste of effort. His hand remained firmly in place, and she heard a small sound of frustration from him.

"One meal is hardly cause for an interrogation. Release me and I shall sup as I intended to do."

His forehead furrowed. "As you intended?"

"Quite so." Now her voice was firm, her chin steady as she glared at him. "You are making far too much of such a simple matter."

"Only because you seem so intent on denying me the truth of the matter. I see no reason why you cannot answer me directly."

He released her, frustration darkening his features. The action surprised her, yet also threatened to shake her composure as well. She was far too aware of how warm his touch had been, too knowing of the fact that he chose to release her and that she was not strong enough to force her will upon him.

Or was she? Marie's words suddenly rose to mind. Challenging Curan's strength with her "strength" was unwise. Drawing a slow breath, she pushed her pride aside and sweetened her voice. She forced a soft smile onto her lips and lowered her eyelashes so that her eyes were partly veiled.

"It is only a trifle. What is a bit of bread and cheese when I have done little the entire day? For certain there are more important matters for your attention."

He hooked his hands into his belt, his lips pressing into a hard line. "Do not try to placate me, Bridget. It was two meals missed, for you never broke your fast this morning."

Stubborn man, so determined to have his way, but his keen observance of her was unnerving. This attention felt so intimate. Drawing a deep breath, Bridget continued smiling at him. His eyebrows lowered; the hands gripping his belt turned white.

"As you will. The wagon sways, sir. I have not been to sea since I was a girl, but I found the sensation quite similar. It was not so great a burden that I felt the need to delay the progress of your entire army by telling you that it unsettled my stomach."

Surprise crossed his features at the simple honesty of her response.

"I am quite hungry now, I do assure you." With another soft flutter of her eyelashes, she turned and resumed walking down the hill. It was a bold move, but she kept her chin level and her pace even. Marie had been confident and smooth. Still, Bridget felt his eyes on her.

She made the bottom of the rise, and the sounds of men talking grew. The horses were quiet now, the animals eagerly chomping on their feed. Smoke teased her nose, coupled with the scent of roasting meat. That smell drew a rumble from her belly, loud and long, betraying just how empty her stomach was. Now that she thought about it, she had not supped the night before, either. The scent of food actually made her quiver. Her pace quickened; the desire to make it through the last screen of trees became intense. Was there truly fresh meat? Her belly grumbled once again.

"We need more practice on how to deal with one another, Bridget."

Curan spoke next to her ear. She felt his breath, warm against her skin, and shivered. He caught her once again, this time sliding a solid arm around her waist to stop her. He plucked her out of her steps and pulled her against his larger frame.

"I, for one, am most curious to discover just how well your confidence holds up when there is nothing to prevent us from being completely intimate."

He stood flush against her back, his body hard and large behind her. Every little sensation intensified because she could not see him. The idea of him was far more powerful than the man she saw when facing him. Gooseflesh raced across her skin, and she couldn't quite decide what to do with her hands. Her fingers released the fabric of her dress and sought out the hard arm holding her in place. But without gloves, her fingertips seemed more receptive. She felt his body heat through his clothing, and her hand abandoned his arm.

A soft chuckle shook his chest, and she recalled it from when she had bathed him. A moment later his fingertips gently stroked the bare skin of her neck.

"Uncertain, Bridget?"

Though his voice was teasing, the inference of his comment

annoyed her. There was no thinking through her actions; she was too agitated by the proximity of his body. She jerked against his hold, her hand clawing at the arm imprisoning her.

"Of course I am. What think you? That I have been free with men?"

Her efforts to free herself were wasted. Too much strength rested in him, yet he controlled it, his embrace remaining solid without hurting her.

He stroked her neck again. She was keenly aware of each fingertip. Her own skin, sensitive to his lightest touch, bloomed with warmth under his touch. The chill of the evening quickly became soothing as her body heated.

"I wonder about what you have been doing with a courtesan."

He spoke the words softly, but there was no mistaking the sharp edge to his tone. Bridget froze, standing still in his embrace.

"My mother told you about Marie's lessons?"

He grunted, which was no true answer. A moment later she was free. She could still hear his men on the other side of the trees, but she was too curious to know the answer to her question, so she turned to look at Curan.

"Lessons? What sort of a mother has her daughter tutored by a courtesan?"

His tone implied that he disapproved, yet his expression remained unreadable.

"Why didn't you ask my mother that question?"

His eyes brightened with his temper. "If I had known of it while still beneath her roof, I would have." Thick determination edged each word. "My men found your teacher on the road, intent on spending another day instructing you."

"Didn't you ask Marie that question, my lord?"

His expression tightened. "She refused to speak upon the matter. So I ask you, Bridget. What manner of lessons were you taking from her hand?"

Even Marie's soft instructions to stroke men's egos didn't keep Bridget calm. Her annoyance burned bright. Her neck was still warm and tingling where he'd stroked her, driving home how well he knew a woman's body. Yet he was displeased that she might know a thing or two about how to touch him.

The arrogance of it all.

"Frank ones, sir. So that I would not find myself quivering like a ninny when my groom removes his nightshirt. Somehow I doubt that you are unaware of what I look like beneath my stays, and yet you stand there displeased by the notion that my mother made sure that I was ready to take my position as wife with confidence instead of dread. If that displeases you, set me back on the road home. I am sure you can find some bride who will sniffle like a frightened child, since that appears to be what men think they desire from marriage."

His unreadable mask transformed into an incredulous expression. "You play the docile lady well, yet I see it is not your true nature."

"If you do not wish to hear me speak plainly, do not address me in private. Be assured that I know how to appear meek so that the egos of my male relatives are not bruised while others watch."

His lips curved up into a grin that was anything but comforting. Instead the expression sent a shiver down Bridget's spine.

"Yet in private is the only true place for us to discuss what a courtesan taught you." His eyes narrowed. "Show me."

Bridget plucked at her skirt nervously. He was playful once

more, but she couldn't miss the warning bell ringing in the back of her mind. "I do not know what you mean."

One of his eyebrows rose. "Show me what manner of instruction prompted you to stroke my cock."

His words were intended to prod her into making a hasty confession. Bridget felt her face heat. She pressed her lips into a hard line as her hands fisted in the fabric of her surcoat. A memory of Marie and her steady poise rose to mingle with her temper. She rubbed her fingers against the wool fabric of her dress to distract her from her rising emotions. She needed her poise now, more than ever before, for this man was deadly accurate in the barbs he cast.

Bridget drew a slow breath before answering him. "Since it vexed you so, I will refrain from doing such again."

Her words did more damage than any slap from her hand might have. For a moment his eyes were filled with yearning and disappointment. Yet he recovered quickly, a soft snarl coming from him.

"On the contrary, madam. I am looking forward to giving you ample opportunity to perfect your skill." His face darkened, hunger drawing his expression tight. Had she truly affected him so? Part of her enjoyed thinking such. His dark eyes suddenly glittered.

"Be careful, Bridget. Look at me like that and you will not arrive at Amber Hill a virgin."

There was thick promise in his tone, but also hunger. A soft laugh spilled out of her mouth. "Your mood appears to change rather abruptly, my lord. I find myself confused as to your will."

"My will? My will remains unchanged." He scanned her from head to toe, missing nothing. "I intend to take you home and to my bed."

He was trying to shock her. Or perhaps test her was a better way to consider it. Challenge was etched into his features, and it drew a response from her pride.

"Ah, but I believe I am now unsure how you prefer me to behave once you have placed me where you will, since you appear unhappy about my dealing with Marie. Hmm . . . I suppose I can remain still and quiet."

His lips curved up again. "Not unless you have the strength of Diana, you won't."

There was a smug confidence in his voice that taunted her, but it also reminded her of the look in Marie's eyes. Bridget recalled the sultry confidence that had surrounded the woman when she was sharing intimacies with Tomas. Curan seemed to understand it, too, and the reason was plain—the man was no virgin. Bridget found herself battling envy.

"What do you mean?"

His lips parted to show her even teeth. It was a roguish smile and one that transformed his face into a handsome vision. Curan clicked his tongue in reprimand.

"What is this, Bridget? Playacting? Do you really expect me to believe that a courtesan neglected to divulge the knowledge of just how much pleasure a woman can experience?" He stepped closer, and she tipped her head back to keep their gazes locked. Something dark in his eyes beckoned to her, hinting of that final lesson Marie had promised her.

"I promise you, as my wife, I intend to make sure you experience as much delight as possible."

Her mouth was suddenly dry, but she wanted to know what he meant, if it was that same thing Marie had promised to teach her but never got the opportunity.

"She said it would be better if I allowed myself to enjoy your touch . . ."

Her words trailed off into a whisper because her lungs were

having trouble keeping up with the racing of her heart. Bridget looked away in order to sort her thoughts, but a large hand cupped her chin and brought her eyes back to his. Her cheeks burned at the probing intensity of his gaze, his dark eyes seeming to sear right into her thoughts.

"But she didn't demonstrate any of those touches?"

Alarm raced through Bridget, and she jerked her head out of his grasp. "You mean upon me, with her own hands?" Revulsion flooded her, and she shook her head.

His arm captured her once more, sliding across her back to secure her against him.

"I am pleased to see that look on your face."

Confusion needled her, and she spoke before thinking about how unwise her words might be. "Do you mean to say that she might have touched me?"

"Exactly as I have done, madam." His arm held her steady when she would have jerked away. "Some women enjoy it. Even prefer it to a man's touch." His eyes flickered with hard resolve. "I wonder if you do."

"She did not touch me. Save for a hand beneath my chin once. I did not enjoy it as I do your—"

She shut her jaw so fast her teeth clicked together. Embarrassment heated her cheeks, but what made her belly tighten was the flicker of heat in Curan's dark eyes.

"Stop toying with me." She was ashamed of how close her tone was to begging but could do nothing to change it. Her entire body was twisting and tightening with needs she was losing the ability to control. His eyebrows lowered.

"I do not mean to be unkind, Bridget. Yet I am as drawn to you as you are to me."

He lifted her and moved her back until she felt the thick trunk of a tree pressing into her back. His huge frame held her against it while one of his knees boldly pressed between her thighs. His free hand smoothed down her body, over the curve of her hip and onto her thigh to grip it and pull it up.

"I find myself battling the urge to bind you to me." He spoke through his teeth, his control clearly stretched thin. He pulled her thigh up until it rested against his hip, allowing his leg to press firmly against her sex. The fabric of her dress was no shield. At least not one up to the task of protecting her from the rush of pleasure that assaulted her.

You could couple in more positions than just on your back . . .

The position he held her in was enough to allow him to penetrate her right now, and she felt the night air brush her ankle as he began to tug her skirt up.

"Curan . . ."

"Yes, Bridget?" Her skirt rose higher, that cool air teasing her knee. She clamped down on the panic trying to flood her. It would be better to know what he intended; then she would not shiver while she waited to discover his will. Yet that did not mean she would simply bow to his command. She flattened her hands on his chest and listened to the soft snort that passed his lips in response to her touch.

"What do you want of me?" Her voice was firmer, and that gave her satisfaction. "Is it your intention to shame me in front of your men by lifting my skirts like a doxy?"

His hand fisted in the fabric of her gown. She could feel how tightly he gripped it, and her chin rose with defiance.

His face was becoming harder to see as night wrapped around them. In a way, the darkness deepened the mood gripping her, making it even harder to ignore the need pulsing through her. Though the night made it much simpler to surrender, her pride refused to remain silent.

"If you choose to challenge me, Bridget, be very sure that I will take up the gauntlet." He pulled her gown up farther.

"I did not cast out any challenge, sir."

His hand found the back of her thigh, skin against skin, and she gasped as hot sensation shot up her leg.

"Ah, but I disagree, sweet Bridget. Your very demeanor challenges me to claim you." He smoothed his hand along the back of her thigh, sending little waves of enjoyment through her skin. Her breath felt almost too heavy in her lungs, and she labored to exhale.

"So the fact that I am not simpering like a foolish chit makes it correct for you to treat me disrespectfully?"

His face was hidden half in shadow, but she still noticed the tensing around his mouth as her words impacted him. His hand froze on her thigh, granting her a reprieve from the delight his touch inflicted on her.

"You are my wife. Touching you is my right; there is no disrespect."

"Indeed, my lord? With my skirt hiked above my knees and my thighs on display to any of your men who cares to watch?"

She felt his fingers tightening on her thigh, but they relaxed almost as soon as she felt the tensing.

"None of my men would dare."

"Or would they simply not admit that they were enjoying the sight, my lord? By the time you were ready to protect my modesty, they would likely have slipped away."

Her words were bold, dangerously so, because now she was casting a challenge. Maybe it was the darkness, or the overwhelming need he provoked that made her want to allow him to do what he pleased with her. . . . Whatever it was, there was no tempering her words.

The hand on her thigh left, and her skirt fell back down to cover her legs.

"You are correct, Bridget. You are not a girl, but more of a woman. One that knows full well how to tease a man."

His tone told her that was not a compliment. His breath was raspy, and he didn't move away, but remained with his body pressing her tightly against the tree. There was a look in his eyes, one that told her he wanted her to feel his strength, know that it was greater than her own.

A shiver of what she now knew to be arousal skittered down her back, because she did indeed enjoy his embrace. He was her opposite, hardness opposed to her softness, and the contrast was alluring.

"I will look forward to a full rendering of your studies once we are encased in the privacy of my chambers at Amber Hill."

His mouth captured hers in the dark, his lips boldly taking a hard kiss from her. But the shocking thing was how much she enjoyed the way he commanded her mouth, his lips pressing hers until they opened and he could thrust his tongue inside her mouth. The invasion drew an insane need to press her body against his. She didn't want to be his prisoner; she craved something different. Her hands slid up and over the hard muscles of his chest until she found the top of his shoulders where her fingers might curl around and hold him. She tilted her head to the side so that their mouths might fit more completely against one another. A low growl rumbled through his chest before he cupped the back of her neck.

"Meet me, Bridget. Give me your tongue."

Yes . . .

That was the only thought her mind seemed able to hold. Her mouth opened for his kiss, and she sent her tongue toward his, stroking along its surface. Another growl came from him, and he pressed her tighter against him. She could feel the hard outline of his cock against her belly, and it tore her away from the pleasure of the kiss. His hand left her head, smoothing along the column of her throat and down to boldly stroke the swell of her breast. Excitement made her shiver, and her nipple begged for his fingers to travel lower so that she might feel what it was like to have his hand on them.

You yearn for it so much . . .

She retreated, letting her body fall back against the tree instead of pressing so feverishly up against his, the force of her desire shocking her. Watching Tomas and Marie had not prepared her for how her body was demanding she allow Curan to claim her.

"Enough, Curan. We have agreed that this is not the place to . . ." Her voice was too husky, shocking her further, so she shut her lips while her hands gripped the rough bark of the tree behind her.

He allowed her retreat, but only a few inches. Her breath came in pants, but his was labored, too.

"I see that your tutoring did not include true kissing, even if you were shown what to expect."

He drew in a deep breath and stepped back. "We will wait until we reach Amber Hill."

Each word sounded as though it were forced through his teeth. But she understood why. Her entire body was pulsing with needs so great they were rapidly transforming into demands. She fisted her fingers in her skirts while fighting off the urge to reach for him once more.

She longed to, actually craved having their skin meet again. The urge to shed her dress and press against him pounded through her so loud and hard it drove almost every other thought from her mind.

"These . . . feelings. They cannot be right."

Her words were a mere whisper, a vain attempt to regain some measure of control over the weakness that seemed to have taken command of her flesh. How did one kiss destroy so many years of practice and instruction on proper behavior?

Curan snorted. "I see why the courtesan was on her way to

you again." He reached out and clasped her wrist to draw her
slowly away from the tree. With a turn he began leading her
down the remaining distance to where his men were camped.

"She hadn't finished your lessons." He stopped just short of
breaking through the trees and cupped her chin in a warm
hand once again. To her starving senses, the contact was jar-
ring and she shivered.

"I will look forward to introducing you to the pleasure intimacies can produce in a woman when her partner takes the
time to make sure she is satisfied."

Satisfied . . .

Curan was as far from that as possible. He stopped when
they broke through the tree line and allowed his bride to leave
his side. He had to hook his hands into his belt to keep from
taking her back up into the night for enough privacy to relieve
the ache in his cock.

Yet he did not suffer passion's burn alone. That bit of
knowledge drew a stiff breath from him while he watched
Bridget make her way back toward the wagon she'd traveled
in. Her step was hurried and her hips not nearly as steady
now. Her poise was deserting her in the face of the flames licking her body.

It was astounding—the way they were attracted to each other.
How had he missed it three years ago? He had chosen her for
many reasons, always understanding that celebrating his union
would be another duty required of him. Something stirred inside him, and he realized he was happy for the first time in a
very long time. There weren't many possibilities for personal
happiness while earning his spurs of knighthood, or in the
service that was required of him after he became a knight. The
years since he'd left his father's house to begin training
stretched out in a cold trail of completed tasks. For sure, he

had been proud the day he received his knighthood and like-wise during the times he had ridden in the midst of other lords who respected him for what he had proven on the field of battle.

The feeling settled in his chest, and he stood still to enjoy it. Bridget climbed easily into the wagon in spite of her dress and bulky surcoat. He was rather grateful for the over-garment that hid her form from his gaze. It would seem his self-discipline was inadequate to the task of resisting her.

There was a confidence in her he admired. Truth was he had no patience for helplessness even if he had spent many hours tempering his judgment to expect his bride to need some coddling. His lips curled up. Somehow he doubted his bride would enjoy hearing his thoughts. She was stubborn, a trait he didn't find at all repulsive. After all, he was not some polished gentleman of court. Amber Hill did not need a lady who was despondent over being denied the court atmos-phere. They would not live without comforts, but there would be work aplenty for his new wife to see to.

Yet he wondered if she would be happy. He had little taste for dealing with those who could not adjust to the way things were. Too many times he'd seen noble sons sent off to earn the respect of their king by riding with him, only to hear them whine about everything that wasn't up to their standards. Spoiled. There was no other word to place upon them.

Well, his bride was neither a child nor spoiled. He allowed the grin to remain on his face as he walked farther into camp. It was a fine day in spite of the circumstances that had almost seen him having to fight for his rights as Bridget's groom. He would have fought for her, and the devil take whichever man thought to claim her away from him. Maybe the throbbing cock in his britches was a result of the years he had carried the image of her face in his dreams. On countless nights he had closed his eyes and allowed himself to enjoy the vision of her face, the way she moved or the shy manner with which she had sneaked glances at him. Now that he thought about it, the happiness warming his heart wasn't very surprising at all. He had considered her his for three long years, enjoyed her in his dreams, and taken his only leisure while thinking of her.

They would both be happy. Her brazen kiss was proof of that. Stoking her passion would be the perfect place to begin demonstrating just how content she would be as his wife.

It was a situation he was eager to begin showing her.

Chapter Five

So this was passion.

It was as much a torment as it was delightful.

Bridget tried to hold her head steady while covering the space between the trees and the wagon. She couldn't recall being so ill at ease before, not even when she was younger and first placed in a position of authority over the household. Tonight, it felt as if every man watching her could tell that her nipples were hard behind her stays. Her cheeks colored because she was very sure that Curan knew it.

She certainly understood that he was the one causing her such upset.

Passion . . .

Hot and thick, moving through her veins like strong cider. The sort that her mother had insisted she sample so that she would know how potent it was, just as her mother had brought Marie to show her the power passion might yield over a man. At the moment Bridget found herself longing for that final lesson Marie had promised her.

Curan seemed very willing to instruct her; that was as clear as a summer day. To be honest, she was enjoying his tutoring. Watching Marie and Tomas had not been nearly as enjoyable as having Curan's hand on her thigh.

What did it feel like to be touched on more sensitive parts of her body?

She was sure her blush was burning bright enough to illuminate her shame now, but the men around her only looked away when their gazes connected with her. It was a reflex, something they did without thinking because they turned their attention to any motion near them. Once they realized it was their lord's bride, their eyes shifted. That was true respect for the man they followed. She reached the wagon and climbed in, only pausing on the tailgate to unlace her boots lest she track dirt into her bed. The evening air was chilly on her stocking-clad feet, and she scooted into the back of the wagon where she might pull her toes up into the folds of her clothing.

Someone had laid out one of the rolls of bedding. Considering that ninety percent of the men making the trip to northern England would be passing the night on the hard ground, the fact that any of them had even taken time to see to her comforts was an extreme luxury.

"Beg pardon, lady."

Bridget looked back at the foot of the wagon to see one of Curan's officers. She recalled his face from those who had stood nearest him when he had first arrived. This was the man who had moved her mother. He had light blue eyes that seemed to make his gaze sharper.

"We downed a few deer today, and your mother had her kitchens bake bread for us as well."

He stretched out his arm and placed a large wooden bowl as close to her as his arm length allowed. Even covered with a linen cloth, the rich aroma of roasted meat teased her nose.

"Thank you."

"I am Synclair, first in command. You may look to me when

Lord Ryppon is not present; he has charged me with your welfare, lady."

"I see."

Synclair inclined his head but did not lower his gaze. There was a firm confidence in him that reminded her of Curan, but it did not send a jolt down her spine. This man was just as hardened, just as polished in his skills, but there was nothing drawing her closer to him.

At least it would appear that she was not wanton. Or only when it came to Curan, it seemed. A curse with a blessing attached, now there was a paradox if ever she had heard one.

"You should eat, lady."

Her thoughts had distracted her yet again. "Yes, I shall."

She reached for the bowl and had to force herself to do so calmly. Her belly rumbled low and long, berating her for losing sight of how hungry she was. The night would seem endless if she neglected to fill her stomach.

Synclair watched her silently. His armor breastplate was missing, but a gold knight's chain sat proudly over his shoulders. It was a symbol of his years in service, and the intense focus of his eyes on her felt misplaced because every other man had spent the day looking away from her. This knight appeared to take the matter of her not eating as more important than the need to allow her privacy. That spoke of command and grooming to rise in rank. Unless she judged incorrectly, this knight was one whom Curan relied upon to help command his men. One of his captains, his helmet would have feathers that proclaimed his rank. He was one that she would have to watch if she planned to escape.

"It is not necessary for you or Lord Ryppon to give so much attention to my eating habits."

She found it difficult to consider taking even one bite while being scrutinized so closely.

"The pair of you are treating me like a prized mare. I am not some child who must be monitored."

Surprise registered on Synclair's face, but he remained firmly in place for another long moment, clearly considering her words against those of his lord's.

"Yet you are prized, lady. The border land is an uncertain place. Attention must be paid to ensure your safe arrival at Amber Hill." His gaze shifted to the wagon cover that was tied securely in place along the sides of the wagon now. "It is not my intention or Lord Ryppon's to see your modesty bruised."

But keeping a close eye on her would be their way, no matter her feeling on the matter. Bridget saw that truth clearly illuminated in his eyes. A firm, unwavering set to his expression confirmed his opinion of her position as his responsibility. Her mother's words returned.

"Trust no one with a sword . . ."

Wise advice, indeed. Synclair did not move until she uncovered the meal he had brought. The way he watched her definitely bruised her pride. She felt the sting of this hurt even after the knight inclined his head and left her to eat in privacy. Escaping would not prove simple. She resisted thinking that it might be impossible. She resisted thinking that she would prefer it to be impossible.

Then she truly would be free to enjoy what delights Curan promised her.

She scoffed at her own ideas. The man had more threatened her with those pleasures of the flesh than promised her them. She recalled very plainly the look in his eyes and the feeling of his hand tugging her skirt up. Firm purpose, coupled with the same passion she felt burning her as well. A passion that removed any conscious choice in the matter because her body had already decided to yield.

She had to remain firm; to falter would see her ruined. No

matter how much Curan desired her body, the man had contracted her for the connections and dowry that came from her father. If her sire cut her off without a shilling for disobeying his command to marry Lord Oswald, she would be less fortunate than a whore, for she would have nothing for the favors she gave to Curan.

Not only would she have nothing at all, but possibly a child in her belly. Her best option was to beg to remain as his leman when he took another wife who brought him everything he desired from marriage.

She stopped eating before finishing the portion given to her, her grim thoughts killing her appetite. When had life become so dim? Truthfully, she had been spoiled. Never had there been such a lack of hope in her life. Now there was only the very difficult task of somehow escaping the diligence of Synclair and Curan, before attempting to cross the border into Scotland while avoiding any Scots who might decide to slit her throat simply because she was English.

These thoughts were quite dark indeed, crowding her mind and giving her little peace throughout the night. She huddled beneath the bedding and woke several times, keenly aware of the howl of the wind. It sounded colder and lonelier than she could ever recall. The only mercy came when the camp began to stir at the very first hint of dawn. But the day was gray; the thick clouds massing above them were black with the promise of rain.

The precipitation began to fall before noon, but there was nothing to do save continue onward. The wagon cover was well oiled, providing her with a haven of dryness that none of her escort enjoyed. From the opening at the foot of the wagon she could see the water turning chest armor shiny. Drops dripped off helmet edges, and the horses' coats darkened. The steady clop of their hooves became a sloshing sound when the road turned to mud. The wagon began to sink, and the team pulling it snorted as they tried to drag it through the mire.

Bridget truly tried to temper her thoughts and recall that appearing docile would serve her intentions best, but when Synclair or Curan did not appear at the rear of the wagon and the team continued to struggle, she lost the resolve to not challenge Curan's authority publicly. Sliding to the edge of the wagon, she made sure her shoes were tied well before jumping to the ground. Her feet instantly became cold, but she turned and stepped out of the way of the mud being flung by the wagon's wheels.

Horses snorted and jostled at her appearance, making the knights riding them struggle to control them. More than one annoyed glance was shot at her, but the grumbling was kept low. The felted wool of her surcoat absorbed the rain quickly, making it necessary to grip the front and hold it up to avoid tripping. The clouds were pressing down on them, creeping along the sides of the hills to promise her a long day of chilling rain.

"Get back into the wagon."

Curan was angry with her. A side glance showed her an expression that was tight and inflexible. He held the reins of his stallion in one gloved hand while the other rested on top of his thigh in a hard fist.

"You will stay where I place you, madam."

"I will walk, for I shall not add to the burden of the team pulling that heavy wagon. My legs work as well as any man marching under your command."

"You have the concept of being under my command quite correct." His words were still hard and edged with anger, but he shut his mouth before finishing. His gaze rose to the wagon and the way it sank into the mud. His lips turned white from being pressed tighter, but his eyes were full of displeasure over her questioning of his will.

"I suppose I should admire the fact that you are wise enough to notice need around you. That is a good trait in a wife. Yet I do not favor your manner of acting on your impulses when it places you in jeopardy."

"There is no danger here, only mud."

His gaze settled on her, and one of his dark eyebrows lifted. In a smooth motion he slid from the saddle to land next to her. She shivered, but it had nothing to do with the water reaching her skin. He fell into step alongside her easily, while maintaining a firm grip on his stallion's bridle. Another shiver went down her spine as she noticed just how much taller he was—her eyes were not even level with his shoulder. He tucked his chin to angle his face so that their eyes might meet.

"Be assured that there is plenty of danger on this road, Bridget. The Scots cross the border now that word has reached their ears that the king is nearing his final days." He broke away and scanned the horizon. "Do you not wonder why I am being given permission to maintain such a large number of men?" He looked back at her. "I am being charged with maintaining the border. The Barras clan resides on the other side of the land that I call mine. Their clan laird would pay a large reward for you if someone were brave enough to attempt to snatch you away."

"Are you saying you wanted to hide me inside that wagon?"

"Exactly. A ploy that has been rendered useless by your impulsive action."

His tone attempted to condemn her as a foolish girl who should know enough to trust in the men around her, but Bridget held her chin level.

"Anyone intent on stealing me would already know that I

travel with you. A wagon cover would not blind them to my presence, which makes it ridiculous to burden the horses with my weight when I am able-bodied."

He swept her from head to toe with a quick, yet efficient look.

"A simple boast to make when you have not yet spent hours in the rain."

Her pride flared up, chasing the chill from her. "An easy enough matter to prove as well, Lord Ryppon, since I see no castle in front of me to announce the end of this journey."

His attention was on her once more, and she shot a hard look straight into his eyes. A flicker of male enjoyment lit then, drawing a soft sound from her. Men made no sense. In one breath he demanded obedience, and yet he appeared to enjoy it when she refused his will.

No sense at all.

A soft chuckle teased her into returning her attention to his face. His lips were curved up now, smug male enjoyment making his expression far less imposing.

"You ruffle too easily, Bridget."

He rolled her name, lingering over it as his gaze dropped to her lips.

"I wonder how well you shall rise to my suggestions when we are alone. Although I confess to looking forward to your rise in passion quite a bit."

She jerked her attention away from him and set her sights on the road in front of her. "An unimportant question when we are where we are." She cared not if she sounded surly; the man was being obnoxious.

"I find the topic drives away the chill, leaving me quite warm."

She found herself agreeing.

In spite of wanting to shun him, she turned to fix him with

a narrow look. "Begone if all you want to do is toy with me. I have not practiced the art as much as you clearly have."

The grin melted until his lips were a hard line once more. "Good."

His tone was hard and edged with possession. He held her gaze for a long moment, and she felt the heat ripple across her skin in spite of the chilling rain. "I find the idea of you flirting with other men very displeasing."

She laughed at him. There was no stopping the rise of amusement; not even the hard glint in his eyes was able to warn her sufficiently enough to remain silent.

"Ah, and yet you are so practiced in the art of, as you said . . . ruffling me. Where have you practiced such skills?" Bridget leaned closer so that her next words would not carry. "Perhaps with a courtesan?"

"How better to make sure I understand how to keep you satisfied in my bed, Bridget, than to take lessons from a woman who might instruct me on the very intimate details of her body?"

"That is—" Words failed her as she felt her face burn scarlet. He leaned even closer until she couldn't seem to keep her eyes on his but stared at his mouth instead.

His kiss was intoxicating . . .

"My solemn promise to you."

A moment later he remounted his stallion. Settling atop the huge animal, Curan resumed the role of commander. She clearly saw the change, actually felt it. The man who had been verbally sparring with her now hid behind the polished exterior of his command.

The transformation was complete, except a slight flicker of heat in his eyes. Deep in those dark eyes was a flame that promised he was not finished toying with her. In sooth, the man appeared to consider her his favorite plaything.

"We shall make Amber Hill sometime tomorrow."

There was a finality in his tone that sent a shaft of fear through her heart. She cast her attention forward and heard him make a sound of frustration before the stallion moved away.

Tomorrow.

So close and unavoidable. It felt as if someone had their hands locked around her neck, squeezing and tightening their grip until she couldn't breathe. That idea persisted the rest of the day. With nothing but rain and mud to look at, her thoughts churned like the swollen rivers they crossed. It grew colder the farther north they traveled, but it wasn't the location she dreaded. It was the groom who intended to claim her on the morrow who was the source of her concern.

Crawling into the wagon at dusk, she gratefully took shelter in it. Curan's men sought out the trees, pulling the lower branches down to drape oilcloth over to form crude tents. The blanket of leaves that had fallen beneath those trees last fall gave the men a drier place to pass the night. They scraped aside the moist top layer, and soon there was the scent of smoke in the air. She did not have a fire, but the wagon was by far drier than anything else. Bridget pulled her shoes off and even stripped off her stockings because they were soaked. One of her trunks was sitting near, and she was able to open it slightly. The cover prevented her from raising the lid very far, so she reached in to pull what she might from inside. A chemise came out first, and then a light dressing gown. While she wouldn't have normally considered wearing so little while surrounded by an army, the night was cooling down rapidly. Getting out of her wet dress was imperative before she caught a chill. Reaching up, she untied the flap that would cover the back of the wagon and act as a curtain to give her privacy.

Removing her dress proved difficult. Her fingers fumbled

the hooks, and the knot in her laces stuck tight. She couldn't help but notice the difference between the practice disrobing she had performed for Marie and the struggling efforts she had to use to strip the wet garment from her. She shivered when her bare skin was exposed. A quick look at the tail of the wagon showed her that the curtain was still in place. Tugging on her wet chemise, she pulled the wet fabric over her head. She used the linen cloth that had covered her supper last evening to dry off as best as possible. Her teeth started to chatter, and she clamped her jaw tight to keep them still. Even lightweight clothing that was dry would be welcome. Besides, she could use the bedding to provide the additional warmth she craved.

"Lady?"

Synclair's voice came through the curtain, sending Bridget beneath the blankets before she even had the dressing gown tied.

"You may lift the flap."

Pulling the covers up to her chin, she watched the knight use one hand to open the flap. He still wore his helmet for the protection it might provide him.

"It is cold fare, but I found you a bit of wine to cut the chill."

"I am grateful, but you need not pamper me, sir."

"You are not alone. Lord Ryppon has opened the stores to ease the aches this rain brings."

So Curan was a generous lord. Somehow she found that bit of information heartwarming. Synclair pushed a wooden tray toward her. A wineskin was sitting in it, too.

"Good evening, lady."

The knight offered her a quick nod before the flap fell back into place and she was left in privacy.

She was being kept in luxury and felt a surge of guilt for the dry wagon bed at her disposal. Her intention to flee made her unworthy of such comforts, for they were being provided to her because she was the mistress.

In the bowl, her fingers found little droplets of water clinging to the bread and beading on top of the thick slice of cheese. Feeling the little drops of water made her realize that she was dry for the first time since leaving the wagon that morning. While it was still cold, the air lacked the bite of winter ice, making her count her blessings that they were not traveling in the dead of winter. Having anything to eat was welcome; even simple fare would be filling and a comfort to enjoy. The wine truly did chase the chill from her nose, warming her cheeks, while the bedding helped relieve the bite of cold from her feet. Her legs ached from pulling her feet out of the mud all day long. A throbbing pain bit between her shoulder blades from the weight of her soaked surcoat hanging on her shoulders. She shied away from thinking about getting back into her wet clothing at dawn. Better to enjoy the warm, dry bed, even if it was hard against her back. She slipped into sleep but found dark eyes watching her there.

Eyes that flickered with passion while they came nearer. She felt his hands on her, first only a single brush of fingertips and then his entire hand stroking her until she yearned for his possession. She twisted away but couldn't escape her own passion. It slithered across her skin, giving her no reprieve until she threw herself out of the bed she lay in.

She hit a hard body and opened her eyes to stare into pitch blackness.

"What troubles you, Bridget?"

"Curan?"

"Aye. No one else would dare approach your bed. Even if you did cry out."

His voice was husky and edged with concern. There was also a hint of tenderness she did not expect from the imposing man. Her hands pressed flat against his hard chest while she tried to decide if her nightmare was over or simply beginning.

"What are you doing here?"

The arms around her shifted, moving her so that she was once again lying on the bedding that was unrolled inside the wagon. Curan was beside her, propped on his side, but his larger body dwarfed hers, and she was keenly aware of it.

"As I said, you cried out. Softly, yet 'twas enough to carry past the wagon cover."

He stroked a hand over one side of her cheek, sending a shiver down her chest and across her breasts.

"I am well."

She wasn't, but keeping her voice lower disguised that fact. A soft grunt brushed her ear before she felt the press of his lips against her temple.

"You are not."

One large hand pressed down in the center of her chest, directly over her heart. There was no hiding the frantic pace of it, but it was the feeling of having his fingers so close to her nipples that sent her rolling away from him. She was keenly aware of how simple it would be for him to touch one of those soft tips. It was almost as if she longed for it.

"I am, and know myself better than you do." She tried to sit up and push him away from her. She needed some space between them for her mind to begin functioning once more.

He snorted softly and pressed her back down.

"I know that you enjoy my touch." His words were edged with frustration now. "So lie still, Bridget, and do not act as if you do not like my hand upon you. No one sees us, and there is no other way to begin my education of you, for you are correct—I do not know you well enough at all."

"You said you would wait until we reached your holding."

"To possess you, yes, I would wait until we have a bed beneath us. A maiden deserves such respect from her groom. That does not mean I will not begin the process of learning more about you before then."

He found her mouth in the darkness, claiming her lips with a hard kiss. She was suddenly aware of how thin the dressing gown was and how exposed her natural shape was to his hand. Strangely, his kiss was perfect coupled with the darkness encasing them, as though she had never truly understood what the night was made for. The dark hours were crafted for veiling lovers, the lack of light allowing her to feel every touch more deeply. Without her sight, her skin was aware of each touch, each stroke. She noticed what his skin smelled like and detected the scent of rainwater clinging to his hair. So many little details suddenly grabbed her attention. She turned her head and drew in a deeper breath that brought the scent of new spring grass with it. She could smell the faint traces of bread that clung to his fingers where he held her head in position for his kiss. But most of all, she noticed how warm his lips were against hers, the way they slid across the tender surface, producing a friction that was sweetly enjoyable. His weight was even pleasing. Part of her enjoyed knowing that he had her pressed down for his pleasure. Hidden deep within her own thoughts was some unexpected longing to feel him completely on top of her.

It became impossible not to reach for him, her hands longing to seek out the warmth of his chest. Each fingertip ultra-aware of the moment when they made contact with him, first one and then another until her hands were resting lightly against him.

Bridget shivered, and he pressed her lips wide for a deeper kiss. The tip of his tongue slipped gently over her lower lip in a slow motion that sent ripples of sensation through her. He was tasting her, lingering over her lips like fine French wine. Her confidence swelled as she felt the power of her own attractiveness. Her jaw relaxed, allowing him to penetrate her mouth with a slow thrust of his tongue. It wasn't the bold invasion she expected from him, but that did not mean it was soft. Steady and sure, he stroked her tongue with his until she mimicked his motion, kissing him back.

"Sweet Bridget, I must thank you for having mercy and giving me an excuse to join you. I confess I've been discarding reason after reason to come in here since you lowered the flap and shut me out."

"I didn't mean to disturb you."

A low chuckle drifted over her. In the dark she felt it as much as she heard it. His fingers threaded into her hair, slipping through the strands to rest against her scalp and cradle her head. He turned her face up to his, but all she saw was a shadow. Her sight failed her, but her other senses were keenly aware of him. She could feel his warmth and smell his clean male scent. It sent her heart racing once more, as if she had fallen back into her dream and his arms.

"Yet you enjoy having me here as well." His hand trailed down to rest over her heart once more. He tapped against her chest in time with the frantic tempo her heart was keeping. "The proof is plain. Besides, you should be happy that you have snared my attention."

"Why? Because you believe that all women thirst for male admirers?"

He chuckled again, and his opposite hand moved, sliding gently over the soft mound of her breast. She shucked in a harsh breath, her body attempting to roll away from the sheer abundance of sensation that touch produced. But he denied her any escape, his body leaning over hers and the hand cradling her head keeping her firmly in place while his hand gently fingered her breast. Soft strokes made the breath freeze in her lungs.

"I think it is time I demonstrated just how much you may expect to enjoy being admired by me, Bridget."

"You shouldn't—"

"I disagree wholeheartedly."

And he wasn't going to continue to debate the issue, either. His fingers circled her breast, sending ripples of delight through the soft flesh. With naught but two thin layers of linen between his fingers and her skin, she felt the heat from his hand scorching her. A soft sound made it past her lips, but she honestly didn't know if it was born of distress or delight. She felt suspended between the two emotions, but her body was rapidly losing the will to protest. She wanted to arch up and offer her breast to his grasp, to his will.

"I believe I made a grave error in leaving our union uncelebrated. The knowledge of how close I came to losing you sticks to my thoughts like tar. I find myself jealous of even the idea of another having you."

His voice turned husky and deep, drawing her closer to him to ensure that she heard each word. She felt his breath against her cheek, and his hand closed gently around her breast. A soft sound came from her that she didn't recognize as her own. The night air was no longer chilly, Curan's body warming her until she was hot. Her racing heart warming her more completely than a summer day.

"Perhaps it was best, though, else I might never have been able to complete my duty knowing how sweet you sound with my hand upon you. Knowing how soft your flesh was might have turned me traitor to my king's will just so that I might lie with you again."

His hand moved away from her breast, and disappointment surged through her. A tiny groan came from her, but it became a gasp when he slid his hand beneath the neckline of her chemise. Delight raced across her skin, startling her with its intensity. Excitement twisted through her belly so tight she jerked with it. He controlled her easily, moving with her as though he understood what his touch was doing to her.

"You shouldn't—"

"It would be a sin against the flesh nature gifted us with not to show you what delights await you as my wife."

She lost track of what she was trying to forbid him to do as his hand cupped her breast. Skin against skin, it flooded her with pleasure. It seemed as if she were finally experiencing what her breasts had been created for. With them contained behind stiffly boned stays for years, she had never realized how much the mounds of flesh might feel.

"Disagreeing with you is becoming an enjoyable thing, sweet Bridget." His thumb glided across the hard peak of her nipple, wringing another gasp from her. "I believe it is time to crush this desire you have to tell me no so often. Maybe you doubt my ability to make my bed a place you will eagerly look forward to sharing."

"You mustn't say things like that. What would the church say?"

He pinched her nipple, the harder touch shocking her with how much she enjoyed the sensation. She pushed against his chest, but it was more reaction than a desire to be free. Curan didn't move; he remained solid and hard beside her, resting most of his weight on one elbow. His fingers remained closed about the hard point of her nipple, gently rolling the woman's tip.

"I have followed their teachings and taken you as my wife. I expect the church to bid me well and leave me to enjoy my bride, in every manner I desire or you do."

"Your words are far from humble and quite lustful."

He grunted and tightened his hand on her breast. "You begin to know me better, Bridget. A task I believe we shall delve into deeper."

His hand left her breast, and this time he grasped the tie that held her dressing robe closed. With a sharp jerk it opened, and he grasped the edge of her chemise to pull it down and bare her chest. She felt the brush of the night air against her hard nipple a mere moment before he leaned over her and captured the puckered tip between his lips.

Another cry crossed her open lips, but she was not intent on escape. Her body arched, offering her breast to his mouth. Sweet delight flowed from that point of contact, his mouth hotter than anything she might have imagined. His hand moved from cradling her head to the center of her back, where he lifted her to him so that he could suck more strongly on her nipple. The pleasure bit into her, sharp and hard, racing through her flesh to the spot hidden in the folds of her sex. A throbbing began there that spread to her sheath. It became a needy ache that made her twist, because remaining still was impossible.

She wanted to touch him, spread her hands over him just as boldly as she had witnessed Marie doing. There was no forcing herself to do it. She reached for the hard shoulders that her attention had rested on so frequently and muttered with enjoyment as her fingertips glided over the hard ridges.

His knee dropped over her thigh, locking one of her legs in place. He teased the hard top of her nipple with his tongue, lashing it with soft motions that set her heart racing faster. Her blood felt as though it were on fire, and she didn't truly protest when he tugged her chemise up to bare her thighs. The cool air was a relief and so freeing, she shuddered. Her eyes opened, and she realized how overwhelmed she was. She wanted more than that, craved the same level of involvement she had seen Marie taking.

Curan released her nipple, and the night air turned it cold where her skin was wet. Slipping her hands up to his face, she held him cupped in her hands and lifted her head up to press a kiss against his mouth. He shook slightly, surprised by her boldness, and that filled her with confidence. She held on to him and pressed a firm kiss to his lips. He didn't take command of it, only allowed her to push his lips apart so that she might deepen the kiss. His hand cupped her breast lightly, tenderly, before slipping down her body to her belly, where it rested.

Sensation twisted beneath that hand. An insane sort of excitement made her kiss him harder. Curan abandoned his relaxed demeanor, his lips meeting hers with equal passion while his hand ventured lower to where his knee kept her thighs slightly parted.

She gasped, and it broke their kiss. Knowing what happened between a man and woman did not completely prepare her for the first touch on the top of her mons. The throbbing increased, and she was suddenly aware of her passage being empty.

His cock would fill you . . .

It was a wicked thought, but her mind was filled with the memory of the way Marie had so confidently lowered her body onto Tomas's hard flesh. Curan was watching her, trying to gauge her mood, but her expression was hidden in the dark. He kept his hand on her mons, as sure and steady as he did everything else. There was no retreat in this man, only steady, onward progress that would win the day.

She could be taken on her back or rise to meet him . . .

Stretching up, she pressed a soft kiss against his neck. His skin was not as rough as she might have thought it would be. Her hands on his chest felt him shiver slightly in response. This tiny vibration filled her with a sense of victory.

"You tease me, Bridget."

His voice was rough, but she detected a note of admiration in it.

"Because I do not remain still and simply allow you to cover me, while I lay still in submission?"

She relaxed and did exactly that, forcing her limbs to go limp. "Is this better?"

He growled at her with a low sound that practically defined the idea of frustration. Bridget laughed softly at him, but her amusement died swiftly when his hand moved lower until it was resting directly over that spot that throbbed so incessantly between the folds of her flesh.

"Two may play the game of taunting. Be careful what you begin. I enjoy victory a great deal. It might be interesting to pit our wills against one another, to see exactly how long you might remain still while I tried to entice you into responding."

His fingers moved, rubbing her directly on top of her sex. Pleasure shot up into her passage so fast she cried out. She quickly lost her ability to remain in place, her body bucking with the amount of sensation his touch produced. His chest rumbled with his amusement as his fingers continued to move. He covered her lips with his, smothering the sound while his larger body held her on her back and at his mercy.

"I believe the victory goes to me."

"You are arrogant. Why do you torment me?"

Yet it was a sweet torment he inflicted upon her. His fingers rubbed, working in a slow motion that produced as much pleasure as need. She felt torn by the twin emotions, each so opposite from one another but being created by the same action. Her hips wanted to lift up to his hand and increase the pressure. She felt compelled to strain toward him, seeking some form of release from the aching need filling her passage.

"Have you ever been pleasured?"

"What?"

That single word sounded hoarse. She shut her mouth and swallowed to try to force herself to recall how to answer in a smooth tone.

"You have never fingered yourself?"

"Of course not." She tried to twist away but was pinned quite securely. His fingers continued their slow and lazy motion. Her taut muscles began to ache. It seemed impossible to relax or to even be completely still.

She wanted to be filled. Wanted it so badly she almost cried out in demand.

"Release me. You promised we would wait."

Her words sounded sulky, as though she wanted to taunt him until he lost his own control and gave her what she craved. In the night, it seemed right to feed the desire tearing at her. The darkness hinted at absolution for any sins committed while hidden in its velvety folds.

He leaned down and bit her neck, a soft nip that sent a ripple of pleasure down her spine.

"I don't want to wait, I want to fill you tonight and feel you clasping me with your thighs. I can feel the need shaking you, Bridget. Tell me you desire release."

His tone was gruff, and part of her rejoiced. His lips found her breast again, and he nuzzled the soft mound before teasing the nipple with little kisses. It was too soft for what she needed, and she arched up to press against him.

"I will not." The words felt as if they were torn from her. Her body shivered in disappointment.

"I shall not make it such a simple thing for you, Bridget."

His finger continued to torment her, building more hunger

beneath its slow motion. She wanted something more, but she was powerless within his grasp to obtain it.

"You are my wife; there is no shame in taking pleasure from my touch."

He loomed over her again, and she could feel the change in his mood. Tension felt thick in the air when his fingers stilled. She shuddered, her body reacting to the lack of motion. She still needed more. Needed something harder and faster to satisfy her.

"Tell me you desire pleasure from my hand."

Hard and unyielding, his words drew a sharp gasp from her. She shut her jaw so fast her teeth clicked against one another, but he chuckled at her response and gave a sharp tug on her chemise. The lightweight fabric rose up her legs quickly, baring her to the top of her thighs.

"Begone, Curan." She didn't care if he took exception to her tone. He'd been warned to avoid her in private if he wanted properness from her.

He snorted, sounding as frustrated as she. "And leave you hungering, sweet Bridget?"

He pulled on the fabric of her clothing again. Even her weight did not prevent him from raising it above her waist. A soft sound came from her lips as she felt her sex being touched by the night air. She shivered just a tiny amount as the first layer of her innocence was stripped away.

"Where has your confidence gone?" The trace of amusement in his tone chaffed her pride.

"You shouldn't jest. Would you rather I was a slut? Well accustomed to a man's touch? Eager to follow my lustful impulses the moment I laid eyes upon a man who pleased me?"

His fingers gently returned to her mons, petting the soft curls that grew there in a gentle motion before seeking out the cleft that lay beneath them.

"I would rather you accept that I am your husband. The man you will willingly welcome into your body without further hesitation or excuse." His fingers penetrated the folds of her sex, sinking down until they connected with that point that was keeping pace with her heart rate.

"I want to hear you say that you are mine."

She wanted to. The need was clawing at her insides. Her hips were begging to lift once again and press her clitoris against his fingertips. She felt desperate for that contact, so intensely hungry that her body shivered while she battled against her pride. But she would not submit so simply. Reaching out, she touched his thigh and trailed her fingers across it until she found the hard bulge of his cock.

He drew in a sharp breath that whistled through his clenched teeth.

"And what about what I desire, Curan? Submission is quite boring when it is the only thing allowed."

His finger moved on top of her clitoris, sending a bolt of white-hot pleasure up her passage. This was what she had craved. Direct contact, his flesh against her own.

"This is very much about what you desire, sweet Bridget. Submission to my will has rewards."

His finger rubbed the sensitive little point, drawing a moan from her. She had never made such a sound before but seemed to be a stranger unto herself at that moment. Stripped away were the polished manners and poise she had spent years perfecting. There was no set of rules that she understood to follow as his finger drove her into a mindless state where nothing mattered but the need twisting tighter and tighter beneath his touch. She clamped her thighs closed, but his hand remained in place. He leaned down over her to pin her shoulders flat, filling her senses with his warm, male scent. It was intoxicating and impossible to ignore. Her thoughts dissolved into impulses that all centered on having him pleasure her, the hard body pressing down on her adding to the moment and increasing the frantic need pulsing through her.

"Submission can be sweet. So sweet because it feeds what you crave."

He kissed her hard and with a demand that she struggled against but found her will bending to accept. His finger moved faster, applying more pressure, and it became impossible to remain still. Her hips strained up toward his hand, her thighs grasping his forearm now out of the need to keep that hand exactly where it was. Her thighs burned because she strained up so strongly, but that only added to the pulsing sensation gripping her. It all centered under his finger. Her passage begged to be filled, but her clitoris became white-hot a moment before pleasure squeezed her in a grasp so tight it felt as if she were shattering under the pressure. Delight raced through her, burning along her muscles and limbs without missing a single inch of her body. She cried out into their kiss, his lips smothering the sounds. Time ceased to exist. She found herself suspended in that moment, with pleasure glowing in her belly like a flame. There was no thinking, only feeling.

"And that, my sweet wife, is the reason for submission. The pleasure my touch can give you."

She lay willingly on her back now. Every muscle in her body feeling lax and limp. Exhaustion clouded her thinking while delight still warmed her passage and clitoris. He trailed his hand up to rest over her womb, gently massaging the quivering muscles. Her hand still lay near his cock, and her fingers brushed against it, telling her that he was still hard and unsatisfied.

He shifted away from her touch, a snort brushing past her lips.

"We shall sleep beneath my roof tomorrow night and I shall be happy to allow you to stroke my cock as much as you like . . . wife."

"But—"

He growled, the sound full of impatience.

"There is nothing further to say, Bridget, unless you wish to discuss exactly what delights we shall share tomorrow. I, for one, am dwelling on the idea of you clasping your thighs about my hips as you just did to my forearm."

He was being blunt on purpose in an attempt to intimidate her. It was strange how she noticed it. Her body was basking in a glow of contentment, but her wits had returned. He tucked the bedding back around her, and the wagon rocked as he left it. When he lifted the flap, enough light illuminated him to show her the rigid set of his face. She suddenly understood what Marie had meant when she spoke of power over a man when he was hungry.

Curan was hungry for her. Yet he had pleasured her and left unsatisfied. She tried to dwell on that fact, but slumber stole her away, her body happily slipping into its restful embrace now that her passion had been fed.

Chapter Six

Morning broke, but it was hardly noticeable. Dim light was the only thing the dawn offered. The rain had stopped, but the clouds massing directly above rumbled with thunder, making the horses irritable.

Everyone walked, including the knights, to avoid being thrown from the saddle by the powerful horses. They held on tightly to their mounts and led them up the road while lightning began to flicker. The only saving grace was the fact that it was not night. It was much harder to soothe a stallion during the dark hours.

Bridget's first sight of Amber Hill was dreary, to say the least. The stone fortress rose up from the landscape, almost the same color as the black and gray storm clouds. The clap of thunder only seemed to add to the foreboding nature of the moment. Three towers were built near each other. A wide curtain wall connected them, and they reached up into the clouds to provide good sight over the Scottish border. Bridget shivered, certain she could hear the voices of generations past who had met their death along this disputed strip of land.

Her gaze shifted to the man who intended to take up the post of guarding this plot of English soil. Curan was back in the saddle, his powerful thighs gripping the stallion with confidence. No hint of unease marred his expression; in fact, the man looked smugly pleased while drinking in the sight of his home. His attention shifted to her, and a deeper shudder shot down her spine. Thunder cracked above them, and she had to fight the urge to make the sign of the cross over herself.

For certain she had never felt so threatened before. It was not fear of pain that sent that sensation rippling down her back; it was the memory of just how needy he had made her while wrapped in the dark cloak of night.

"We'll be dry soon, Lady Ryppon."

Synclair sounded glad even if he remained the image of a properly dutiful knight to his lord. Still, there was no disguising the note of relief in his voice. When Bridget glanced at him, she saw that pleasure flickering in his eyes.

"Forgive me, lady, I should have begun by telling you that Amber Hill is the fortress ahead of us."

"I recognized that from the looks on the faces about me."

His elation faded a bit, lines appearing beneath the edge of his helmet. "Returning home is normally a time of rejoicing."

"Of course."

He did not care for her lack of enthusiasm. His expression became tight, his lips pressing into a hard line.

"You will come to think of it as your home. Soon would be best." He paused for a moment, clearly attempting to soften his comment since he was addressing a woman instead of a man. Obviously the knight had spent far more time in the company of men and found the task difficult. "In time you will adjust."

"Of course."

She did not care that she was repeating herself. The fortress standing so coldly in front of her resembled more of a prison, not an unusual thought considering that an army surrounded her, and the choice to enter was not resting in her hands. She might have been a stolen heiress instead of a negotiated bride. Someone watching would never know the difference.

She wasn't sure if she wasn't both, considering that her father had made the match.

She sighed, chastising herself for her thoughts. Railing against the way the world was would bring her no gain. Besides, she liked Curan well and good, and that was a solid truth. He was no old man who wanted young flesh, and he was no coward who paid others to fight in his place. He was absolutely everything that she should be thankful for in a husband. This acknowledgment made it doubly hard to recall why she had to stick to her course and deny him.

Synclair gave her the briefest of nods to accept her response before he mounted his horse and rode toward his commander. They made quite a pair, both men embodying the image of strength.

Her mood turned surly. It was not the rain or the fact that her toes felt swollen from being wet for two days. What needled her was the way the sight of Curan instantly revived the memory of what he had done to her last night. Her cheeks turned hot with a blush and her nipples began to tighten just from the thought of it. But what truly turned her mood dark was the fact that she recalled just how much she had wanted everything he had carried out.

There was no choice, not even control, Marie's example seeming so impossible to reproduce within herself. The courtesan had always appeared in command, but Curan reduced Bridget to a weak and needy creature after nothing more than a few kisses.

But such hot kisses . . .

A soft growl made it past her lips. Amber Hill rose higher in front of her, darkening her mood further. She was torn between duty to her father and desire for Curan. Never once had she thought to be in such a dilemma. Only daughters who were foolish enough to get carried away in romantic verses full of love found themselves struggling to follow their fathers' dictates when the time to become a wife was at hand.

Resentment boiled inside her for the position in which she found herself. She had been obedient. Even if the church would berate her for thinking harshly against her father, she still did. She desired Curan only because her father had made it possible for her to.

That is not so. You would have desired him no matter what . . .

She snorted again, annoyed by her own thoughts.

"I assure you, in spite of its exterior, Amber Hill is a modern building."

Bridget jumped, startled by Curan's deep voice. The man seemed to have materialized directly out of her musings.

"I do not doubt such."

He frowned at her tone. "You would prefer a crumbling castle complete with a moat half full of century-old sewage?"

"What I would prefer—" Something gleamed in his eyes, and she shut her mouth. The man was baiting her.

One dark eyebrow rose. "Yes, my lady?"

He rolled the word "my," giving the word more emphasis, and that pushed her demeanor over the edge into angry. It had been so long since she had allowed herself to be so unpolished that the burning emotions stunned her.

"Finish what you began saying, Bridget."

Now he turned her name into a warning that further agitated her.

"I shall not." She lifted her chin and shot him a full look of fury. It took him by surprise, his expression breaking the unreadable mask he so often wore when verbally sparring with her. She gained a glimpse at his true thoughts and the frustration lurking there. She found a measure of calm in the sight of that frustration because she felt just as unsure.

He reached down and plucked her right off the road like some Scottish marauder. A sound of rage got past her lips before she smothered it, drawing the attention of the men around them, and the guards jerked their eyes to Bridget and Curan while reaching for their swords, proving that the two days of rain had not stolen any of their sharpness.

They looked away even faster once they saw her lying across their lord's thighs.

"Let me up!"

Bridget didn't soften her words and did not care if Curan took offense. The man was insufferable. Since his saddle didn't allow for her to roll toward the neck of the stallion, she ended up curled around his body with her legs flopping on one side of the horse and her head and arms on the other. Her wet skirts stuck to her ankles and calves, snapping with the motion of the animal.

She heard him make a sound that resembled a chuckle too closely for her comfort. She was past behaving the way everyone expected of her. Far past it. Planting her hands on his thigh she pushed her body up without concern for the fact that she just might end up in a heap for her efforts.

Curan did not take exception to her actions. Instead the man hooked her about the waist and lifted her up above the saddle, so that he might lower her bottom onto the saddle in front of him. She ended up sitting upright and riding side-saddle with his hard body flush against hers. Her cheeks heated again, and that heat licked down her skin, touching all the places his hands and lips had the previous night.

"Are you more pleased now, Bridget?"

His tone was disgruntled, but it suited her mood well enough.

"Pleased that you haul me off the ground in front of your men like a whore?"

"More like a reluctant bride." One of his arms was holding her in place against him, and it tightened with his words. "I treat you as your surly behavior deserves. Yet I wonder why you want to avoid my touch by using such comparisons. It sounds as though you wish to keep yourself from my touch completely."

His eyes flickered with frustration, but shame made her lower her eyes. He was correct. She was using barbed words to attempt to place distance between them. Obedience to her father did not make her behavior less disgraceful. She heard him sigh.

"You are my wife. Your father has given his blessing to our match. Be at ease."

"Not according to my father's last letter home. Can you not see that I must question our union?"

His nostrils actually flared with anger, his gaze becoming so sharp it felt as if it might cut straight into her mind. But his lips curved in a sensual fashion, sending a pleasant shiver over her born from the memory of how they felt latched onto her nipple.

"And what of last night, sweet Bridget? Are you not my wife because of the way you let me taste your tender breasts and stroke your slit?"

His voice deepened until it was brassy and husky such as it had been in the dark. He leaned down close to her ear, and she felt his warm breath against her skin.

"You clung to me, and I felt you shiver when my hand gave you pleasure."

I have . . .

Her body shivered, and he chuckled as he felt it. Along the side of her body that was flush against his, she felt the unmistakable rise of his erection.

"Only after you pressed your suit. It was not your bed I snuck into."

He frowned but took a moment to raise his gaze to scan the horizon. His attention lingered on the fortress growing larger and more impressive with each jolt of the horse's hooves. The hand resting over her belly tightened.

"It shall be my bed you lay in tonight."

Hard certainty coated each word. Her temper resumed its fury as she became bone-weary of being considered his property. May the rest of the world be cursed, she did not care if it was the way her entire life was structured, she was sick of being a man's chattel. Her mother's lessons on poise and being clever suddenly became quite useful. Men did not know as much as they thought . . . at least not about women.

"I must disappoint you, my lord." Her voice was smooth and devoid of anything that might be considered anger. "My monthly courses are due. I cannot possibly assume my position in your bed tonight."

He growled at her, the arm lying around her contracting. Bridget raised an innocent look to him and actually enjoyed the appearance of frustration in his eyes. Let the man taste what it was like to be told what would be instead of informing her what he desired. A taste of humility would do him good.

"And why did you wait until now to tell me this?"

"You have given me little enough time to share conversation with you that allowed for personal topics."

He ground his teeth. She could see the muscles along his jawline drawing tight. "You have had ample opportunity to mention something of that importance, madam."

Bridget lowered her eyelids. She suddenly understood exactly what Marie had meant about her power over a man only being effective while he hungered for her. The hard cock pressing against her hip transmitted exactly how much appetite Curan had for her at that moment. Confidence filled her, and she lifted one shoulder in a delicate shrug.

"I am not accustomed to sharing intimate details with anyone. It has even been years since I told my own mother when my courses were upon me. It is a private thing."

"Not between husband and wife, it is not."

He sucked in a hard breath, and she heard it whistle through his clenched teeth. "It is not something that I choose the time of. Why do you think that it is the duty of the mother of the bride to set the date of wedding celebrations? An experienced woman knows what details to confirm with her daughter."

She raised her eyelids and stared him straight in the eye. Indecision flickered in his, but she did not lower her lashes and give him the opportunity to question her honesty.

"Are you positive, madam?"

She shoved her guilt down deep so that it couldn't reach her expression and foil her plan. "It is not something any woman mistakes."

He muttered something under his breath that sounded like a curse. His body jerked, and he dug his heels into the side of the stallion. The horse quickened his speed, eagerly trying to cover the remaining distance to Amber Hill.

"You should place me back on my feet."

His arm remained firmly in place around her.

"I believe I have heard enough of what you would have me do with you this day, my lady." He gestured at his fortress. "I intend to have you seen sitting on my saddle when we ride beneath the gate." Rich possessiveness coated his words. "At least that will leave no doubt as to whom you belong to among the inhabitants of my holding."

She smothered a snort. But not quite enough. A chuckle rumbled through his wide chest, raising her ire.

"Still so determined to avoid taking your place, Bridget?" He leaned close to her ear once more. "I thought I proved my worth quite well last night. However, I shall be most happy to persevere and apply my full attention to the task of keeping you satisfied."

She did not doubt him, and that sent another chill down her back, but it was followed by a flood of heat that touched off a yearning that chewed on her thoughts.

Staying sounded more enticing than ever. Her mental debate took far too much of her energy, leaving her almost relieved to see the gate growing closer. It was so tempting to simply surrender and allow Curan his way.

She still heard the warning in her mother's voice, however, echoing inside her head and refusing to allow her to relinquish her misgivings.

Time was something she needed. Time in which to flee to her cousin Alice before she consummated a union that might just enrage her father. There was also the growing concern that Chancellor Wriothesley might seek retaliation against Curan for taking her. If the king truly was dying, Curan's friendship with him would not protect him or her if she chose to celebrate their union.

So she would not, even if he could not see the wisdom in agreeing with her.

Disappointment raked its sharp claws across her heart. The pain was shocking, drawing a shudder from her. The arm around her tightened, the hard muscles securing her tighter against Curan. The first of his men reached the arched opening in the curtain wall.

"Welcome to Amber Hill, *my lady*."

There was no missing the deadly edge to his words. Coupled with the imposing stone walls, despair closed around her like the thick clouds pressing down on them. But there was something else. A longing to have fate simply lift the burden from her by making it impossible to avoid being claimed completely by the lord holding her so securely against him.

That surely would bring disaster to them both, and her heart protested. Casting a last look at the hills rising up behind the thick stone walls, she set her thoughts on her cousin Alice.

She would go there soon. She had to.

The household was turned out in full force. The staff must have seen the riders approaching a good hour past because the inner courtyard was filled with servants. Bridget didn't know where to look first. Amber Hill was quite a surprise. The inner yard was covered in stone. Neatly laid cobblestones and mortar filled in the space between the curtain wall and the towers. It was very modern and very expensive. Not many families spent the money to cover the inner yard, but it kept the mud from being tracked near the doorways and into the towers.

"Your staff awaits, my lady."

"They await you."

But they were staring at her and the way their lord had her clamped against his body. Maybe three hundred years ago, brides had arrived in such a manner, but today it was rather misplaced.

Curan didn't appear to think so. The man looked quite

pleased with himself, pulling up on his reins and keeping her securely in front of him while he turned to look at his men filling the courtyard behind them. He didn't dismount until the last of them was through the gate.

"True enough." His keen gaze returned to hers, and she stared at the heat smoldering there. By the look in his eyes no one would know that the man was sitting in the chill of an early spring storm.

"And I eagerly await being able to finish the task of bringing you to my home."

"I am here."

Bridget tried to slip from the saddle, but Curan held her in place with that strength that fascinated her. Feeling it was by far more enticing than just tracing the bulges of his shoulder muscles. Her belly twisted with excitement, and she wriggled away from him, but he didn't allow her any space to avoid his embrace.

"Not yet, you are not." He cupped her chin now that a younger boy had arrived to grasp the bridle of the stallion. His eyes focused on hers, cutting through all the reasons she had to leave him, and finding the answering flare of passion that flickered inside her in spite of her logical needs to leave him.

"My task will not be complete until I place you in my bed."

She shivered, hot need licking across her skin. Her cheeks turned scarlet because she was certain every person watching them knew exactly what Curan was saying to her, no matter how low his voice was.

"Stop it. Someone might hear."

He lifted one eyebrow, mocking her attempts to remain proper.

Bridget frowned at him but couldn't quite stop herself from enjoying the fact that he found her attractive. She suddenly understood why women enjoyed flirting at court; it did stroke the ego quite well. "You are acting like a boy with a new toy."

"Exactly what I intend, Bridget." His eyes narrowed, and a hungry curve transformed his lips momentarily. "To play intimately with you as often as possible."

Her eyes widened, but he released her and resumed his commanding stature.

"Yet such will be done in the privacy of our chamber, as befitting the mistress of my holding, because you are correct. I place too much of our relationship on display."

He grasped her forearm and lowered her to the ground. Somehow the stallion seemed a lot taller as she was slipping over and down its velvety side. But Curan held her steady, his strength amazing her.

Her feet touched the cobblestones, and he swung his leg over the horse's neck in a swift motion. She only had time to back up two paces before he was standing beside her. He captured her hand and kept her beside him as the stallion was led away, to leave them facing the assembled staff. Bridget lifted her chin. She was not unaccustomed to being alongside her mother when she addressed the servants, but Curan had a much larger household.

"What shall be done here is you and I making a united entrance into our home."

There was a note of relief in his voice that surprised her. He was watching her face, and one eyebrow rose in response.

"Can you not believe that I am happy to be home, Bridget? I have been gone many years."

At his words, she felt guilty because she had been laying her head in a safe and secure home while he was out serving his king—a duty that his wife would share the fruits of but none of the sufferings.

"Forgive me, my lord. You are correct. It must be delightful to be returned home."

His eyes moved over her face, lingering on her features while everyone waited on them. Curan didn't allow that fact to hurry him. He reached out and offered her his hand, with the palm up for her to lay her own in.

"It is very pleasing to bring you to Amber Hill, Bridget. I have spent many hours longing for this moment."

Shame colored her cheeks for the promise her mother had extracted from her. She raised her hand and placed it against his. For just a moment, happiness surrounded them both. Tenderness shone from his eyes, and it touched her heart.

"Too many hours."

He spoke beneath his breath, almost as though the words slipped out in defiance of his strict composure. He pressed his lips into a hard line and turned her to face his staff.

But her thoughts remained on his words for a moment. The tone of his voice intrigued her. He always appeared so strong that it was very humanizing to discover something so basic as a longing for home in him. This trait was also endearing in a manner that confounded her. She knew full well that the man desired her flesh, but those few words hinted at him needing her for something else entirely.

Something such as affection.

That opened up her heart, and it sent a sense of vulnerability through her. She felt exposed and in danger of having her heart broken by the man.

The thought was ludicrous. No sane person allowed themselves to fall into romantic love. It brought nothing but insanity. For someone in her position, romance would bring only misery. She had to cast the memory out of her thoughts and resist the urge to dwell on them.

Lined up in front of the main entrance to the largest tower

were more than a dozen maids, all of them wearing matching livery of blue wool with topaz edging. Their hair was covered with linen caps, and there wasn't a rumpled apron in sight. On the opposite side of the path leading to the tower was an equal number of male servants. Their doublets were buttoned to their collars, and every pair of boots was clean and reflecting the sun.

"May I present Bridget Newbury, my bride and your mistress?"

Every single head lowered. Bridget felt her resolve waver before the staff finished offering her their respect. Curan did not have to say she was their mistress. His bride, for certain, but most noble brides did not gain such public displays of respect until they had performed at least a few of their expected intimate duties. That tenderness returned to assault her heart, and this time it proved impossible not to notice how much the man was giving her.

And recall in vivid detail the fact that she had lied to avoid the duties that went with the position Curan was publicly announcing her in.

Shame wrapped around her as thick as tar. It felt impossible to keep her chin level with dishonesty dragging her down. Curan began leading her down between the waiting lines of his staff. A great deal of tension showed as they looked on their lord and new lady.

The head housekeeper stood at the base of the stairs, a large ring of keys hanging over her clean apron. The thick keys were a badge of her status and fit into locks that secured the more costly items, such as silver plate ware and spices.

"Welcome home, my lord."

She curtsied and kept her gaze lowered, but her lips were pressed into a hard line. Bridget felt empathy for the woman. Who knew what mood Curan might be in when he returned after so long away? His staff likely expected the worst, to be demoted from their positions because they displeased a lord whom they had no clue how to serve because he might have changed during his absence.

But you know how to please him . . .

Her memory erupted with the recollection of Marie sucking Tomas. The man had looked pleased, all right. But could she truly bring Curan to such a state? Shifting her gaze to him, she worried her lower lip when she noticed how much larger and hardened he was.

But there was a part of her that rose to the challenge of it. *Oh, stop it!*

Such curiosity would land her in trouble if she did not stem such ideas. She had to recall all of the logical reasons why she could not celebrate her union with Curan. Her growing passion for the man would lead her to ruin if she was not disciplined enough to ignore her weak flesh.

"This is May, head of the house. I will leave you in her care while I attend to making sure Amber Hill is secure. A task I will be happy to see done so that I may focus on welcoming you personally." Curan's voice dipped down into that brassy tone that seemed to melt through her resolve to think of their union in only logical ways. When she raised her eyes to meet his, she found a look of satisfaction on his face, but it lacked the arrogance that normally irritated her. Instead she was fascinated and humbled by the sight of a man who looked very happy to be home.

She could discover herself growing affection for this side of his personality. It would be so simple, so very completing . . .

Bridget realized that he was still staring at her.

"Yes . . . thank you, my lord." Her own curtsy was shaky.

"So, you are finally home. I'll die of your strict nature for certain."

Curan cleared his throat and glanced up the stairs. Bridget did as well and felt her jaw drop. One of the most beautiful girls she had ever set eyes on stood there. She was slender and petite and everything poets wrote about. Her skin was creamy and fair, her hair a perfect complement in lightest brown that was almost blond. She watched them with honey-brown eyes that sparkled with mischief.

"This ill-spoken girl is my sister Jemma."

Jemma performed a perfect curtsy, but her lips remained in a smile that made light of her respectful gesture.

"And my dearest brother Curan keeps me secluded here to avoid having my behavior shame the family at court."

Curan climbed the steps and stood towering over his sister. Bridget marveled at the size difference. Curan caught her staring.

"We have different mothers."

"I am much younger." Jemma shot Bridget a smile with her comment. "Which accounts for my brother's lack of understanding of me. The old rarely comprehend the young."

"I understand too well the court and what such a pretty face would gain there."

Jemma waved a hand in the air. "Well yes, and there is that bit of fact. Yet I am not as dim-witted as those other noble girls. Sweet words do not lead me so easily."

"Gossip is all that is needed to ruin a person at court," said Curan. "I was glad to turn my back on it."

Jemma's smile grew larger. "You mean to say that you were eager to claim your bride."

Curan shook his head. "Enough out of you, Jemma. We are soaked, and I do not wish my bride to think she has a shrew of a relative to tolerate along with learning to be a wife."

"Compared to you, I am an angel."

"A truth if ever I have heard one." Bridget spoke before

thinking. Jemma's teasing nature reminded her very much of Marie and what the courtesan had tried to teach her.

Curan lifted an eyebrow at her. "I was hoping you might set a fine example for my sister on the virtue of marrying."

Jemma scoffed at her brother. "Only if God has managed to create a man who is not boring, and able to gain your agreement to court me. I have abandoned hope of such a coincidence ever happening in my lifetime."

She reached out and caught Bridget's hand. "Come out of the rain. My brother seems to have forgotten that you were going to bathe." She smiled widely once more. "Another trait of the old."

Curan snorted, but his sister paid him no mind. She tugged on Bridget's hand and led her away, but Bridget felt his eyes on her. Peeking back over her shoulder, she allowed her eyes to narrow with passion. It took no playacting on her part, for her body truly did desire him. His expression instantly transformed from the stern one he wore so often. Surprise covered his features, but it faded quickly into a mask of dark passion. He'd looked like that last night, she was sure of it. A shiver raced down her spine, touching off ripples of recalled sensation all along her body. She felt it travel over her skin, up and over the mounds of her breasts until her nipples tingled as they recalled exactly how hot his lips were. It did not stop there but slipped lower, across her belly and into the folds of flesh that covered her clitoris. A soft throbbing began there, a hunger that whimpered for satisfaction.

She must deny that urge. Turning her head back around, she focused her thoughts on absorbing the path that Jemma took her on. She would need to memorize how to escape when the moment presented itself. Her flesh wailed against that thought, but her heart also lamented it. She wanted to stay and learn more about the part of Curan that was happy to be home. In truth, she longed to share that feeling with him.

Yet she must not, for both their sakes. The world was an unforgiving place, full of men who would not give mercy. Her mother was correct; she must not celebrate her wedding because Curan's honor would not allow him to see the logic in obeying her father's letter. He was a knight, and in all honesty, part of what softened her heart to him was his unfaltering sense of honor. Without it, he would be weaker. That left the task of protecting him to her.

She would, as much out of duty to her sire as a gift to Curan.

She refused to think too long about why she felt that way. A week ago there was nothing in her head save duty and logic. The reason simply was, she wanted to celebrate her wedding and not because Curan insisted that she do so.

She wanted him. Passionately and with a growing need that threatened to consume the only part of her that was hers alone: her heart. She couldn't allow him to claim that, couldn't trust in a future that was riddled with uncertainty. He would discard her if ordered to by the king's advisors. No knight would refuse his king.

So she would flee over the border to the sanctuary of her cousin Alice. *If* she could escape. There was a part of her that warmed to the challenge. The sounds of Curan's men filtered into the hallway, confirming that it would be no simple task to slip past them. The only thing that would make it possible was their arrogance. None of them, including their lord, considered her anything but a prize they had claimed. Such pride would be the key to outwitting them, exactly as Marie had said. Stroke their egos and claim what she wanted. Wise advice indeed.

Chapter Seven

D ry feet were a blessing, one she had been very neglectful in noticing.

Bridget took several additional swipes at her toes with the toweling because her skin was so wrinkled and swollen from hours in wet shoes that she was feeling water that was no longer there.

"You're not used to having servants attending you."

Bridget jumped, grateful she'd slipped a chemise on and laced her stays to keep her breasts from hanging free before working on her feet again. Jemma wasn't smiling in her playful manner now. The girl was more woman than she had first appeared. Her gaze was keen just like her brother's, and Bridget felt it sliding down her length. It was very clear that her wits were sharp in spite of the teasing nature she had displayed when her brother arrived.

"My mother raised me to be frugal and mindful of how many tasks there were to be completed every day. Having servants stand about, looking after me, takes hands from those chores."

"Hmm, perhaps that is the best answer, but I like privacy when I bathe as well. Maybe that is a maidenly need." Jemma moved farther into the room. "You must tell me if your opinion changes over the next few weeks."

The girl delivered her question in a smooth tone, but Bridget caught her shy look over the top of the dress she picked up. There was a hint of uncertainty in her eyes that Bridget understood all too well.

"I will not be assuming my wifely duties this week."

The dishonesty needed to speak such words almost choked her, but her resolve was firm. The overall good outweighed the small sin of lying.

"That is a surprise." Jemma sounded suspicious, and a glance at her face showed Bridget a familiar raised eyebrow.

"You look like your brother just now."

Jemma looked shocked and then she laughed. A soft and low sound of feminine amusement. "Lord, I hope not. He's an ugly creature, like most men. Poor, pitiful things."

Now Bridget discovered herself stunned. "Your brother is quite handsome."

"Is he?" Jemma lifted Bridget's dress high over her head to help her dress. "I hadn't noticed."

"Good."

Curan spoke from the doorway, the sound filling the small bathing room that sat behind the large baking ovens. Heat filled the room from the morning baking in spite of the window shutters being left open.

"On both accounts." He moved into the room, filling it with his larger size. Jemma laughed again.

"You find it pleasing that I think you are ugly or that I think all men are devoid of attraction?"

Curan actually looked playful as he lifted one hand and fingered his jaw. "Both, dear sister. The idea of you turning your ever-so-delicate nose up in the face of your rather large number of suitors brings me peace."

His gaze shifted to Bridget, who felt her cheeks heat instantly. Passion flickered in his dark eyes along with pleasure.

There was a part of her that enjoyed knowing that she had pleased him, because he was worthy of that.

"And hearing that my bride finds me handsome is very pleasing indeed. Do be a kind soul and leave us in private, Jemma."

His sister blew out a long sigh while she gave Bridget's dress a little tug to set it in place before she turned to her sibling and lowered herself very prettily.

"Excuse me, I am suddenly feeling ill."

Curan grinned at his sister, and Bridget stared at the way the slightest curving of his lips transformed his face. Her words to his sister had been true—he was quite attractive, this facet of his persona even more than any other she had encountered. Jemma swept from the room with another dramatic sigh.

"What surprises you, Bridget? Do you not think I can be affectionate?"

She worried her lower lip while watching him through her lowered eyelashes. He stared at her, waiting for her to answer, but for once his expression lacked its commanding expectation. Instead, there was an ease about him that led her to think that the gleam in his eye was actually a flirtatious one. A similar need suddenly awakened inside her. The blush deepened on her cheeks.

"I wouldn't dare accuse you of being unpolished in anything, my lord." She spoke the respectful title in a husky tone. He pressed his lips into a tight line that turned them white.

"I believe it well that I sent Jemma on her way. I find myself longing for the chance to woo you." He moved closer, and she felt him closing the space between them as much as she witnessed it. Awareness rippled over her skin. He paused when he was close enough to lift one hand and reach for her. The breath froze in her throat, her lungs suddenly suspended while she anticipated his touch. When his fingers met her flesh, it was hotter than an August day at noon. She drew in a stiff breath and felt sensation shoot lightning fast down her body. The feeling was almost too sweet to endure, but she refused to move away because it was too delightful. He stroked her cheek, sliding his fingertips along the side of her face that felt as though it were aflame.

"Sweet Bridget, your blush is by far the greatest compliment I have ever received."

"False flattery is not necessary between us." Truthfully, she found it difficult to think when he was behaving so charming. The hard expression that he wore when sitting in command made it much simpler to find no reason to disobey her mother.

His fingers moved up into her hair. It was still half wet and hanging loose, just as her dress was. But her stays were tight, and her breasts felt as if they were straining to be free from the stiffly boned undergarment.

As you were last night, when that hand cupped the soft mounds and his lips tasted your nipples . . .

"Because you are bound to surrender yourself to me?" A hint of arrogance colored his voice again. She lifted her eyelids to stare at him fully.

"Because you believe that is my place."

He chuckled. The amusement surprised her. His face didn't become clouded with pride; instead he stepped closer so that she could feel his body heat. The scent of soap clung to his skin, and she realized that his hair was damp like hers. His hand cupped the back of her head, tipping it up while he took the final step left between them.

A soft sigh left her lips when his body touched hers.

"It is your place, Bridget, for so many more reasons than the agreement I made with your father."

He pressed a hard kiss against her lips, but she enjoyed his strength. It was the shameful truth. Her mouth opened, and she tilted her head before he used his hand to move her. The tip of his tongue traced her lower lip before thrusting into her mouth to toy with her own. Sweet delight filled her, burning through the last of the chill that lingered from the freezing journey on the road. She reached for his shoulders, eager to touch him. His lips left hers, wringing a soft cry from her, but it turned into a sigh as he trailed soft kisses down the column of her neck.

Never once had she noticed how sensitive was the skin covering her throat. His lips were hot against it, making her shiver and press her body closer to his. He locked a hard arm around her waist, holding her tightly. Her hands tangled in his half-wet hair, threading through the strands. Every inch of her was alive with new awareness. She felt more, noticed more than ever before. She could smell his skin and knew his scent apart from others. It twisted into her senses, bringing an enjoyment that rose up from some dark corner of her mind. Just as a baby smelled sweet, Curan's skin brought her enjoyment when she was close enough to smell its scent.

Her blood felt heavy as though she had drunk too much wine, but she did not care. She wasn't close enough to him. Her hands moved over him, seeking to touch every part of him. She slid one down over his chest, over the hard flesh she craved. Her fingers curled around his erect cock, and his powerful body shuddered. She gasped, stunned by the ferocity burning in his eyes when he lifted his head to lock gazes with her.

She did not abandon her grasp. Confidence surged through her, awakening the need to command him just as completely as he had done to her last night.

"Do not toy with me, Bridget."

She stroked his cock through his pants, refusing to shiver at his tone. In his eyes was a need that flickered in spite of his warning.

"You mean as you did with me last evening?"

The hand on her nape tightened and his voice deepened. "I left you very satisfied."

"You assume I would leave you wanting, Curan."

She spoke his name in a sultry voice that drew a husky groan from his lips. She kept her hand moving up and down over the hard bulge covered by the fabric of his britches.

"Or is it the idea of losing control over me that truly drives you to reject me?"

The hand around her waist slipped lower, over her bottom, and clamped her tightly against him. Her hand became trapped between their bodies, his hard cock against her palm.

"Gaining satisfaction with you has been my wish since I arrived to claim you, Bridget. You are the one who insists on telling me that you must obey your father."

He leaned down and pressed a hard kiss against her mouth, taking a bold taste of her that sent heat throughout her body. But he broke the kiss and stepped away from her. "You accuse me of toying with you, and yet you remind me that our union is not valid in your own eyes." All hint of playfulness had departed from his face, leaving her facing the hardened side of his nature. "Yet I think you mean to toy with me, Bridget. To practice some of those lessons your mother had you given, only to take your practiced knowledge off to Lord Oswald."

Her eyes widened, shock making her curl her fingers into a fist and hug her hand closed to her chest. "I told you it would be better if you left me with my mother." Because she truly hadn't meant to play with him. He was correct to be wounded. Shame choked her.

He reached out and cupped her chin. "And I have told you, Bridget, that you are mine."

His eyes were lit with anticipation and determination. She witnessed the raw power that made him the knight who had earned a title. There was no faltering in him, only solid purpose.

"I will have satisfaction from you, my bride, but it will not be so simple as a trick you watched a courtesan perform. I desire more from you, and I swear that I shall have you as my wife."

A knight always kept his vows.

Bridget shivered, her body tormenting her with how much it craved Curan. Except he'd left her directly after firing his words at her.

Her temper did not save her this time. How could she be angry when in truth she was behaving shamefully? The maid always cried foul when a man trifled with her while intending to leave her.

Was she not committing the very same transgression? Taking her ease with Curan, touching him and sharing her kisses with him all the while thinking that she would leave.

Harsh and laden with guilt, her thoughts cut into her for the rest of the day. She found it hard to focus on the housekeeper May and her introductions to Amber Hill. Bridget found that her resolve to resist Curan had dwindled. Her heart ached, which confounded her the most, that small glimpse into his relaxed nature having snared her tender emotions. Hidden inside him was a heart she could love, tempting her beyond everything else to stay and disobey her mother.

Yet to what end?

Amber Hill was truly a remarkable castle. Three main towers rose up from the border land. The stone was solid and sturdy, while inside the roof of the great hall was supported with timber covered with slate tiles. There were no damp corridors. Whoever had drawn the plans for the towers knew his art well. Windows were placed to capture the most light possible, even on such an early spring day. From the third floor the hills of Scotland were visible as well as the patches of snow that dotted them. Alice lived far over the rise, her husband performing a similar duty to his overlord that Curan would for England. Both of them helping to secure the border.

A curtain wall surrounded the towers, but every inch of the yard was covered in cobblestone. Curan clearly had his financial affairs in good order to be able to afford such a fine fortress. Many border holdings were little more than mud piles that boasted well-armed knights.

"My lady?"

Bridget jumped. "Forgive me, I was lost in thought."

May inclined her head, but her eyes held a knowing look that such a demure action could not conceal.

"There is no hurry."

Bridget drew herself up straight. "Spring is upon us. No one will have time for a lack-wit trying to run things."

"It is not so upon us that you may not take a small amount of time to celebrate being a bride before the duties of mistress take you away."

"Yes, well, my mother raised me to be diligent to my chores."

The housekeeper looked like she wanted to argue, but Bridget did not give her time.

"Show me where the spices are kept."

May turned and walked down the hallway without a comment. There was no escaping the unspoken words lurking in the woman's eyes, however. Bridget followed her and forced herself to take note of the portions of herbs and spices stored in the still room. Rows and rows of stores kept Bridget's thoughts centered on the task at hand. She didn't dwell on the fact that she needed to gather such knowledge only if she intended to remain at Amber Hill. She had to appear as though she were, so she remained in the still room for hours. The shadows grew long across the floor before May spoke again.

"My lord."

She lowered herself and stopped opening locked drawers.

"Supper is on the table. You should have told my bride."

May offered him a smile. "I have had too many days of idleness when supper was the only thing for me to spend my time on. It has been a delight to assist the mistress with getting to know Amber Hill."

She dropped another curtsy to Bridget before leaving the still room.

"I didn't mean to keep her from her meal."

Curan was fully dressed now, but her memory recalled him vividly in naught but his shirt. His doublet was good English wool and lacked any trim. He hadn't dispensed with his boots, either—they were still pulled up above his knees—but the leather was cleaned and recently oiled. They suited him, and she decided that he would most likely never wear the smaller slippers that were fashionable for gentlemen of the court.

"The cook hoists the blue flag when she is beginning to serve." He walked across the still room and pointed out one of the windows. A flag was fluttering in the evening breeze. The horizon was scarlet and gold, the sun sinking below the mountains.

"You will learn to look for it near sunset."

He reached into the window and pulled the shutters in. The thick wood covers blocked out the light, casting the still room into semidarkness. The dimness sent a tingle across her skin because her memory of what Curan did to her in the night was a passionate one. He grasped her hand and she jumped, far too aware of every touch he laid on her.

He clicked his tongue at her in reprimand.

"I do believe this might be the longest week of my life, waiting for your courses to be finished." His face was cast into shadow and his voice was dark and husky while his hand clasped her warmly. His thumb found the center of her palm and rubbed it gently.

"Week?"

"Aye. I have come to understand that is the longest that a woman's courses might last." His thumb sent shivers down her spine and drew her nipples tight. "But some are shorter . . ."

He leaned down and placed a kiss against her lips. "Dare I hope you will come to me sooner . . . Bridget?"

His voice was soft, too soft. He was testing her. Tension knotted in her belly, and she squeezed her hand tightly against his to still his teasing thumb.

"I must be sure that I am clean . . ."

"Ah . . . of course."

Silken and smooth, his voice didn't betray anything, but she could feel him circling her like a hunter looking for the weakest spot on his prey.

"That is nothing to question me over, my lord. It is—"

"We are alone, Bridget."

His voice rose, and she clearly heard its sharp expectation. He pulled her closer by their joined hands, twisting their forearms to bring her nearer.

"You shall use my name when we are in private."

It was the command in his tone that tempted her to do as he said, but it was the flicker of need in his eyes. Lurking in the dark pools was something she had difficulty defining, but her heart seemed to understand. A desire to know you were treasured. It was hidden behind the stiff expression of the warrior, shoved down behind the mask he wore when being dutiful to every part of his life.

She knew that burden, too, always hearing the lingering echo of what was expected of her.

"As you say, Curan."

He didn't respond for a long moment, remaining frozen, but her heart accelerated and she became aware of each one of his fingers wrapped around her own. He suddenly drew in a deep breath.

"I suppose I must learn to ask you for what I wish in private." He placed a soft kiss against her hand before allowing their hands to lower between them.

"We should attend supper. I suspect the clergy will refuse to bless the meal until you and I appear."

The look in his eyes told her he could care less about the meal awaiting them. But the guilt that had assaulted her earlier resumed its tearing at her.

"We should not keep others from eating."

"I suppose you are correct. You will have to teach me the appropriate manners for a household. I believe they are different from commanding an army."

Bridget smiled and then laughed. There was no holding back her amusement. They were closer to the door now, and the fading daylight illuminated Curan's expression. Back was that easy expression that he used with his sister. Her lips rose higher and parted to show her teeth.

"You do not smile enough, Bridget."

"I do not? I do not believe I have seen a single one gracing your lips." At least not one that wasn't mocking.

He shrugged, his powerful shoulders relaxed but still looking so strong. He pulled her out into the hallway.

"A commander needs to be focused on what is happening around him, not finding things to make him smile."

He maintained his grasp on her hand, a grasp that seemed such an intimate thing. Her mother had held her hand, but this was vastly different.

"I suppose that is what makes you so competent in your position."

He titled his head and studied her from a sidelong glance. "Yet it does not please you, does it, Bridget?"

She tried to pull her hand from his. The smile faded but only for a moment before his lips curved back up and his fingers gently massaged her hand.

"You are too tense. Our arrangement is three years old. I find it odd that you are still so ill at ease with me."

"I have not been in your company these three years. Thinking about something is different than doing it."

He nodded, but suspicion glittered in his eyes. Bridget pulled on her hand again but gained nothing. Frustration made her temper heat.

"I have been in the company of only my mother as well. If you wanted a wife who was used to being in the company of men, perhaps a court lady would have been a better choice for your wife."

He stopped and turned to face her. But the man did not remain still. He released her hand and reached for her face. She tried to command herself to remain firmly rooted in the face of his imposing stature but failed miserably. Her feet retreated before her mind was able to order them to stand in place. She bumped into the wall and hissed with frustration.

"I am such a ninny . . ." The words slipped out.

Curan laughed. Only it wasn't the sort of amusement heard when the players were performing well. This was a deep rumble of male enjoyment. He pressed his hands flat against the wall on either side of her body, caging her with his muscular limbs while his body faced her.

"I see the correctness of what you say, Bridget. You are not resisting our union, merely skittish now that the moment is here."

"Horses are skittish, sir!"

His eyes narrowed as he angled his head down to look at her. Her muscles were twitching with awareness now, her skin warming and becoming sensitive once more. His eyes focused on her mouth, and the tender skin of her lips actually tingled. She licked her lower lip before realizing that he was watching her mouth so intently. His smile melted away as his mouth became a hard line of hunger.

"So are you, Bridget. If you do not like the term, I suggest you take action to change."

"You are the one who left me earlier, my lord."

She used his title on purpose. He was too close, and it was awakening her passion for him. She needed space before she weakened further, before her resolve to follow her mother's words melted in the flames of need.

"If I hadn't, I would have taken you up against the wall without a care for how unclean you think you are."

It was harsh and blunt, but she witnessed the truth simmering in his eyes. He meant each word.

"Then you should back away from me now, before your control is tested beyond your endurance."

His lips rose into a grin, a teasing glint mixing with the hunger in his eyes. "There is wisdom in your words, but I confess that you often have a way of encouraging me to behave illogically . . . Bridget."

He bent down and captured her mouth with his. His hands remained pressed against the wall beside her shoulders, but that did not lessen the impact of his kiss. It was bold and demanding. His tongue teasing the seam where she had her lips pressed together. His hands left the wall, coming to cup the sides of her face and angle her head so that he might apply more insistence to the kiss. Her jaw opened without thought. Need led her forward, refusing to allow her to ignore the pleasure. She wanted it and reached for him, her hands slipping up and over the hard muscles of his chest to hold on to his shoulders.

The touch was pure bliss. Delight flowed through her and excitement tightened her belly. Her clitoris throbbed and she enjoyed it. Her tongue stroked his, laying with it as the kiss continued.

Someone cleared their throat, a loud sound meant to interrupt them. The hands holding her head tightened a fraction before Curan lifted his mouth away from hers. Her body lamented the loss of his touch, and frustration at the interruption whipped through her. An answering flare of displeasure met her from Curan's dark eyes.

"Forgive me, Lord Ryppon, but a party is approaching the gate." Synclair's voice was gruff.

Curan's face instantly became a mask of command once more. He turned and placed his wide back directly in front of Bridget. It was a protective posture that struck her as gallant. She was grateful for the small bit of privacy as well, lifting a shaky hand to her lips because they felt swollen and shiny. She did not want the other knight to see her blush.

"What colors are they flying?"

Synclair drew in a stiff breath. His face was unreadable when Bridget peeked around Curan to question why he hesitated with his answer.

"It is the Lady Justina."

Tension rippled along Curan's features. A muscle actually

began to twitch on the side of his jaw. He was not pleased; in fact the man looked angry.

"The hell you say." Curan growled out his comment.

Synclair retained his serious expression in the face of his lord's displeasure. Curan pushed his body forward on quick strides, his boots actually making sound on the stone floor because of how agitated he was. His body was tight with displeasure. He didn't slow down, and Bridget found herself scurrying to keep pace with his longer legs. Using a doorway that led outside, he climbed the stairs built into the curtain wall. They were steep, making it necessary for Bridget to yank handfuls of her skirt up in front of her to avoid stepping on the fabric.

With the sun gone, the night air was bitter. It blew down from Scotland with an icy touch that sent a shiver along her spine once she stood on the top of the wall. The soldiers welcomed their lord with inclines of their heads while they maintained their posts at the open spaces. The wall was topped with large stones that were equal to the open spaces, providing each soldier with something to hide behind during attack. The men looked at her with astonishment. Curan spun about to shoot a deadly glare at her.

"You do not belong on this battlement, madam. Ever."

All traces of the playful man who had been kissing her vanished. She faced the impenetrable commander who had taken her from her home. He flicked two fingers, and she felt her forearms grasped from behind.

That infuriated her beyond every lesson in poise she had ever learned. "I can remove myself, my lord."

Shrugging off the hands, she turned without looking to see what sort of response her words gained her. She refused to care. The man was callous beyond endurance.

Which made it pure torment to know how well he could control that brute strength when they were in private. May was waiting at the bottom of the stairs, her hands twisting her apron.

"My lady, you must never go up onto the battlements."

"So I have just been told."

The housekeeper was startled, but she recovered quickly, her face becoming stern. "As it should be. Lord Ryppon is thinking of your safety. You cannot take offense at that."

Bridget bit her lip. Yet another thing that she must not take offense over. God, she was sick unto death of should nots and could nots. The look on May's face, however, drew her attention.

"What is it?"

The housekeeper tried to herd her through the doorway and into the hallway instead of answering.

"May, I asked you a question. I see that something is troubling you."

May clasped her hands so tightly her fingers turned white.

"I suppose there is no keeping it from you." She huffed before drawing in a deep breath and pegging Bridget with a direct stare. "The Lady Justina is . . . or I should say *was* . . . the lord's mistress."

Chapter Eight

Bridget felt the blood freeze in her veins. She stared at May and knew that she was gaping at the woman but couldn't seem to correct herself. The housekeeper looked flustered, wringing her apron between nervous fingers.

"Of course, Lady Justina is a widow, which does not make it respectable, but she isn't an adulteress at least." The housekeeper seemed exasperated and at a loss as to what to say further. She sighed before reaching out to pat Bridget on the shoulder.

"I am sure Lord Ryppon will make it clear that you are mistress here."

But nothing further than that, and she had no one to blame save herself if he sought out another woman's bed. It was entirely possible that Curan had sent for Justina. Cold and bitter, the truth stuck in Bridget's throat. The sound of the gate being raised sent a chill down her back. She rubbed her hands along her arms as she felt her skin growing colder.

You could go to his bed . . .

She could and then what? Discover herself chasing the man as his mistress was now doing? Doomed to be gossiped about even as she hoped for shelter in that same house?

That was the plight her mother was attempting to save her from.

"May, go and tell everyone else to begin their supper without Lord Ryppon. It appears he has a guest to attend to."

The housekeeper offered a slight curtsy before moving away. She looked relieved to do so, for it was an awkward moment. Bridget breathed a sigh of relief, too. She needed no one witnessing how unhappy she was.

She shouldn't be.

And still her heart ached. It was there, in her chest, an agony that refused to listen to logic. There was no denying the fact that she was jealous. She wouldn't be the first bride who shared her home with her husband's leman.

She was quite sure, however, that she would be the most unhappy out of the three of them.

Supper no longer interested her. The light was fading rapidly and the hallways becoming dark corridors that looked more friendly to specters than the living. Bridget moved toward the wide double doors she had entered the first tower through and watched Curan stride across the cobblestones of the inner yard toward the arriving party. Lady Justina pushed back her cloak's hood to reveal a face that was quite pretty. Her hair was the lightest blond and her teeth even when she smiled.

Bridget was too far away to hear what they said, but Lady Justina's features remained radiant. She never frowned or even lost the curve of her lips. She reached out and laid a familiar hand on Curan's forearm without a care for any stares directed at her. Instead the lady kept her eyes on the man in front of her, just as intently as Marie had done with Tomas.

Bridget turned her back. She did not have the right to watch, not if she intended to leave. Drawing in a stiff breath, she went searching for the supper hall. There would be no escaping without food in her belly. Even if her appetite had vanished, she needed to be practical.

Practical . . . dutiful . . . she hated the world and all of its rules. Yet most of all she hated the fact that Curan was welcoming another woman that held the dear, so very dear, option of choosing whom she would lay with.

May bustled about the chamber where she had taken Bridget after supper was finished.

"Of course, we didn't think to ready a separate chamber for you, seeing as how you are so newly wed, but I run a good house, and everything you need for the night should be here."

It was a good-size room with a solid door and even two windows that had glass set into them. May pulled large sheets off the bed and handed them to two maids who stood nearby. If there was any dust, Bridget couldn't see it in the candlelit room. May was clearly not lax in making sure that the maids were cleaning all the rooms assigned to them. More than one lord had returned to a tower that was ankle deep in dirt with a staff that was fat on the coin he had paid them to maintain his home while he was away.

"The bed is strung tight. You'll sleep well." May turned back the covers and cast a knowing look at her. "Sleep you'll be needing come next week, my lady."

There were a pair of stifled giggles from the maids.

"Thank you. I will attend to my prayers before retiring."

The maids took their leave, eager to be finished with their duties for the night. May hesitated, the housekeeper clearly expecting Bridget to want help disrobing.

"I am very accustomed to putting myself to bed, May."

May lowered herself, but there was still firm determination in her gaze. "As mistress, there will be many changes in your life."

"Yes, well, they may wait until I take my place."

The housekeeper nodded. "A pleasant night to you, mistress."

May had a light touch, for Bridget never heard the door close. She sighed with relief as she looked around the chamber to ensure that she was alone. Hiding the fact that she was not having her monthly courses was going to take diligence on her part. The staff were loyal to the lord, for certain.

"That isn't the bed I wanted to see you in."

She jerked the covers up to her chin as Curan's voice cut through the darkness. Gooseflesh rippled down her limbs as she strained to see him in the dark. She didn't hear him, but his shape materialized from the night anyway. The bed shook as he sat on the side of it.

"Why . . . why are you here?" It would be far too simple to have her lie discovered.

He blew out a hard breath while watching her.

"Is it not a poor groom who fails to toast his bride on the first night they begin their life together?"

The bed rocked and he was gone, but she still felt his presence in the room. A spark brightened the room and then another as he struck a flint stone. A single candle began to cast its golden light over him a moment later. It was quite magical, the way that single source of light softened him. He appeared very gallant, and she stared in awe at the relaxed expression on his face.

But he frowned when he looked back at her.

"I did not imagine you sleeping in any chamber save my own."

"This chamber is very nice."

He reached for a small bottle that rested on the table. She did not recall it being there earlier, so he must have brought it with him. He lifted the bottle and tipped it until fluid poured

out of it and into a small silver goblet. The light sparkled off
the pouring liquid, and she smelled the strong scent of strong
drink filling the room.

Wine. French wine—an expensive item. The aroma of it
teased her nose while he filled a second goblet.

"My chamber is nicer and will be even more so when you
are sleeping in it with me. I did not marry to endure a cold
bed."

He left the bottle and the candle on the table. The bed itself
was far enough from the table to be cast into semidarkness. It
set a romantic mood she had only read about in poetry.

Yet this was very real.

The bed rocked again when he sat down, confirming that
she was not lost in any girlish fantasy. Her cheeks heated when
she noticed his gaze aimed at her with no hint of wavering.

"If I had not been distracted, I would have had May take you
to my chamber in spite of your courses."

"What?"

She nearly fumbled the goblet, spilling the wine onto the
sheets. Curan merely offered her a firm look while holding the
stem of the goblet steady until she recovered and grasped it
solidly.

"I do not mean to have us sleeping in separate chambers."

He lifted his own goblet to his lips but watched her over the
rim of the glass. He was judging her once more, reading her
face for clues as to her thoughts.

"Most noble unions do not share a chamber, my lord."

He lowered his goblet and frowned at her. "We are in private, Bridget."

She took a sip from her own wine to cover her indecision.
To allow his name to slip across her lips seemed so intimate.
This action opened the door to other, even deeper intimacies
that were dancing through her mind. Never once had she spo-

ken with a man while in a bed, and she was having difficulty recalling exactly why she needed to keep him away.

Her body held no reservations about welcoming him closer. "I will have to have more time to become accustomed to addressing you in a familiar manner."

"Hmmm." He took another sip from his wine but lost a great deal of his judgmental expression. "I suppose that is to be commended. Your lack of comfort in the company of a man."

He reached out and laid a hand on top of her knee. "I will enjoy giving you ample opportunity to become at ease in my company."

She jumped, the wine sloshing up toward the rim of the goblet. A quick motion from her wrist rotated the cup enough to avoid staining the sheets. Curan chuckled, rich male amusement filling the chamber while he took another sip from the goblet.

"That is, if I survive this week." He stroked her knee and up over her thigh as hunger began to flicker in his eyes. "I confess that the temptation is driving me insane."

His gaze settled on her lips, and the sensitive skin tingled, warming beneath the attention of those dark orbs. She wanted to taste his kiss, wanted to have it combine with the sweet taste of the French wine . . .

"You should go . . . now." Bridget looked away and drained the remaining wine in one, long swallow. The sweet elixir burned a path down her throat and pooled in her belly like liquid fire, but it was nothing compared to the need licking at her.

The hand resting on her thigh squeezed. "I want to stay . . ."

Her body liked that response. Excitement flared up, burning away at her resolve to refuse to celebrate their union. Once she had lain with him, Lord Oswald would reject her.

She liked the sound of his words, full well, and the firm grip on her thigh told her that Curan enjoyed it, too. She lifted her face to make eye contact. She felt it right down to her toes. His dark stare was piercing and consuming, making it impossible to ignore how much she wanted exactly what he craved, too.

He growled and pushed up to his feet. His lips pressed into a hard line while his grip around the silver wine chalice threatened to destroy its delicate shape.

"You are being more logical than I am, and yet I am not sorry I came to this chamber tonight." He moved over to the table and refilled his goblet. This time he tossed the wine into his mouth, draining the liquid in two quick swallows. He paused for a long moment before leaning over to blow out the candle.

She instantly felt alone, yet watched. A shiver raced along her back as she strained to hear his steps in the dark room. Instead she felt his fingers sliding along her hot cheek.

"You tempt me beyond measure, Bridget, yet that is nothing to lament."

He pressed a warm, wine-flavored kiss against her lips that she eagerly returned. But he pulled away, leaving her with only the sound of his breathing to know that he still remained near.

"Are you quite certain you will not take your place beside me in my bed tonight?"

Her fingers gripped the bedding. "There is no doubt."

No doubt that her parents had forbidden her this man.

She heard him sigh, a soft sound that betrayed his disappointment. It wasn't arrogant or demanding such as she expected from him. But it cut her deeper than any words he had spoken.

"Until dawn, sweet Bridget."

Until I discover a way to leave you . . . or cast my fortune to the wind and embrace what I really long for . . .

Such was a tantalizing idea . . . rich with the promise of pleasure and even affection.

She heard the door softly open and close behind him. The scent of candle wax drifted into the bed curtains, making her eyes burn with unshed tears for what was not to be.

"So, you're the bride Curan spent so much effort contracting."

Bridget turned in surprise but more so for the way her temper flared. Before she even turned around she knew who was in the chamber now. A small lantern hung from the woman's gloved fingers, casting a welcoming glow through its costly glass sides.

Lady Justina was even lovelier up close. Her complexion was flawless and her eyes the blue of a summer day. Her lips looked like new spring berries, and she knew how to carry herself well. She looked down her nose, clearly judging Bridget.

"Yes, I am."

Justina blew out a little snort. "You needn't take such a tone, Bridget. After all, I have traveled a great distance to assist you."

"What do you mean?"

Justina sighed. "Your father was most concerned when he heard that Lord Ryppon had left court with his full contingent of men. He made no secret of the fact that he intended to claim you on his way north. Since you had not arrived yet at court, your father feared that you might be caught before you could obey his summons."

So her mother was correct. Her father had changed his

mind about her match with Curan. The walls suddenly felt thicker and even more impossible to escape, while her need to do exactly that grew.

"I fail to understand what manner of help you bring me." Bridget lifted her hands to indicate the walls around them both. "You are as much a prisoner as I, now that the gate is lowered for the night."

Justina's eyebrows rose slightly. She pressed her hand against the door to make sure it was closed before moving closer. Her voice lowered when she spoke once again.

"I know Amber Hill. There are two escape routes built into the walls in case of the castle being overrun. Your father sent me here to make sure you do not celebrate your wedding. Lord Oswald is not a man to disappoint. Thank God you sent Curan away even if you had to lie to do so."

Bridget felt her gaze lower for being caught. "How did you know I wasn't suffering my courses?"

"You did not ask the housekeeper for more linen. She will report such a suspicious thing by tomorrow, for Curan is her lord."

Bridget snorted with frustration. "I am not accustomed to being dishonest."

She slapped at the bedding but suddenly looked up at Justina.

"Did you say escape routes? Ones that would lead outside the curtain wall?" She should have considered such. A border castle would be exactly the place for such a consideration to be built into it, under the strictest of silences, of course.

"Yes. I left most of my escort outside the walls where the passage leads. They will take you across the border to your cousin Alice and then on to a Scottish port where a ship will take you south. You must not try to ride for London. Curan will run you down on the road. His men can travel much faster than you."

"Of course they can."

Justina was correct about the housekeeper, too. By tomorrow, she would not be able to hide that she was very fit indeed to take her place in Curan's bed. Her father was wise to send Justina, and yet she felt tears burning her eyes. Bitterness filled her mouth as she looked around the chamber and stared at the bottle of wine left on the table.

"There is no time for you to sleep. You must go now while Curan is engaged with his officers. They will meet for only a half hour; they do so every night before he seeks his own bed, and I do suggest that you slip out while he is busy. The man has a keen sense and does not leave the running of his men to others. He walks the walls himself. Besides, I do not hesitate to think he will return here once again. He is drawn to you."

As you are to him.

Justina pulled Bridget's surcoat from where it hung near the fire. "Come."

There was an urgency that cut through her grief. Bridget rose from the bed and began dressing. Justina helped with hands that were quite steady despite the tone of her voice and the way she kept looking at the chamber door.

"I will distract the guards at the escape gate while you slip through. Head south by the moonlight and your father's men will be there to help you."

All too simple.

Bridget lifted the lid of her trunk and pulled the small bag of coin from it her mother had given her. At least she need not fear who would be taking her to Alice. Her father's men would be trustworthy.

Justina took the two plump pillows at the head of the bed

and stuffed them beneath the coverlet. She pushed at the lumps they made until they looked like a person curled up in sleep. She lifted one pane of glass in the lantern and pinched out the candle. The chamber became dark, but Bridget heard the woman walking across the wooden floor.

"Come on, your eyes will adjust. We dare not risk a light to draw attention to us."

Justina opened the door a mere sliver and looked out into the hallway.

"Synclair has the same keen senses Curan does. The man is always appearing when you do not expect him to. I had hoped that Curan would give him his leave to return to his holding, but I saw him on the walls."

Justina opened the door slowly to ensure that the iron hinges remained silent. With a wave of her gloved hand, she motioned Bridget out of the chamber. There were few candles burning in the hallways, and that suited her mood. Bridget cringed when they came close to one, the orange and scarlet light illuminating her and Justina and casting their shadows onto the stone walls. Tension tightened across her shoulders, and her mouth went dry. She wasn't sure if she feared being discovered or succeeding in her flight. It would be so simple to fail. Even Curan's anger would be easier to bear than the cold separation from him forever.

Justina had not lied to her. The woman knew her way through Amber Hill very well. Envy rose in Bridget because it proved that the housekeeper had not lied when she told her that Justina had been intimate with Curan.

Justina knows her way about Curan's flesh, when you are to be denied such a pleasure . . .

Her jealousy returned to mix with the tension that filled her. Never had she felt so unhappy.

"There, do you see them standing near the wall with no

light? The gate will allow you to move away from the curtain wall without being seen from on top of it. There is a small tunnel cut through the earth on the other side. Very clever roofing has been placed there with soil and rocks placed on it to cancel it. Once I have the guards' attention, slip through and move quickly."

"What will you do if Curan discovers me missing too soon?"

Justina drew in a stiff breath. "I will go to him as soon as you are away."

Bridget felt her blood freeze. Justina stared straight back at her, a knowledge in her eyes that was devastating. Justina reached out and gripped her upper arms, shaking her.

"You must go, Bridget, just as I must help you escape. Neither of us dare disappoint Chancellor Wriothesley. The man holds terrible power, and he uses it. Do not be foolish enough to think there is any mercy in him. I assure you, there is not."

For just a moment, Justina lost her composure. Her eyes became pools of yearning, and her lips took on a pinched look. Bridget felt pity for the woman, for though not many years separated them, Justina seemed much older.

"Don't move until both guards are occupied with me."

Justina shook off her melancholy and restored her sweet expression. She squared her shoulders and pushed her cloak open to reveal a low-cut dress. The swells of her breasts were in clear sight. She didn't flinch or cower but walked down toward the guards with a sure confidence that reminded Bridget of Marie. There was a clang of metal against metal as the guards moved, and their armor shifted quickly with the motion.

A soft chuckle came from Justina.

"Do forgive me, good sirs. I was simply taking some of the night air and meant no harm. It is a lovely night. I confess that I enjoy the dark hours more than I should."

Justina's voice was soft and husky. She appeared to float on delicate steps, the moonlight glimmering off the creamy swells of her breasts. She leaned forward, just the correct amount to display her charms, and the guards became her disciples. Both men moved toward her, and she fluttered her eyelashes while twirling back a few paces. Her cloak and skirts spun up, giving the men a tantalizing glimpse of her ankles and calves. Her laughter floated upward.

"The moon is so large. I simply cannot help but long for May day. I want to dance and sing and enjoy the spring."

She began singing a catchy tune while grasping the hands of one guard and leading him around and around in dance. His comrade was eager for a chance to touch her as well, and crowded closer, taking him even farther away from the post the pair had been assigned to watch.

Just as Marie had shown you with Tomas . . .

Bridget shivered as she ducked through the gate. The tunnel leading through the thick curtain wall was pitch-black. The air within it was dank and stale. Thankfully there was no mud beneath her feet because even rain didn't make it past the first few feet. The ground was dusty and dry, so hard beneath her shoes because it had not seen the elements since construction of the wall. High above her head were men diligently guarding the castle, but she slipped beneath their boots as easily as a ghost.

Panic tried to steal her courage, but she resisted its icy grip. Pushing herself forward even as the stone walls felt like they were stretching out longer, Bridget kept her feet moving. She had to rely on herself and her family. Curan wasn't her family, not yet. Her heart ached for how close she had been to having the man to husband. There was no doubt that she would prefer him to Lord Oswald.

She pushed onward until her eyes detected a faint glow of starlight. The brightness grew more enticing as she hurried to reach the end of the tunnel. She hesitated at the exit. The trees and plants grew thickly around the tunnel end. Gooseflesh rippled down her limbs as she searched the darkness.

"Mistress Newbury?"

It was a mere whisper, but Bridget flinched. Tension held her body so tight, the sound felt as loud as thunder. The impulse to edge backward toward the protection of the castle lord was strong.

A shadow emerged from the darkness. The moonlight cast its glow on the blue and green colors of her father's retainers' uniforms.

"It is Captain Brume, mistress. Sent by your father so that you would know his will."

Brume. One of the oldest captains in her father's guard. She had grown up knowing the man. He drew close enough for her to see his long beard. In the poor light, his face remained a mystery, but the soft whistle he blew was something she recalled very well.

"Come away now, mistress. We don't want to be discovered. There is a ship waiting for you up the coast of Scotland. We've a fair bit of land to cover."

More shapes moved in the night. Bridget felt her heart freeze as cold as the patches of snow on the hills of Scotland. To be sure, she was away now, the night providing the perfect cover again.

Only this time, it was helping to ensure that she would never see Curan again.

Time was often so cruel.

It twisted like a dull knife into the mind, while a person waited for punishment to begin. Justina did not sleep, could not have closed her eyes if Chancellor Wriothesley had ordered her to. All she would have done was pretend to do as bid. Her lips twisted into a bitter line. Always she pretended. There was only one thing that was real in her life, and that was the thing that she played her role to protect.

Her son.

She allowed herself to think of his face when he smiled. Brandon was six now and his mind inquiring about everything. Every letter he sent was clearer, his spelling and command of the quill becoming more practiced. She smiled at the memory but felt it shatter when steps sounded outside her chamber. Sure and hard, they announced the arrival of one of Curan's men. There was no knock upon the door; it swung in, telling her that her guilt was already known by her former lover.

"Lady Justina."

Synclair's voice was grave, but Justina expected such. She turned to look at the knight and stared at the harsh accusation being aimed at her. The sun had risen, and she'd heard the bells begin ringing across the walls. Bridget was well and truly away now, and Curan was no fool.

"Lord Ryppon would have words with you."

Synclair was not alone. More knights waited in the hallway, their expressions grave. Justina sighed and moved toward the escort awaiting her. They fell into step around her, reminding her all too clearly of the way Queen Catherine Howard had been escorted to the boat that took her to the tower after running down the palace hallways to beg her husband for mercy. In spite of that event being many years in the past, Justina recalled it clearly. She had been there, in the palace to watch it, of which Chancellor Wriothesley reminded her often.

He threatened her with the same fate if she dared to disobey him.

But she would not have betrayed Curan for him, hadn't

taken the man as her lover because she was ordered to, either. She had been drawn to the man the first time he cut into her with his dark eyes.

Today, those eyes were filled with hard displeasure. His hands were hooked into his belt, the fingers white from gripping it so tightly.

He glared at her, harsh reprimand etched into his features. "Where is my bride?"

Each word made her flinch. His men surrounded her, and she lifted her chin. There was power in his stare, but she refused to crumple. Maybe it was because she had been intimate with him, she didn't know, but there was still a trust deep inside her that refused to believe that he would harm her.

There was no other man alive she felt such a thing for.

He snorted but flicked his fingers, and she heard his guards retreating. Only Synclair remained, his eyes burning into her back.

"Do not force me to break you, Justina. It would grieve me."

Yet he would do it. Justina saw that truth reflected on his face. She shivered, feeling the last of her tender emotions for him dying.

Good. She didn't want to even like any man. It was much better that way.

"Tell me where she heads and who sent you to assist her. I do not wish to raise my hand against you, but I will not order any man to do it, either. You know the only way out of this fortress. I trusted you with that knowledge. Curse you, Justina, for using that against me." He stepped toward her, and Synclair appeared in front of her, too.

"I am already cursed, you need not apply more to me." Fury edged her words, and both men looked stunned by her outburst.

"I am cursed with this beauty that prompts men to possess me like a fine bit of jewelry, all the while trying to use me against their enemies."

"I never treated you as such." Curan shook with his anger but kept his hands on his belt. "Yet I never deceived you with false promises, either. What have you done with my bride?"

The truth of his words undid her. Tears fell from her eyes for the friend she was losing in him. "I have restored her to her father's men, as I was sent to do. They waited outside the walls for her. One of her father's captains, he had a letter with the baron's seal upon it."

Curan looked stunned for only a moment before his face became a mask of rage, but it was Synclair who cupped her chin and turned her to face the flames of anger brightening his eyes.

"Are you mad to involve yourself with that bastard Wriothesley?"

Justina shook off his hold and stepped away, snarling fiercely. Synclair reached for her again, his expression furious.

"Hold."

Even Curan's voice wasn't enough to stop Synclair before the knight had advanced another few paces. He drew himself up with a great deal of effort and turned to look at his lord, his body quivering with rage.

Curan stared back at him. "Think upon it, Synclair. There is only one thing that drives a woman to these lengths, and it is not affection for me."

Synclair cursed. It was a vicious grouping of words that made Justina's eyes widen, in spite of her sordid life.

"That bastard Wriothesley has your son." Rage darkened Synclair's face. The knight drew himself up stiffly. "You should have asked for my assistance."

Justina shook her head. "There is nothing to do save obey. He is the Lord Chancellor, named by the king to remain in control even after the king's death. Bridget has been promised to his compatriot. You cannot keep her."

"I will have her back, Justina, make no mistake about that. The church will support my claim. Bridget is my wife."

"To what end? Wriothesley will strip you of everything if you attempt to reclaim her. You will have nothing left if you resist. The church will offer you nothing save confirmation of your marriage, yet where will you live? How will you feed your children? What will become of them when they are grown and labeled with the stain of your disobedience to those in power? The king is dying now."

Curan snorted. "That is my concern." His voice softened. "I would have thought you would have more faith in my ability to defend what is mine."

"Against the future that includes the chancellor ruling in all but name because Edward is a child? Trusting in that is foolish, and you are the one who needs to adjust your thinking. No one will call you Lord Ryppon if you persist in defying the will of the chancellor."

Curan moved closer but stopped and looked at Synclair. "Leave us. Prepare the men to ride."

The knight did not like the order, and his face showed his displeasure, but he turned and left after a barely noticeable inclining of his head. Curan waited until his footfalls had faded.

"Did Wriothesley order you to my bed?"

There was no hint of emotion in his voice, but Justina saw it lurking in his eyes. Just a mere flicker of injured feelings. Of course she had known that he did not harbor more than gentle affection for her, but that did not seem to change how he felt about her deceiving him. Anger she was accustomed to; this was something far different.

"It was the first time I did not feel like a whore since my husband died."

He sighed, a soft male sound of frustration.

"I never suspected you." He shook his head. "I believed I seduced you away from Synclair."

Justina raised her chin. "Of course you did. My circumstances do not allow me to fail at the tasks demanded of me."

Curan's features hardened. "Then you will understand that I feel the same way about Bridget. Tell me where she rides to and trust that I will not allow your son to suffer."

She couldn't see the towers of Amber Hill at dawn. Bridget turned to look behind her, but the travelers were already too far north. Sometime during the night they passed a crumbling section of Roman wall that had been raised to keep the Celtic tribes out of Britain. Now the hills of the highlands rose in the distance. Before dawn chased the night away, she had been certain she heard the wailing of all the men who had died fighting over the ground she rode across.

In spite of having a king, Scotland was still divided. Clan lairds maintained the loyalty of their men even above the king. James the Fifth had his hands full with keeping his isle lords from stealing his crown, and while his attention was on them, the lairds often raided one another. Her cousin Alice had been terrified when her father negotiated a match for her on the other side of the border. But it had been done to help maintain peace, for Alice had only a single brother who was fifteen years her junior. Her father had needed his neighboring Scot to stay on his side of the border.

And now Bridget would be sent to Lord Oswald for a similar purpose—a pawn to be used to a father's best advantage.

She sighed and tightened her grip on the reins of her mount. Captain Brume and his men were silent, their eyes moving constantly. They wore only chain mail, instead of armor, to better blend in. Without armor, from a distance they might be mistaken for Scots if you didn't look at their pants too closely. The English cut their britches differently than the Scots made their trews.

"Up there, my lady." Captain Brume pointed at the horizon. A single round tower was materializing as the sun burned some of the clouds away. Relief rang through his voice, and his men urged their horses faster. He turned to look at her.

"We'll be sheltered soon, mistress. With something to ease our empty bellies, I'll wager. Kin is kin, no matter what side of the border it lives on."

"Indeed, Captain Brume, I believe you are correct."

She gave the expected reply. One that she pushed past her reluctance, ordering herself to recall that she must make the best of her coming marriage. Just as all daughters were expected to do. She cradled her feelings for Curan deep inside her heart, where no one might view them. There was no further point in attempting to ignore the affection. It was like an infection, just as she had always been warned such tender feelings were. Now that these feelings had taken root, she was at their mercy.

They drew closer to the tower, and they heard the gate closing with the harsh grinding of the metal chains. The Scottish captain looked down on them while his men pulled their bows tight with arrows in the notches and aimed at them.

"We seek shelter for the Mistress Newbury, cousin to your Lady Alice, come with a letter from her father seeking shelter," Captain Brume called out to the Scots while they waited.

"You'll have to be proving that, English, and do nae expect it to be a simple matter. These walls were built to keep you English out."

"I've a letter that the Lady Alice will know is true."

The Scots lowered a bucket in which Captain Brume was instructed to place the letter. Time seemed to stop while they waited, unknowing if they would be denied entrance and struck down where they waited. But the chains suddenly groaned, and the thick gate inched upward. When it had risen completely, they faced over a hundred steel-edged pikes aimed at them while the archers maintained their posts above them. On the far end of the yard, Alice squinted as she tried to recognize Bridget. She suddenly nodded, and a shrill whistle went out across the men threatening them.

"Come in, English, and don't be making any fast motions."

Captain Brume muttered something under his breath as he eased his mount forward. Bridget followed, feeling the stares of the Scots upon her.

"Bridget? Oh, Bridget, it is so wonderful to see you."

Alice waved from where she stood at the base of the entrance to the tower. The gate groaned behind them, lowering once more.

"Come in, Bridget, it is going to storm."

There was nothing else to do, and her cousin was correct, the clouds were turning dark. A brisk wind had whipped up, cutting through the wool of her surcoat. Her cousin wore a Scottish dress complete with arisaid pinned over her shoulder. It was hard to see the girl who had spent many years with her sharing her tutors before being sent north to the match her father had arranged for her.

"Go on, mistress. All will be right now." Captain Brume was out of the saddle and reaching up to offer her a hand with relief shimmering in his eyes. "We'll take shelter here for the night and head out at first light."

Until then she would hide behind the walls of a Scottish tower. Bridget took slow steps toward her kin, the muscles of her legs protesting. Alice smiled warmly at her, continuing to wave her forward. Clutched tightly in Alice's other hand was the letter Captain Brume had placed in the bucket. The wax seal was broken, but Alice held it against her chest as though she cherished it. There was no missing the sparkle in her eyes.

"You must come inside with me, dear cousin. I am so glad you have come to me."

Alice reached out and clamped a strong hold on to her wrist. She pulled hard, surprising Bridget.

"I thank you, cousin, for your hospitality."

"You must be hungry. Come . . . come. We will eat. Inside now."

Alice pulled her inside and toward a set of stairs that rose to the upper floors of the tower. There was the loud sound of the doors shutting behind her that drew a startled sound from her lips.

"It's going to storm, Bridget. We need to shut out the rain, you know. Here in Scotland it rains like heaven's fury."

"Yes, of course." But two burly Scots took up position on either side of the front door, and she doubted that they were needed to hold it shut against nature's fury. Suspicion clouded her mind, but there was little to do about it.

She would have to trust in her kin.

The day became a long string of hours in which everyone she met smiled and welcomed her. The night-long ride made it harder and harder to think every action through. She was longing for a bed well before Alice showed her to a chamber, which was high in the tower up too many stairs to count. But there was a fireplace and coals already blanketed with ashes to help keep her warm. She collapsed into the bed while Alice watched.

"Rest easy, cousin. You are very secure on Barras land."

"Thank you, cousin . . . Alice."

Her words slurred and her eyelids fluttered shut. Every

muscle felt limp and lacking strength. It was strange and odd. She had been tired before, but not felt so drained of strength. Suspicion began to grow in her thoughts, but she slipped into slumber unable to act upon her mind's musing. In her dreams, Curan stood just beyond her reach. She strained toward him, desperately needing to touch him. Just a brush of her fingertip would satisfy her, but no matter how much she tried to make such a connection, she failed. Bitter defeat filled her, sweeping her away into a nightmare where she was tormented by the thought of him lying with another bride. Tears wet her cheeks as she fought against the bedding, trying to fight her way free of the chains holding her. She turned her face up to see him riding away with another bride clinging to him.

In her dreams, her heart broke.

Chapter Nine

Her mouth felt as if she had eaten wool when she awoke. Sunlight was streaming in through the thin window on one side of her chamber. It was little more than an arrow slot, and the shutter had been opened. The sun was bright, confirming that morning had come and gone without waking her. Her entire body ached, as though she had spent the night struggling instead of resting. Her hair was a tangled mess, lending more evidence to the fact that her slumber had not been natural.

"I'm glad to see you rising. My husband is home and eager to have you brought below."

Alice wasn't consumed with good cheer today. A calculated look on Alice's face and something in her eyes instantly revived the suspicions had begun when Bridget fell into sleep last evening. She stumbled when she tried to stand, and her cousin frowned.

"You'll have to shake it off now, Bridget. Laird Barras is below and we don't want to be keeping him waiting."

"Who?"

Alice snapped her fingers, and a maid gripped Bridget's wrist and pulled her over to a chair. There were suddenly hands on her everywhere, brushing her hair and wiping her face with a wet cloth. The cool water against her cheeks helped sharpen her attention, her mind beginning to function once more. A dryness in her mouth confirmed that her suspicions were well founded. It coupled well with the look of anticipation on her cousin's face.

"What goes on here, Alice?"

Her cousin frowned and looked down at her clasped hands for a long moment. Not a single maid allowed their eyes to meet hers, and her anger stirred as she felt more of her head clearing.

"You poisoned me yesterday."

Alice's head lifted immediately. " 'Twas not poison. Just a bit of sleeping draught is all. You'll be right as can be in another hour."

Bridget pushed the maids away when they tried to resume tending her. One had even brought forward a powder box and was holding a small face brush.

"You are my kin, Alice; we are blood."

Alice drew in a stiff breath. "And I am married to a Scot. You have no concept what that means, cousin. Life is harder here. My husband has to maintain friendship with the laird or we'll be overrun by another clan, and he will refuse to protect us." She shook her head. "I have my children to think of. Their inheritance must be kept secure."

A sickening dread began to twist in Bridget's belly. She turned to look at the maids and found every one of them looking as resigned as Alice did. Firm resolve shone from their eyes, but what made her belly fill with nausea was the pity mixed in with that determination.

Alice shook off her remorse, taking a step forward. "Laird Barras is below and waiting on you. It's best not to test the man's patience."

"And I'm to be painted up for his pleasure as well, cousin?" Bridget used the family term on purpose, but she maintained a tone of voice that was sweet as springtime honey. Alice flinched, but Bridget gave her no pity. "By all means. Let me not keep the great man waiting. Far be it for me to expect my own gender not to offer me up like a roasted lamb. Or a painted harlot."

"Bridget, do not be so hard upon me. Life is different in Scotland. The king does not have as tight a control on his clans. Raids happen here, and they change lives forever."

"Alice, do not be so traitorous as to slip potions into my cup if you do not want me to tell you plainly that it is shameful behavior. The circumstances do not remove that stain from your actions, and I am no coward to look at the floor and refuse to say such straight to you."

Her cousin paled. Bridget grabbed a hairbrush from the frozen hand of one maid and pulled it through her hair herself. She didn't clamp down her temper but allowed it to burn away the sickness pooling in her belly. She needed her courage and her wits now. It took only moments to restore neatness to her hair.

"Keep your paint away from my face. If your Laird Barras doesn't care for my face as it is, that much the better. I am no wanton doxy."

Alice snorted. "Your temper will make things worse for you, Bridget. Better to use every weapon you might to lull a man into dealing softly with you. A pretty face has led more than one man to doing what a woman desired of him."

Just as Justina had done last evening. The memory burned through her anger, allowing her to recall how much Justina was like Marie. Both women play acting the role of temptress to steal the wits of the men holding power over them. It was unjust but at the same time very effective. What truly mattered? Her pride or her future? Men did not take well to being challenged by women, or to being shown that women had in-

telligence equal to their own. Queens of England had lost
their heads on the tower green for forgetting that fact. Bridget
sat back down.

"Keep it simple and light."

Laird Barras was a large man. He wasn't an old man, either.
Alice's husband was sitting at the high table with the man
when her cousin escorted her into the great hall. His eyes
moved to her the moment she appeared. Sharp and keen, his
stare declared him to be a man who was more than a roughly
raised peasant. Over his shoulder rested a length of plaid
wool in rust and orange. He wore no doublet at all, and the
wide sleeves of his shirt were actually tied up to the shoulders
of the garment, baring his forearms. The cool air of early
spring didn't seem to chill his bare skin. A knitted bonnet was
hanging at an angle over his dark blond hair and he kept his
blue eyes on her in spite of Alice's husband talking to him.

"He's a powerful man, Bridget. Take heed of that. He can
lock ye away and no one will challenge him on it."

Alice mumbled beneath her breath while she made a curtsy
and pulled on her to follow.

"Clearly you have never met Curan."

He would challenge the very devil if the fallen angel had
something he desired. But she had fled from him, and it was
very possible that he would simply wash his hands of her for
the insult. She would have to deal with this Scot and do it
well, or suffer the fate he dictated.

Bridget lifted her chin and remained standing while all the
women with her lowered themselves before the laird. Eyes
widened at her behavior, but the only change in Laird Barras
was a slight tightening of his fingers around the cup in his
grasp.

"They do nae teach manners in England anymore, Mistress Newbury?"

She stepped forward, maintaining eye contact with the man. He was an arrogant one, but she didn't think it was unearned. His forearms were cut with muscle, declaring him to be a man of action.

"I do not lower myself in front of those that drug me into compliance."

One of his fair eyebrows rose as he crossed his arms over his wide chest.

"I take it ye prefer to be chained then?"

Amusement coated his words, and a few snickers escaped from the men surrounding her. Bridget allowed her lips to rise into a small smile that was mild and unworried.

"What I prefer is honesty. Slipping potions into drinks is the age-old skill of traitors, is it not?"

All traces of amusement left his face. His hands landed back on the tabletop with a firm sound that betrayed how little liking he had for her veiled accusations. The hall was silent, so much so, she heard the hounds' tails thumping against the floor. One of the dogs whimpered, clearly feeling the discontent in the room.

"I did nae order such an action." His voice was hard as steel and bounced off the wall behind her. "Will ye offer me courtesy now, mistress?"

Bridget made him wait for a response. His eyes clouded with displeasure before she turned in a wide circle, her skirts flaring out as she went. Turning back to face him she sunk into a low curtsy and remained there with her hand spread wide. Several gasps came from the women watching, but most of the men took to stroking their beards while they waited to see what their laird would make of her mockery.

Standing back up, she lifted her own eyebrow at him. "Be assured that my mother had me schooled in the art of soothing arrogant egos, even of those that intend me ill."

Laird Barras stood up. He was a large man, and he flattened his hands on the tabletop. "Be very sure that I do nae hand out abuse where it is not warranted, lassie. I protect those wearing me colors when needed, and I would nae accept those words from any man."

"You face those men with honor, not with poison slipped into their cups while you smile in false welcome as has been done here. My cutting remarks have been earned, and I am not given to speaking lies for the sake of being polite."

"Bridget, mind yer words," Alice whispered, but it was so silent in the hall that Bridget was sure half the people watching her face down their overlord heard.

"I believe I am finished with minding you, dear cousin Alice."

Bridget cut a quick glance at her kin to see her cheeks turning scarlet. But a chuckle from the high table drew her attention back to the Scottish laird watching her.

Laird Barras suddenly grinned at her, and the expression transformed his face into a handsome one. "I do believe I understand why Ryppon would be wanting to get ye back. Ye're a fine bit of spirited lass, to be certain."

"I have not promised you that there is reason to think Lord Ryppon would wish me back. If it is gain you seek, take me to the ship my father has sent so you may receive a reward from my father's gratitude."

Laird Barras left the raised platform the head table stood upon to stride down toward her. The plaid was pinned in place by a large gold broach that kept the fabric flattened against his shoulder. A wide belt went around his waist, holding the back of that plaid in wide pleats against his waist, too. As he came closer, she noticed why he wore the belt over the fabric. Strapped to his back was a large sword. The pommel rested behind his right shoulder, and the tip of the scabbard was tied to the belt near his left hip.

"I am Gordon Dwyre, Laird Barras, and since ye've made a point of saying ye prefer honesty, I'll tell ye straight that I intend to take ye home with me, Mistress Newbury."

"I am quite sorry to disappoint you, Laird Barras, but I have been summoned by my father and cannot linger in your country. To do anything else would be to disrespect my parents, which is something the scriptures forbid."

There were several outright laughs in response to her words. Laird Barras tilted his head slightly and grinned at her. The man had a devil's grin, for it made him too handsome when he allowed his lips to curve.

"Ye'll be doing a wee bit more than lingering, and that's a fact. Yer a woman grown, and it's time for ye to be giving obedience to a husband."

He reached right out and grasped her forearm. With a quick tug, she stumbled toward him, and the man bent over so that she collided with his muscle-packed shoulder. He rose and lifted her right off her feet, her body falling over his shoulder with the help of a solid whack that landed on her unprotected backside.

Bridget snarled, but the man laughed and strode from the hall with her over his wide shoulder like a sack of grain. Humiliation rose thick and choking up her throat while the blood rushed to her head. The snickers of those waiting in the yard only intensified her shame.

There was no sign of a storm today. Bright sunlight streamed down to illuminate her undignified position. He tossed her up onto a horse without any more effort than he might have used to toss a child. Bridget sat up in a huff, her face red from hanging over his back.

"You are a brute."

He swung up onto the back of a stallion standing near the horse he'd placed her on. Someone held the reins of the animal and tossed them to him. Bridget looked at the ground, tempted almost beyond endurance to dismount simply because he had placed her on the horse, but that would only see her standing in her cousin's yard, which she detested more. She muttered something beneath her breath that would have shocked her mother before tightening her grip on the saddle.

Laird Barras chuckled, drawing her attention back to him.

"I am a Scot, mistress, and ye should have expected to run into a few of us when ye crossed so boldly into me country." His eyes darkened. "We have a reputation of keeping what we find on our land."

"I am a person, not some possession." Bridget realized that her skirt was flipped up, exposing her legs. With a growl she sent the fabric down into place. Gordon was grinning at her when she looked back at him.

"What ye are, lassie, is a fine bit of fortune, and I'm nay going to quibble about the details. Ye'll be riding with me, if I have to tie ye over that saddle. So think a wee bit afore ye slip off that animal. I'll no give ye the chance to sit upright again." He tossed the reins at her, and she caught them with a firm hand, determined to show him that she was not beaten by his crude handling.

"Barbarian. Your threats do not intimidate me. Even an Englishwoman knows that a Scottish laird would not keep a woman who brings him nothing. Not unless you are a fool."

He smiled, flashing even teeth at her. "Careful now, ye'll be turning me head with such flattery." His words may have been teasing, but there was a hard glitter in his eyes that warned her he was not pleased.

"We'll have to be talking about it once we reach me home. I've a yearning to tuck ye behind the very sturdy walls of Barras castle."

The stallion he rode tossed its head, eager to be on its way. Gordon clamped hard thighs about the animal and remained solidly in place atop it. He was the picture of strength, but she didn't feel any heat licking across her skin.

Not as she did when she watched Curan . . .

Men mounted all around them, and the gate was raised. Bridget cast one look back to see Alice watching her, but her husband stood one step in front of her, his hands propped on his hips and his face in a set expression that told her not to expect any leniency from him.

From the side of the stable, her father's men appeared, every one of them stripped of their chain mail and swords. Their horses were strung together with thick rope to keep them from having command over the animals.

"I'll be getting a bit of silver from your father, too. Just no in trade for you."

"You sound like a Viking raider."

Gordon reached up and tugged on a curling lock of his blond hair. "Of course I do, lass. Don't ye ken that we Scots are Norse blooded?"

He sent his fist into the air, and the mass of horses and men made for the open gate. Her horse followed without any guidance from her. They raced out of the yard and into the rocky hills that made up the border land. Gordon had a good sixty men riding with him, over half of them remaining outside the keep. They joined their laird now, their plaids bouncing with the motion of riding. The sun was warm on her face and the wind just brisk enough to keep her from becoming too warm.

There was a certain spark of life in the moment, a sense of freedom that made her want to smile. The men kept her surrounded while they headed overland. Within an hour a fortress came into sight. This one put Alice's home to shame. It rose up into the sunlight as proud as Amber Hill. But she felt a touch of sadness for the fact that Curan was not there waiting for her.

Thinking of the man killed her enjoyment of the ride. She took a sidelong glance at Laird Barras, and in spite of his well-muscled body she did not feel any passion for him, only a slight annoyance for the arrogance he seemed to radiate.

Well, that was what she could expect from tender feelings. Dissatisfaction forever because she had been foolish enough to allow her passion to rise for Curan. She looked down toward England with a longing that sent a shaft of pain through her heart.

"Ye've no given me any time to press my suit, Mistress Newbury. Do me the favor of no looking so forlorn."

She snapped her head about to discover Gordon watching her. He wasn't mocking her now, but there was a deep consideration flickering in his eyes that warned her to be careful how much of her true feelings she allowed him to see. He was a man who would make the most of an opportunity.

"Ye'll find me home quite comfortable, I assure ye."

"Please do not think it is my nature to argue over every point, but I disagree with you."

"Because Ryppon isnae inside? Dinna worry too much on that account, lass. I expect the man soon enough."

Confusion crowded her thoughts. "What do you mean? I have no such confidence, nor have I given you any reason to believe he would chase me. I ran away from him and the vow I made to wed him. It is an insult that he does not have to suffer. He can easily find a more obedient bride."

Gordon shrugged. "Well now, if the man doesna show his face soon, I'll just have to marry ye myself."

He offered her one of his grins again before kneeing his stallion and moving ahead to the front of his men. They cheered as he took his place among them, and the pace increased. They embodied the legend that she had so often heard about Scots. There was a wildness about them that was balanced by their homage to their laird and the plaids they wore that gave them enough order to not become lawless bandits.

That did not mean she wanted to marry their leader. In fact, the idea of wedding anyone save Curan sent a twist of nausea through her. She tried to remember her duty, but the attempt failed. Her passion was rapidly taking her past the discipline instilled by her mother. The longing to return to Curan was gaining ground inside her, becoming hotter and more uncontrollable.

But that was assuming a great deal. The man would be unlikely to welcome back any bride who had fled from him. His pride was most likely wounded too greatly for her to resume her role. There was also Lord Oswald to think about. Bridget suddenly felt tired. More weary than ever as Gordon's men sent up a cheer and their leader took them through the open gate of his fortress. The castle was built of solid stone, and that fit her mood.

Cold and dead . . . exactly as she felt.

She wasn't placed in a cell, or even in a chamber with a door that might be barred to keep her prisoner. Instead, Bridget discovered herself following two burly Scots through a maze of hallways and staircases. They kept her going in circles until she blew out a frustrated snarl and stopped, refusing to take another step.

"Enough of this game. I am confused. The only way I can think of to make it back into the yard is by slipping out a window. Are you satisfied?" They watched her from brooding expressions that didn't give her a hint as to their thinking. Bridget shrugged.

"Well then, I have thought that the gossip I have heard concerning just how lazy Scottish men are was false. However, if you have naught better to do than lead me through hallways, I must rethink my opinion on that matter."

"This way."

The words were spoken with a great deal of irritation, but at least they led her to a destination instead of another set of hallways. This was an older portion of the castle, and the room she was in did not have doors. Of course, that was most likely the reason she was placed there. Candles burned in the center of the large round room, but the light did not allow her to see what was beyond the arched doorways. It was a solar, simply one floor built across the expanse of the keep. She was in one of the four that she had seen rising up to form Barras Castle. Arches surrounded her, helping to hold up the floor above her. In spite of the bed and furnishings that were present, she doubted that the solar was used very often. If it were, walls would have been built to create hallways, but such was more of a newer construction technique. This keep was just as it had been fifty years ago when it was expected that the surrounding villagers might need to take shelter inside it during a siege.

Having the dark arches ringing her was worse than any door. She felt placed on display. The candles illuminated her while the Scots withdrew behind the arches. She heard them walking sometimes and, as the day wore on, listened to them being relieved and replaced by others. There was no way to tell how many guards she had or where they were.

Nevertheless, that was not what weighed heavily on her mind. She walked over to one of the windows and leaned out. Greeting her were a hint of green on the hills and a little nip of chill blowing down from the north. She was too high to consider leaving the keep by the window, which left her with nothing to do but look down toward England, where Curan was most likely drawing up an offer for another bride.

Her heart ached, and there was no comfort to be found in knowing that she had done as instructed by her parents. A maid brought her food, but Bridget had little appetite. So she left it where the girl placed it. The day grew long with nothing but her own thoughts to keep her company. Always there had been work to occupy her hands. She suddenly did not understand how anyone might endure being lazy; it was quite irritating to have nothing to do. Bridget discovered herself pacing simply to have something to occupy herself with. Yet the true torment was the fact that her idle mind had naught to do save think about Curan.

"I thought ye had more spirit, lass. Me men tell me ye've been pacing and no eating. Are ye truly broken in so short a time?"

Bridget turned her head to discover Gordon watching her from one of the arched doorways that led into the solar she was occupying. She bit into her lower lip when she realized how happy she was to see him. She didn't like knowing that one day of solitude had made her so hungry for companionship.

"If you prefer to hear me railing, then you shall have to learn to live with disappointment. The body does not require much nourishment when it is doing little." She folded her hands neatly and offered him a mild expression. "I have no intention of becoming some type of amusement for your entertainment."

"Och now, lass, would ye like to get down to that bit of the business right now then? I'll be quite happy to show you what manner of entertainment I think ye can provide me with."

Gordon was just as large as Curan, but for some reason he didn't have the same impact on her. He moved too close, and she did not have any urge to back away from him. Her belly did not tighten, and no excitement rushed along her skin. Instead she simply watched him close the distance, but her boredom ended when he reached out to touch her. She lifted a hand quickly to slap the hand he tried to touch her with. The blow made a loud popping sound that drew a chuckle from her captor.

"You are quite out of line, sir."

"I'm a Scot, I was never a well-behaved lad. Goes against the entire idea of being Scottish. You wouldn't want me to be disloyal to me own country, now would ye?"

Moving away from him, Bridget turned to shoot a hard glare at him. "Somehow, I doubt that you are quite the marauder that you are attempting to act. I have never understood that being Scottish means you were raised with a lack of honor."

He frowned and crossed his arms across his chest. She was beginning to realize that he did that when he was afraid that too much of his true feelings were on display.

"I will wed ye if it comes to that." Instead of a threat, his words were more of a soothing promise. One that she found distasteful.

"To preserve my honor? Is that it? No, thank you."

He shrugged and allowed his arms to relax. "I'll admit that there's a wee bit of me that would enjoy needling your English chancellor by taking a lass he thinks is his, but aye, I'd wed ye before seeing ye returned to a life of shame since I'm the one who brought ye here."

"You may dispense with that concern. I shall weather the storm well enough."

"Nay, lass. I know the world, and it's a harsh, unforgiving place when it comes to an English lass who has been behind these walls." He moved closer, and she had to resist the urge to retreat from him. Approval shimmered in his eyes when she stood still.

"If Ryppon does nae come for ye, the man is a fool, and I'll be happy to take advantage of what he is dim-witted enough to let go unclaimed."

He reached out and stroked her cheek. It was a simple touch, and she remained still while his fingers made contact with her skin. No rush of sensation resulted from the touch, only a mild enjoyment. Gordon tossed his shoulder-length hair back and laughed.

"I should keep ye anyway, just because that English lord is too fortunate by far to have earned such devotion from ye."

"I am not devoted to him. My father arranged the match." She turned in a snap of her skirt and offered him her back. "What you should do is return me to my father. That will gain you more from this bit of evildoing by my cousin."

He clicked his tongue at her in reprimand. She began to turn, but he slid a hand around her body and pulled her back against his body in one quick motion. Bridget snarled and became a spitting bundle of resistance. Her flesh crawled with revulsion, making her struggles even more violent. She scratched and hit him without a care for the damage she inflicted. He released her with another mocking laugh.

"If ye are nae devoted to the man, why does my touch enrage ye, lass?"

"Because I am not some loose light-skirt slut, you mongrel! You insult me by trying your hand at me."

"As ye insulted me so freely in front of yer cousin's husband."

That hard glitter appeared in his eyes.

"Oh, I see. You are repaying me, is that it?"

He shrugged. "Well, I suppose ye cannae be expected to understand the way respect keeps peace on me land. But it is a way of life for me. The moment I begin letting someone insult me is the day that a new challenge to my authority begins. Those most often end in bloodshed."

"I see."

"Do ye now?"

Bridget offered him a slight nod. "I can understand that our lives are very different and thereby require different actions."

He grinned again, clearly amused by her response. Even knowing it, she still had trouble pushing her emotions down where he could not see them so easily.

"I'll not be content to have any man's hands on me who is not my husband. Yet that is no excuse for being surly this morning."

At least her tone of voice cooperated with her resolve to maintain her dignity. Gordon lost his grin, his face becoming a firm mask of consideration.

"Is that why I hear that you spent most of this day looking toward England? Because ye're longing to join the man ye fled from?"

Gordon snorted when her eyes narrowed at him, but she denied him any comment. The Scot shook his head.

"I ken, lass. I'm a stranger to ye and one that has taken ye in the hope of getting something for ye. There's no foundation for trust between us. But I keep my word. Dinna fret that I'll allow ye to return to England's court. Ryppon will either give me what I want for ye, or I'll take ye to the altar and we'll find a way to make the best of it. I can be a charming man when I put my mind to it."

"Do not bother on my account, sir."

He reached out quickly, succeeding in touching her cheek with two thick fingers before she jumped away.

"Och now, lassie, ye need to stop all that worrying."

Don't worry? The man had a misplaced sense of kindness if he believed he was putting her at ease. Still, it wasn't his place to soothe her. She was a woman, not a lost girl.

"Lord Ryppon will not come for me. I cannot fathom why you believe he will. Best that you return me to my father and gain your recompense from him." And she did hope the ransom was a dear one, for her father was beginning to wear her patience thin with all his demands. It seemed quite fair that someone else in her family should have to suffer as she was.

Gordon's eyes lit with something that made her step back. A burning determination that she had seen in Curan's eyes when he looked at her.

"He'd better show, because I'm nae in the mood to search for another way to get what I want from him."

And it wasn't her.

Bridget knew it. Somehow she sensed that the Scot wasn't any more interested in wedding her than she was in marrying him. He wanted someone else, and the truth of that glittered in his eyes while she watched. "I wish you every success, and it is of course a relief to hear that this is truly not about me."

He drew in a stiff breath and crossed his arms over his chest once again. His expression became hard. Clearly the man didn't care to know that she had read his emotions.

"Good. Then I'll no be hearing that ye refused yer supper. I dinna need to think I'm starving ye."

The laird in him was talking now. Thick authority edged his

words, and his voice rose, ensuring his men heard him. He gave a soft grunt along with a solid nod of his head when he finished. Bridget merely stared back at him, content to let him have the last word.

Soothe the male ego . . . Marie had clearly known what she was talking about.

A moment later he was gone in a swirl of plaid wool. Bridget suddenly felt chilled, as though she stood on the edge of a cliff just waiting to see if her balance would fail. The image was well founded for the future looked bleak.

Would Curan come for her?

Doubt was cruel, and it sliced into her fragile hope. Gordon might believe she was smitten by Curan, but that did not mean Curan would shoulder the blow she had dealt him in fleeing. Which left her standing on the cliff, looking at the fall that would not kill her, but instead leave her suffering from her broken heart for too many years to endure.

"Synclair, you must not do this." Justina tried to dig her feet into the floor, but her shoes slid easily across the stone surface.

The knight offered her no mercy. His hand was clamped about her forearm, pulling her along in spite of her resistance. He suddenly snorted and released her. Relief swept through her, but it was short-lived, for the man boldly swept her off her feet, cradling her against his chest. It shocked her because Synclair had always acted the perfect gallant, never ignoring chivalry. Holding her against his body was a direct violation of those ancient codes.

"Synclair—"

"Enough, lady. I shall do as bid by Lord Ryppon and gladly so. Cease your protests for they gain you nothing."

Doing so allowed her to notice how much she liked his embrace. Justina tried to wiggle out of it, but the knight was far stronger than she. He carried her the last few steps to the top room in the tower and angled her through the narrow doorway. Maids were busy pulling sheets off the furniture and placing candles in the holders.

"Out. All of you."

Synclair's normally controlled tone was strained. The staff scurried to obey him, their steps fading down the stairs quickly. He released her legs, allowing her to stand, but he maintained a solid arm about her waist, binding her against his hard body. He had never been so forward with her. Always the knight had maintained tight control over the urges she had seen plainly in his eyes. It had always been possible to push him away when she felt her emotions rising.

She could not trust any man.

But it was so difficult to recall her reasons to maintain that vow with him so close. He gently stroked her cheek with the back of his hand, allowing her to inhale the scent of his skin. A shudder shook her as a breath got stuck in her throat. Her eyes slid closed because there was so much sensation, she didn't need to see, only to feel. She was suddenly so weak that she could not resist taking comfort in the moment. Only for a few beats of her heart.

A soft kiss landed on her mouth, startling her. It was brief, because Synclair allowed her to jump away from him, his arm releasing her when she tore herself from his embrace. Lifting her eyelids, she discovered him watching her from eyes that were dark and full of desire. Yet he hadn't taken a deep kiss from her, hadn't used his greater strength to impose his will on her. Hadn't acted on that hunger blazing so clearly in his eyes.

Disappointment clawed through her, surprising her with how intense was her own longing for him. She could not afford such reactions. Her circumstances did not allow such feminine weaknesses; she must prevent him from thinking kindly of her because she could not resist him. Lifting a hand, she laid it across his cheek in reprimand. The slap made a harsh sound in the silence.

"Blackguard."

He drew in a sharp breath, a muscle along the side of his jaw beginning to twitch, but his hands remained at his sides.

"I must attend my lord, but I swear unto you, Justina. I shall return to you and you shall confess every detail of how they threaten you."

He turned to leave and pulled the heavy door shut behind him. She heard a bar being lowered into place and the grinding of a lock being set.

"Don't bother! Do you hear me? I care not if I ever set eyes upon you again. You are nothing to me. Nothing. I prefer my circumstances, sirrah!"

He heard her. Justina willed herself to believe that. There was no future with him. She would never be allowed to follow her feelings, never. Worse still, any gallant knight who took up the cause of lending his good name to her would find his honor stained by her soiled reputation. She was a whore. A highborn one, but a woman who used her body to survive nonetheless. Her father had sold her first, and then her husband. Widowhood had not freed her as she had hoped. Instead, the man in charge of her son's inheritance directed her misdeeds. Her sin gained her the sweetest fruit, however, for it kept her child where he belonged.

Tears filled her eyes, and for once she allowed them to drop down her cheeks. Her prison room was as much sanctuary as cell for she could weep now. Weep for the child she ached to hold and for the knight that she would deny.

* * *

Gordon Dwyre knew his land well. He'd ridden it by moon-light and by pitch-blackness, too. He knew what the birds sounded like when there were men hidden in the shadows. He left his sword in the scabbard strapped to his back, in spite of the fact that it tested his discipline. His fingers itched to yank it free, and his palm craved contact with the solid pom-mel.

But that wasnae what he was about tonight, and he needed to remember that fact. Some battles weren't fought using the steel of a man's sword. Sometimes, a man needed to apply his wits if he wanted to win the prize he had his eye on.

He could smell the men on the breeze, and it was a sure bet that Ryppon would notice he was on the prowl, too. His mus-cles tensed, his skin itching with foreboding as he moved for-ward a few more inches.

"You are either brave beyond measure or a fool to venture outside your walls."

Curan's voice was whisper soft. A second later, he stepped into view so that the meager moonlight washed over him. "Maybe you're both."

Gordon straightened up and ignored the impulse to draw his sword. His neighbor was fighting the same urge, but the English baron managed to keep his sword hanging from his hip while he gripped his belt. Tension drew both their fea-tures tight. One false move and there would be a bloodbath around them both.

Gordon drew in a deep breath and made sure he stood completely still.

"I doubted that ye'd come inside me home for the conver-sation I'm interested in having with ye."

"You are correct on that account, Barras." Curan frowned and gave a flick of his wrist. His men halted where they were behind Gordon, but the Scot merely grinned and gave a toss of his head to indicate his own men behind Curan. There were a few curses muttered around them, but Gordon and Curan maintained a steady lock of their gazes, each man recognizing the cunning of the other.

"I've been wanting a meeting with ye, Ryppon, and hearing that your bride had snuck onto me land was a bit too much of a temptation to ignore the opportunity that capturing her would afford me. I'm out here to show ye that conversation is what I'm seeking, no spilt blood."

Curan snorted. "I've come for Bridget and nothing else until I have her."

"I set the lass up in one of me towers with the hope that ye wouldnae be far behind her." Gordon smirked. "I wouldnae hesitate if I were wearing yer boots."

"She is my wife, Barras, so return her now if you have a sense of honor."

"Well now, the way I hear it, the wedding has nae been celebrated. That makes her yer bride, and those can be stolen, my friend. Even among honorable men."

Curan growled and stepped closer to Gordon so that his words wouldn't drift.

"Name your price, Scot, and do it quickly before my mood turns too dark. Stealing my bride, is not in your best interest. Not if you want me to remain friendly." He was itching to lay the man low just for the fact that he had Bridget, but that wouldn't get him through the walls she was hidden behind. Uncertainty always remained in battle, and having his bride mixed up in that enraged him.

Gordon abandoned his teasing. "Ye don't take teasing too well, Ryppon, so it's a good thing ye are no Scottish. Let's sit for a moment. I've business to talk with ye, and it's a truth that I've been thinking on it for some time. I've nae intention of keeping the lass, only of using her to bring ye up here so that we can talk face-to-face."

"I'm not going into your castle, if that is what you mean by sitting down with you, Barras."

"Ye won't?" He chuckled, gaining a raised eyebrow from Curan. "Well now, I suppose 'tis a good thing that I figured on that already."

"There is nothing good about this entire situation."

"Now is that any way to talk when I've gone to so much trouble to set a welcome out for ye?"

Gordon waved some of his men forward. They actually deposited chairs and struck light to a quickly gathered fire before setting out a bottle of wine on a small end table that one of them set down with a grunt of relief. They had hauled all of it across the hillside, lending weight to the fact that the Scot clearly did have something of importance weighing on his mind.

"I'm impressed, Barras."

Gordon shrugged before untying his sword scabbard and handing it to his captain. His teeth were clenched tight while he did it, and Curan felt his own jaw tightening while he forced himself to give his own sword over to Synclair. It was the only honorable thing to do. He took a seat and watched Gordon pour a measure of the wine into a wooden goblet, then take a large swallow out of while keeping his eyes on Curan. With a soft grunt, he poured another measure into a second goblet and offered it to him. Curan took it and lifted it to his lips, once more bound by honor to not insinuate that the man was trying to poison him when the man had tasted it in front of him.

Gordon sat back in his chair. "We were born enemies, you and I, but it doesna have to remain that way. Times are changing. You English will have a new king soon."

"I've been riding with my current king, Barras, and will not have his name insulted."

"I'm merely mentioning that the way of gaining fortunes is changing. Conquering land is no longer the only way to riches."

Curan paused, thinking about what the man had ordered his men to haul several miles in order to have a conversation with him. "What do you have in mind?"

Gordon swirled the remaining wine around the inside of his goblet. "To start with, you have a port and I've got goods that will fetch a far better price if I can load them onto a ship, instead of taking that cargo across land by cart. I want to strike a bargain that will keep yer port busy and my goods moving towards markets that are hungry enough for them to pay a decent amount. Between us, we can modernize and provide a brighter future for both our people."

Curan narrowed his eyes. "You didn't need to imprison my bride to talk trade with me, Barras. I'm beginning the process of settling down and am thinking along the same lines."

"I didna need to stop her from running away to the ship her father sent for her, either, but I thought it might make a fine gesture of goodwill between us if I tucked her away in me tower to wait for ye. It seems to me that her father is doing a fine job of confusing the lass with all of his mind-changing on just who she's going to be wife to." Gordon offered him a cocky smile. "Why, give me a few days, and I do believe I can convince her that her father has settled on me as the man she's supposed to marry."

"You've already noticed that I don't tolerate teasing well, Barras." Curan watched the man shrug. "But you make a good point. Her father is making a mess of this matter. Be very sure I will hold him to the bargain he struck with me. Bridget is my wife, and I'll challenge any man who tries to interfere with that union."

Gordon lifted his goblet while he considered his next words. "I find it very interesting the way her father is spending so much coin on getting her back to London. Mind ye, having seen the lass, I can see the value in her. She's a sweet little bit if ever there was one."

Curan growled, earning him a snicker from Gordon.

"Relax, Ryppon. I've different taste than ye when it comes to women."

"Is that so?"

The Scot pegged him with a hard glare. "It is. I want to offer for yer sister. I've seen her riding along the ridge like a Spartan when she thinks no one is wise to what she is about. I admit that I have a taste for spirited lasses. Yer sister is untamed."

"My father would have run you through for making that offer." Curan felt his tension ebbing. The Scot was the one who looked stressed now, and that suited him quite well, but there was also a part of him that had empathy for the man. He knew well what it was like to long for a woman and only one woman, while no other would do.

"Well now, you see why I wouldnae ignore the chance to get ye onto my land so that I could place the matter in front of ye. I want a bright future, not more fuel for hatred that has claimed too many lives as it is. But I'm wanting yer sister for my wife, and it's getting a wee bit hard no to snatch her off the back of that horse she is so fond of riding across the very edge of me land."

Curan took a swallow from his goblet. It gave him a moment to consider the man sitting in front of him. The Scot had an excellent point; they didn't need to be enemies, and trade was what would make his own land profitable. A marriage be-

tween their families would forge a solid union, but he would
have to admit to the fact that he held different opinions than
many men in his own society when it came to dealing with his
female relations.

"My sister is no witless girl. I know very well how often she
rides. You would have discovered it a harder task to steal her
than you think, but you are correct about her nature. If I
caged Jemma, she would have strangled on the chain or found
a way to escape. Allowing her to think she slips away from her
escort is a compromise I make to her spirit. As such, I will not
contract her to any man that she is not willing to wed."

"Is that a fact?" Gordon's fingers tightened around his goblet.

"It is also a fact that I would not be opposed to you courting
Jemma." Curan watched his words sink in. "Providing we were
doing good business together. I think a match would be favor-
able to both of us. If you can charm your way into Jemma's
heart, that is."

Barras flashed him a cocky grin at the challenge. Most men
would have taken exception to that look, but Curan recognized that it was quite possibly exactly what his sister needed.
Jemma would never behave meekly, thanks to his father's reluctance to have her disciplined when she was a girl. He had
lavished indulgence upon her, allowing her to grow into a
woman who was firm in her opinions. Women who spoke
their minds were not faring well in England, thanks to the
king's own pride. Any marriage to an English lord would most
likely end with Jemma being broken when the man's ego suffered. The Scot in front of him was a different matter. He
found Jemma's wildness attractive, giving Curan hope that she
would be happy.

Curan stood. Men jerked to attention behind him, but he

made no further moves toward his host except to extend his hand to the man.

"My hand and word upon the matter, Barras. You may court my sister."

The Scot was on his own feet in a blink of the eye. He grinned while he grasped hands with him.

"Let me fill yer cup again, Ryppon. It seems ye have a wedding to celebrate."

Curan felt his fingers tighten around the Scot's hand. All amusement left his face.

"Show me to my bride."

Chapter Ten

B ridget didn't sleep well. She felt too many eyes upon her
to relax. The bed in the solar was encased in heavy curtains to ensure privacy, but she awoke several times when she
heard the guard near the arches changing. She heard only the
brushing of leather against wooden floor, but her eyes opened
and every muscle tightened. Darkness engulfed the room, but
there was a single glow of light, as if someone had opened the
shutters that covered the windows.

Pushing back one of the bed curtains, she stood and saw
that the shutters were indeed opened wide. The night air blew
in, ruffling her chemise and chilling her legs. Loneliness seemed
to go hand in hand with the darkness. Nevertheless, the beck-
oning moonlight saw her striding to the window, the silver
glint bathing her while the night breeze lifted her unbound
hair.

Lovers meet in the moonlight . . .

Heat moved over her skin, licking across the sensitive flesh
while Curan's face filled her thoughts. She felt him so keenly,
it was as though the man was in the room with her. Noise
from beneath the window made her frown. Moving forward
she looked down and gasped.

Horses and men were filling the inner yard. Many of them

lying down next to their horses to sleep while they had the chance.

"I brought my entire army to fetch you back."

Bridget didn't gasp, she didn't make any sound at all, because it felt as if Curan had materialized straight out of her longing for him.

"Does that please you, Bridget? To see that I will place my men in harm's way to possess you?"

"No."

He was half shadow, standing near the wall where only a spattering of moonlight touched him. She felt him more than saw him. Strength radiated from him, making her more aware of how chilly the night air was and how warm his skin would feel against her own.

He struck a flint stone, and the spark was brilliant. It gave birth to the flicker of a candle, the yellow flame bathing him in light. He lacked the mail shirt that he so often wore and stood only clothed in a shirt and pants. She sighed, too full of joy to hold the sound inside her. One of his dark eyebrows rose.

"Are you pleased to see me, Bridget? You will have to forgive me for doubting such." His gaze slipped down her body, the candle flame turning her chemise transparent. Hunger drew his features tight.

"I am pleased to see you, yet that is not a good thing. It is a sign of how weak I am." She moved away from the window and the candle, suddenly recalling the guards who had watched her most of the day. "I am far too happy to allow you to take the burden of obeying my father away."

Curan made a low sound of frustration. "Do not begin trying to twist my thinking. We have received the church's blessing three years past. It is done."

"You know that is not so." Bridget turned in the dark, her

chemise flaring away from her body. "Do not think that because I am a woman raised in the country that I do not hear of
the number of divorces. Women who knelt in front of the
altar, too, yet find themselves cast out without a single silver
piece. You shall suffer along with me if we celebrate this
union. No one disobeys the chancellor. It is time for you to accept reason in this matter."

The candle flame died in a quick pinch, robbing her of her
sight. Bridget didn't hear him, but she felt him closing the distance between them. In spite of every reason, she was still
keenly aware of him, still yearning for one more touch to
savor before she had to live without it.

His hand cupped the side of her face, and she heard a soft
moan rise from her throat. She hardly recognized such a
sound coming from her own lips; it was too husky, too passionate to be hers.

"If challenging a chancellor is the only way to have you,
sweet Bridget, then I shall face him without faltering." His
thumb passed over her lower lip, sending little bolts of sensation down her spine. "But be very sure that I will never allow
you to leave me again."

He growled the last few words in a deep tone that raised
gooseflesh along her arms. His hand slipped into her loose
hair, threading through the silken strands to capture the back
of her head. His mouth pressed against hers, a hard kiss claiming her lips while his hand held her in place. His lips demanded compliance, boldly pressing hers to open so that his
tongue might plunge deeply into her mouth. Passion ignited
inside her so hot the night air became a soothing thing. She
twisted toward him, lifting her hands to touch the hard body
that had so absorbed her thoughts. Her fingertips found his
chest covered in only the shirt. The ties that secured the collar
were simple to open, her hands performing the task without

thought. There was only instinct guiding her, and the need pounding louder and louder until it was the only thing that she heard.

She wanted to touch him, wanted to be touched in return. A sigh broke through their kiss when her hands finally pushed his shirt aside to allow her to touch his skin. It was smooth and hot beneath her fingertips, but so decadent she couldn't contain her delight. His hand still cradled her head, but the hold had become dear to her. Resistance was gone, her body willingly leaning into his. In the dark he was more approachable, and boldness took over as she sent her hands along his neck, pressing her entire palms to his skin.

"Sweet Bridget . . ."

His voice trailed off into a throaty whisper. His hand moved, his fingers combing down her loose hair. She tipped her head back and closed her eyes to allow the sensation to command her. He reached the ends and lifted both of his hands to her head to begin another long stroke through her hair. He closed the gap between them, leaning down to bury his face in her tresses. She heard him draw in a deep breath and make a sound that resembled a contented grumble against her neck.

When he reached the ends of her hair this time, his hands slid onto her hips, cupping them for a moment. The grip sent a wave of excitement through her belly, her clitoris suddenly becoming needy and demanding. The knowledge of what he could do to the little nub hidden within the folds of her sex made her even more eager for his attention.

"Tell me you want this."

He lifted his face away from her neck and stared at her. In the moonlight, his face was cast in silver and black, making him appear more legend than man. Yet his touch was warm, like a man . . . like a lover.

"Tell me you desire me."

His fingers tightened around her hips, the hold feeling more intimate than any she had ever experienced. Her blood was racing through her body, her heart beating in hard thumps that pounded against the inside of her chest. She wanted to press her belly against him, against the hard cock she knew lay hidden behind his clothing. He held her in place, however, refusing to allow her to remain silent.

"I do desire you."

His fingers plucked at the delicate fabric of her chemise, tugging it up until he pulled the entire garment over her head. Her hair floated down once he drew the last of the chemise away from her, the long strands settling against her bare back in a whisper of sensation.

"Good, because I lack any further ability to resist you."

He reached up and yanked his shirt free in one hard motion that betrayed how little control he had remaining. The moonlight cast its illuminating glow over hard ridges of muscle that covered him from his neck to where his pants hid the rest of his body from view. A light covering of hair curled over his chest and down the center of his belly. Bridget was acutely aware of the fact that she was nude, but not because she was ashamed. There was no guilt pressing down on her, only an awkwardness and fear that he would find her form lacking. She felt his gaze sliding over her, lingering on the teardrop shape of her breasts as they hung exactly the way nature had designed them. Her nipples drew into tight little pebbles while he remained silent, and his attention slid lower to her waist and then over the flare of her hips.

"It feels as though I have waited an eternity to see you like this." He reached out, gently stroking the curve of one breast, his fingers tracing the soft globe until they encountered her hard nipple. "It was worth every tormenting moment."

His fingers lingered on her nipple, softly pinching it. Sharp enjoyment shot through her, and she shifted away, unable to remain still. He frowned at her but reached for the waistband of his pants and opened them instead of closing the distance between them. The open garment sagged down his legs, and he stepped out of it in one swift motion. His cock stood up, stiff and erect, with nothing to impede her sight of it.

"I believe you claimed your mother had you tutored by a courtesan to keep you from fear tonight. Is it working?"

"Yes . . ." She answered before thinking. Her mind had long since stopped trying to interrupt her with its ponderings.

"Then touch me, Bridget."

She had never heard him plead, but it was there in his husky tone. A need to have her come to him. There was no choice involved. She reached out, her fingers connecting with his erect member. He stiffened, drawing in a harsh breath. Hearing that telltale little sound flooded her with confidence. She closed her hand around his girth, allowing her fingers to grip him gently. Her memory offered up a picture of how Marie had stroked Tomas's length, and Bridget mimicked the motions.

"Sweet Christ."

Curan clamped a hard arm around her, pulling her against his body and trapping her hand in place.

Frustration sent her chin up. "Now who is timid?"

His teeth were bared at her, but she rubbed the underside of his cock with her fingers and listened to him suck breath through his teeth.

"I believe it only fair that I reduce you to the same weak creature your touch makes me." His lips curved up in an arrogant grin. "I enjoyed hearing you whimper."

"I believe I will enjoy hearing the same from your lips just as much." She rubbed his cock once again. "Unless you are too much afraid of a woman gaining control over you. Somehow I doubt that you have never been sucked."

"Sweet Christ, that woman told you about sucking a man?"

Bridget laughed, a throaty sound that drew one of his hands down to one side of her bottom. His fingers gripped her, the tips curling into the valley between her cheeks. Rising up onto her toes, she placed a soft kiss against his chin.

"She showed me."

He cursed beneath his breath and in French, but it filled her with more boldness.

"Does that displease you? I seem to recall that the subject Marie demonstrated on was most pleased. Or did you want a wife who would lie on her back and submit while reciting her prayers as you serviced her?"

His fingers began stroking her bottom, massaging and gripping the cheek they were holding. Heat licked its way through her passage, making her aware of how empty she was.

"You will be far too busy whimpering with pleasure to pray." His fingers suddenly delved farther between her thighs to touch the entrance of her body. She jerked, knocking her teeth against his chin. He grunted but remained still, one fingertip gently entering her body.

"But we were discussing *me* making *you* whimper." This clear challenge in her voice caused his face to tighten. The arm chaining her to him suddenly relaxed, allowing her to move far enough away to begin stroking his cock once again.

"So we were."

There was unmistakable challenge in his voice as well. But her confidence rose to answer it, determination making her bold. Sinking to her knees, she used both hands to stroke his flesh. It was hard, yet covered in silky smooth skin. Opening her mouth, she licked along the ridge of thick flesh that ran around the head. She heard him drag in another harsh breath, heard it hissing through his teeth. Such a small thing, but from Curan it was a glaring signal that she was affecting him. She longed to be more than a possession; here in the dark she wanted to be his lover. Which entitled her to an equal share of giving delight.

She allowed her lips to close around the head of his cock. Another hiss escaped from him, but his hand appeared at the back of her head, gently cupping while she teased his cock with her tongue. Her heart was still pounding, the frantic pace keeping her warm. Her rapid breathing drew the scent of his skin into her senses. The fragrance was distinctly male and intoxicating when coupled with the way he drew those harsh breaths. Her confidence blossomed, and she relaxed her jaw to take more of his length into her mouth. His flesh felt harder than she'd expected, but it was covered in the satin of his skin.

Bridget felt nothing unpleasant, and she discovered that she preferred doing the sucking far more than viewing someone else perform the deed. Watching had not allowed her to truly experience how much it excited her. She hadn't smelled the scent of his skin or tasted the faint salty drops of seed that collected in the slit that crowned his cock. She had been ignorant of so much while watching, for the act was decadent.

He muttered something that didn't make sense, but the tone stoked her growing pride. She might be on her knees, but there was nothing submissive about her position. Using her hands to caress the portion of his cock that wasn't inside her mouth, she experimented with speed and tightness. She judged the success of her efforts by the sounds he made and the way his hand began to grip her head tighter, as though he feared she might stop.

She recalled that yearning . . . that pounding need to press against the hand giving her pleasure. She wanted to place him in that same position, wanted to know that he was as desperate for her touch as she had been for his. Her hands moved faster, and she took even more of him into her mouth. His hips jerked, thrusting toward her as she heard his breathing become ragged and fast.

"No." He pulled her head back as he snarled that single word at her.

She hissed back at him, her temper flaring up. "You gave me release with your hand. Why will you not submit to my touch?"

"Because I have spent too many hours wondering if I have lost you to take the quick pleasure your lips promise me."

He hooked his hands beneath her arms and lifted her off her knees in a motion that stole her breath. She forgot how much strength he possessed, forgot because he always controlled it so expertly when touching her. Yet it was there in his body, far more strength than she had, plenty to imprison or hurt her if he chose to disregard her comfort.

"I will have my wife, Bridget, and I swear that I shall have you now. There will be no more time for you to spin false tales." He bent one knee and scooped his shirt off the floor. When he pushed back up to tower over her, he captured her head with one hand and held her hostage with his breath teasing her wet lips.

"You are not suffering your courses. Maybe once I have claimed your innocence you will be done with all of this resistance. To be honest, I care about naught save proving that your body craves our union as much as my own does."

He pressed a hungry kiss against her mouth, boldly sending his tongue deep into her mouth to stroke against her own. The hair on his chest tickled her skin, but it felt so very male that she shivered. Passion rose quickly to flood her. Thoughts of taking command vanished as he held her head in place and took a deep taste of her mouth. This kiss was everything she had seen in him the moment he arrived—hard and conquering. His cock brushed against her belly, promising her that he could indeed keep his promise to claim her.

You long for it . . .

"Yet I will say most plainly that your suckling is a delight that I will be most glad to yield to." He placed a soft kiss against her cheek. "Yet not tonight. I have reached the end of my discipline for waiting."

Firm and hard, his tone drew a shiver from her. His hands found her breasts and cupped them, unleashing a wave of heat that washed down her body. He picked her up and sat her on the tabletop with his shirt beneath her, quick and efficient. He pushed her thighs open to allow for his body to stand between them, lending weight to the fact that he truly was impatient to claim her.

She shared that feeling. The time for waiting was past. "I am ready, Curan."

He drew in a sharp breath, and she felt his hands tighten on her for a moment. "Sweet Bridget . . ."

The height of the table raised her so that her body was even with his cock. A tiny bolt of fear intruded on the hunger burning in her. She was a maiden, and losing her virginity would not be pleasant.

Her thighs tried to snap shut, but his legs prevented such. Curan gripped her hips, but he did not pull her toward his erect flesh.

"I would never cause you pain, Bridget, you needs learn to trust in that."

His hands stroked across her bare thighs, back and forth, rekindling the delight that had been consuming her. Skin against skin felt too wonderful to waste her attention on what might happen later. She wanted to immerse herself in the bliss at hand.

"Touch me." His tone returned to the husky whisper that made her think of moonlight liaisons. Her hands lifted without delay to press against his chest.

The next stroke of his hands along her thighs did not stay on top of her leg. He smoothed one firm palm over the top of her thigh and onto the delicate skin of her inner leg. Her passage was quick to recall how good it had felt when he fingered her sex. Hungry and yearning, her body lifted toward his, her knees willingly spreading.

"That's the way, my sweet, trust my touch to pleasure you."

His fingers found the little nub between the folds of her sex that burned for friction to satisfy it. Lightning shot through her at the first rub, and she clutched at his neck to avoid falling back across the table.

"I have waited years to feel your arms about me."

His whisper awoke tenderness inside her. Such soft words from so hard a man. She had never expected them. It almost sounded as though he needed her.

He stroked her slit, running his fingers through the wet flesh from her clitoris to the entrance of her body. Need clawed her, breaking down every thought until she was reduced once again to a whimpering creature.

She craved penetration. No matter how coarse such an idea was, she wanted him to thrust deep and hard into her sheath. Reaching out, she found his shoulders and pulled him nearer. The head of his cock pressed against her sex hot and hard. She muttered approval while he teased the entrance of her body once again. It was impossible to remain still. Her body began lifting to that finger, desperate to take it deeper. Inside her

passage, the walls were sensitive and alight with more pleasure just from being touched.

"Forgive me, Bridget, I would save you this small pain if I
could." His words were too soft for all the yearning churning
inside her.

Her hands became claws on his shoulder, her fingernails
biting into his skin. "Enough. I am not so delicate like a child.
I am a woman grown."

He chuckled, his chest rumbling. "What you are is my
woman!"

Curan's hands cupped her hips, closing around them in a
grip that was as solid as steel. He closed the remaining space
between them until she felt the hard touch of his cock against
her slit. Her folds were wet, allowing his rigid erection to slide
easily between them and into the opening of her sheath.

Hard and hot, his flesh pressed against her, finally breach-
ing the thin membrane and stretching her body until pain
pinched her along every point of contact. She would have
shifted away, but his grasp held her in place for the invasion.
He paused when she drew in a harsh breath, her fingernails
digging in deeper.

"Finish." She hated being suspended in that moment of
dread. Lifting her chin she stared into his eyes. "Now."

His eyes glittered, his lips pressing into a hard line in response to her words. His hands renewed their grip on her
hips before he withdrew from her body. Relief swept through
her, but it was nothing compared to the longing she had for
him to return.

"As you wish."

The words might have been designed to be conciliatory, but
he punctuated them with a firm thrust that didn't stop part-
way into her. His hard flesh penetrated her deeply, and he

held her steady while his cock burrowed into her. Pain burned along every inch of contact, her passage becoming a hotbed of torment that stole her breath. Her muscles drew tight, her back arching away from him, but there was no escaping his grasp.

The pain receded almost as quickly as it had begun. She dragged a deep breath into her lungs and gasped when she realized how deeply her fingernails were clawing into his shoulders.

"Leave them. I enjoyed sharing the moment with you."

"You are coddling me by saying such a thing."

Curan chuckled again. It was a rich, male sound that struck her as somewhat wicked.

"I am not coddling you, Bridget." His hands released their grasp and massaged her hips for just a moment before resuming their hold. "I am making you mine."

He pulled his length free and thrust smoothly back into her. "Completely mine."

Enjoyment edged his words. They were arrogant and possessive, but she was too distracted by how good his cock felt sliding against her clitoris to give her temper any attention. She shuddered, wanting him deeper, willing his thrusts to be harder, but her position did not allow her to move very much, only a slight tilting of her hips toward each plunge of his length.

"That's the way, ride with me, Bridget."

His words were whispered against her ear because she was pulling her body so close to his. Twisting her hands around his neck, her hips curled up to each thrust. Pleasure tightened deep in her belly, more intense than the last time he had touched her. This need was deeper, stronger, and she cried out with the desire to gain release from the mass of need consuming her.

Her lover did not disappoint her. Curan's breath was harsh, and a soft growl issued through his teeth as his motions became more frantic. He thrust harder and faster into her body, his hands holding her hips in place for each penetration. He lingered deep inside her for a moment each time before withdrawing and thrusting once more. Her heart accelerated faster and faster until she was sure it would burst, but she did not care. All that mattered was the brightening flame of pleasure burning beneath the path his cock traveled.

Pleasure erupted deep inside her, spraying up to cover her in thick delight. She bucked toward her lover, pulling on him because she wasn't close enough. Her thighs clutched at his hips to hold his cock deep inside her. Curan snarled and thrust hard a few final times before he stiffened, holding himself rigid as she felt his hot seed flooding her. That set off another ripple of enjoyment, her passage gripping his hard length while she shivered with enjoyment. No words could express this need to remain close to her lover.

Their skin was dewy with perspiration in spite of the night air. Bridget felt his heart hammering as fast as her own, and his breath blew past her ear. He shuddered, his larger body quivering just a tiny amount. Her own became limp, every muscle losing the ability to cling to him. She became grateful for the table and its support. To stand felt impossible. Little ripples of enjoyment ran along her limbs, with only a dull ache to mark where he had taken her innocence.

A soft kiss landed on her temple and then several more. They were mere whispers he trailed along her cheek and across the column of her neck before pulling his flesh from her body. A quiver went through her as pain pinched her sheath.

"It will not hurt like that again."

She suddenly laughed at him. Even in the dark she noticed his eyebrow rise.

"You know so much about virgins, do you, my lord?"

He scooped her up, cradling her against his chest and walking toward the bed.

"I agree that I do not understand you well." The bed shook when he laid her upon it. He pushed the thick coverlet over and leaned far into the bed.

"Yet that is a matter we shall discuss once the sun has risen."

The bed shook once more as he left it. Tears pricked her eyes in spite of how ridiculous it was to feel lonely. She was not some child who needed cuddling. She listened to his feet making contact with the floor and forced herself to pull the coverlet across her body. When it touched her bare skin, she recalled that her chemise was lying on the floor somewhere. With a sound of frustration, she pushed the coverlet back off and sat up.

"Be still, Bridget, you sleep with me."

"With you?"

The bed shook once more as he placed a knee upon it. He reached out and gently pressed her down onto her back with a single hand. Another quick motion and he pulled the edge of the coverlet over her once again.

"Your hearing is excellent."

The light from the window didn't reach all the way to the bed, and the curtains kept most of it out, but Curan was still outside the bed and she watched him lean over to prop his sword against the wall directly beside the bed. As soon as he finished, he rolled over to take the place beside her, lying on his back and stretching his feet out toward the footboard.

"Morning will come soon enough."

He hooked an arm beneath her and pulled her alongside

him. Bridget put her hands out to stop herself from colliding with him but might as well have saved herself the effort. He folded her into his embrace, even raising one of his knees between her legs to keep her near him. She ended up draped along his side, with one of his arms curled around her waist and the hand resting on her hip, while his opposite hand pressed her head down onto his shoulder.

She wiggled, uncertain how to respond. He sighed and pulled the coverlet over them both. She was suddenly so tired, but also keenly aware of how her body adjusted to lie comfortably against his. As though nature had designed the genders to lie just so after passion was satisfied.

Such a tempting idea . . .

Her body liked it well enough. Satisfaction was like the glow of fire coals on a winter night. Her body was basking in it. Curan shifted, his hand smoothing along her waist and hip.

"I need my chemise."

"I disagree." His hand wandered up to cup a breast. "You are not cold, and I enjoy the feel of you against me. I have marched an army across a border to feel you against me, Bridget, so be still."

His fingers landed on top of her lips, sealing her next comment behind them. What was the use in arguing? The man was impossible when it came to changing his mind. She was too tired to attempt to coax him into agreeing with her anyway. Her body relaxed and demanded rest.

Curan did not sleep as quickly as his bride did. Yet that was not a burden. He listened to the way her breathing softened and felt her body become relaxed against his. He was in awe, his fingers lightly skimming over her skin just to test if she were real. Bridget had lived in his dreams for a thousand nights. Three years of thinking of this moment when they would at last be together. He did not begrudge his king his service, but he would be a liar if he did not admit to longing to lay his head down in his own bed with his family sharing the same roof.

Yet his bride was not content by his side. That tormented him. He remained awake, savoring the way she clung to him, for once the sun rose he would have to renew his struggle to keep her.

Chapter Eleven

Bridget jerked awake but discovered that she could not move. She was held in an iron embrace against Curan's body. The window shutters were still wide open, and dawn was casting its first pink stain across the horizon.

A shuffle on the floor drew her attention to the one curtain that was still open.

"Sweet mercy . . ."

Her voice was a mere whisper, and the men standing in the chamber all averted their eyes. Synclair kept his gaze directly on Curan's face, somehow managing to not look at her lying on his lord's shoulder.

Curan suddenly released her and sat up. He tucked the coverlet behind him as he moved, shielding her nude body from his men.

"The proof you seek is on the table."

The men all turned and moved almost in the same moment Curan spoke.

"Proof?"

Curan stepped into his pants that he must have brought alongside the bed last night, and pulled them up before looking back at her. His expression was cast in stone once again, making her wonder just who had slept with her so tenderly all night long.

"The stain will not be on this sheet."

Stain . . . Her face turned scarlet and she cupped her hands over her cheeks, but couldn't stop her gaze from darting over to the table. Synclair held Curan's shirt up to the morning light. In the golden glow, the creamy linen was marked very clearly with a dark stain of dried blood.

"Fly it."

Synclair wasted no time. His boots tapped against the floor as he walked toward the open shutter. He thrust the soiled shirt out into the morning light and a cheer rose from the yard below. Bells began to ring along the walls and even from the chapel.

Curan walked over to where Bridget's chemise lay on the floor. Reaching down, he plucked it up and returned to the bed while his men became absorbed with looking out the window.

Her face burned hotter, if such a thing were possible, but there was no mercy in his dark eyes, not even a shred. Instead there was hard determination glittering back at her. He laid the chemise down where he had slept.

"We have ground to cover, Bridget. Synclair will wait for you with his back turned."

Curan slid the bed curtain closed, and she heard his men walking back across the solar. Yet his warning rang, clear in her head. There would be no trust given to her.

With a sigh, she picked up the chemise and lifted it above her head. She had no right to expect anything else, but still it hurt to know she had a guard waiting upon her. She suddenly detested her father. Never once had she questioned his will, because she had been taught her entire life to be obedient to her sire, but today she felt her temper rise clear and bright against the man who could not seem to settle her future. Where was her reward for being a dutiful daughter?

Where was the lover you felt tenderly holding you in the darkest hours of the morning?

"Mistress? Are ye ready to rise?"

Bridget sighed. Reaching for the curtain, she pushed it aside and let the light chase away the last of her dreams. Illusions were for the night, after all, and the sun had risen now. Just as she had known it would. Her mother had warned her, and yet she had done all that she could to follow her mother's advice.

A maid lowered herself before holding up her long stays.

"There's too many eyes on ye, and that is for sure. Best to get dressed before we tend to yer hair, if ye don't mind me saying so."

Bridget slid her arm into the strap of the corset. "You're correct." Even if nothing else seemed to be right.

Her body ached, reminding her that Curan had done exactly what he wished, and there was no undoing of that now. She was his woman, even if her father might yet argue that she was not his wife. The maid was quick, and her gown settled into place before the sun had completely risen. There was little to do with her hair, save brush it until it was neat and then braid it. Tears prickled her eyes, because she would have enjoyed spending time lingering in naught save her chemise. The freedom was quite addictive as was the tender nature of her husband. She feared that she would not meet that side of him again.

"Lady Ryppon? Are you ready?"

Synclair used her title, and it snapped her back into the moment. Lady Ryppon, indeed. It was a mark of respect from the knight and not one used lightly.

"Yes."

He crossed the solar and retrieved the shirt that was still flying from the window ledge. Bridget turned her back on it and headed toward the stairs. She heard Synclair hurrying to catch up to her and had to force her distaste down for being guarded. Raging against injustice had never changed it, and she knew that well. Her mother had sent for Marie just to show her a way around the imperfect world in which she lived.

It worked remarkably well, though . . . Curan does enjoy having his cock suckled.

She paused at the top of the stairs that led down into the courtyard in front of Laird Barras's fortress. Yesterday's long journey to the solar made her want to snarl for seeing the truth that she had in fact been taken on a merry parade designed to confuse her. Inside the stone walls, it had worked very well. She had never guessed that the exit was so near to where she was being kept.

It was a well-kept place, giving no credit to the rumors she had heard of Scots who wallowed in muck. There were no mounds of droppings or foul odors, either. The yard was not covered in cobblestone, such as Amber Hill, but the dirt was well packed and bore marks from being swept.

"Good morning to ye, Lady Ryppon. I trust the bed met with yer approval."

Gordon Dwyre was a cocksure man, and no doubt about it. The Scot flashed her a bright smile that was followed by a bold wink. "Ye know, I'm quite taken aback by the fact that I did nae get to kiss the bride. A shame that is, considering ye passed the night beneath me own roof."

"Find your own bride to kiss."

There was a note in Curan's voice that suggested he was jesting with the Scottish laird. There was no hint of playfulness on his face, however. He sat on top of his stallion looking every inch the commander. His armor was in place once more, even gauntlets covering his fingers.

Laird Barras shrugged. "From yer lips unto God's ears. Go in peace, neighbor."

A mare was led up to the base of the stairs. Clearly the animal was for her, for it was fitted with a sidesaddle to enable her to keep her skirts over her ankles. The courtyard was suddenly filled with the sound of armor plates hitting against each other as Curan's men mounted. Horses snorted and danced with eager anticipation. Synclair offered her his hand to mount.

So now she was gifted with a horse?

The mare was soft brown and looked healthy. Keeping her chin level, Bridget gained the saddle with all the grace her mother had ensured she had. Bridget discovered herself grateful for lessons she had been forced to repeat over and over until she polished her skills, because today there were more than a hundred stares being directed at her. They were silent but judging looks that weighed her worth through her actions.

Taking the reins, she adjusted her skirts so that they were properly placed. There was only one set of eyes she was concerned with. She shifted her attention to Curan to find him watching her with that dark, keen gaze. He took a moment to survey the way she sat on the mare, judging her confidence. Approval sparkled in his eyes, and she discovered that she enjoyed knowing that he thought her capable in the saddle.

"I hope the mare pleases you."

"Very much so."

Formal and polished, their words might have been exchanged between strangers. Nevertheless she didn't miss the fact that he had recalled that she did not care for being transported in a wagon. Some might suggest that she was clutching at anything to be satisfied, but she ignored those nagging thoughts. There would be plenty of days ahead to worry and battle suspicions.

For the moment she would cradle the idea that Curan had

brought her a mare because he cared about her happiness. Something flickered in his eyes, and she smiled at him. His lips twitched, abandoning their firm line that she had become used to seeing on his face. A brief smile was the result, fading almost in the same moment that it had appeared.

Yet it was branded into her memory.

So what if the man had smiled at her? He possessed a disposition that was impossible to tolerate.

They reached Amber Hill before sunset. The ride had been quite enjoyable with spring in the air. The mare carried her smoothly, and she discovered a new respect being given to her by the men surrounding her. They inclined their heads when she looked at them now. Gone was the rather blatant desire to ignore her.

It really wasn't fair that a woman's virginity was so highly prized when you considered that most men were not virgins when they married. Still it pleased Bridget to know she had brought honor to Curan by being proved chaste.

All of her happiness ended abruptly when they entered the courtyard of Amber Hill. Curan tossed his reins to a young lad who hurried out to greet him. Before she had lifted her knee off the horn set into the side of the saddle to help keep her on the horse, Curan was reaching up to help lift her. His face was set in hard lines, firm resolve flickering in his eyes. He didn't release her when her feet were firmly on the cobblestones. Instead, the man curled his hand around her wrist and turned with her in tow. He pulled her up the stairs that led to the first tower, ignoring the staff that lined the way. His manner irritated her because it reminded her of a child being taken inside for a whipping.

Her throat tightened. A man did have the right to beat his

wife, and she had run from him. Everyone in the castle must know. The slight to his honor was unmistaken. Curan pulled her toward the stairs that led to the second floor, his longer legs making it necessary for her to scurry to keep up while he maintained his stony silence. Her skirts slapped against her ankles, threatening to trip her.

"Enough, my lord. You need not pull me along like an errant child."

He turned to peg her with a sharp glare, but that was not enough to deter her. She yanked on her arm, her temper lending strength to her motion.

"Do you mean to say that you have not earned to be treated as such?"

"I do."

He looked stunned. His lips opened slightly in shock.

"I have obeyed, obeyed, and obeyed until I am sick unto death of hearing what everyone else expects of me. It is far past time for the lot of you to come into agreement on just what is expected from me."

Grabbing a fistful of her skirts, she yanked the fabric up past her ankles and took to the stairs. She didn't know where his chambers were, but a scurry of footfalls on the third floor was telling enough. Gaining the third floor, she faced a set of double doors that were held open. The entire floor was the lord's chamber. The doorway led to a candlelit entry chamber.

A wise choice considering their master stomped into his room behind her.

"Close the doors and be gone."

He snarled his words at the remaining servants while yanking on one of his armor gauntlets. Bridget turned in a flurry of wool skirts and offered him no penance for her sharp words.

"You shall not temper my mood, madam. I marched an

army across a border to retrieve you. Barras could have considered that an act of war."

"And I have told you, my lord, that I am merely obeying my father. An action you told me you would not have me fail at, lest you discard me. I struggle to please both of you while suffering displeasure all about me."

He threw the freed gauntlet onto the table and it made a loud metallic sound as it landed.

"Agreed. Your point is well founded, but you are my wife now, no longer just my bride. Obeying me takes precedence from hence forward."

He stopped himself from throwing the second gauntlet. He dropped it while he struggled to regain his composure.

"Promise . . ." He shut his mouth and took a deep breath. "I understand that you were trying to respect your parents, but our union is celebrated now. Promise me, swear to me, Bridget, that you will stay by my side henceforth. Give me your agreement that this matter is settled."

His eyes were bright, and a muscle along his jawline twitched. He flattened his hands on the tabletop. "I want your solemn pledge of honor, Bridget, nothing less."

She was torn. Her anger dampened in the face of his willingness to accept her word. That was trust and not a thing that came easily for a man such as he.

"I do not know what to do anymore."

His fingers curled on the tabletop. "Why not? You are my wife. Do I not deserve your loyalty?"

She wanted to give him what he sought, wanted to soothe his troubled expression. It was but a few simple words, but she knew they would be false.

"You know the ways of this world. There will be a cry from court if you keep me."

"A matter you will trust me to shoulder, Bridget." He straightened up, much of his anger clearing from his expression. "I ask you to settle into your place and allow me to shelter you as a husband should."

She clasped her hands, trying to maintain her resolve. "And I ask you to recall that husband and wife should work together. That is the reason for marriage, the forming of a union."

Triumph lit his eyes. "Exactly what I desire, a union between us. Give me your promise on the matter."

"The chancellor could take everything you have earned from you." She shook her head. "I will not be the cause of you losing all that you have battled to hold."

Her voice trailed off, and her attention strayed to the bed. It was a huge one, with carved head- and footboards. Thick curtains hung from the canopy. Moving closer, she marveled at the fact that those curtains were made of velvet.

"Henry gave me that bed."

She jumped because Curan was directly behind her. She had not heard even one step. His hands closed around her shoulders, gently keeping her in place while he leaned down to tease her ear with his lips.

"Henry Tudor."

"The king?"

His hands gently rubbed her arms, sending little ripples of sensation down her body. Her skin became more sensitive, eagerly anticipating where his lips would touch next. Erotic anticipation began to burn along her neck at the sight of the bed.

"A gift given in honor of our wedding. Henry had it made by the very same family that made his own." His lips closed around her earlobe, drawing a stiff breath from her.

"Look at it, Bridget. I have imagined you in it from the moment I laid eyes upon it. Swear that our marriage is true and binding in your thoughts, and we shall leave the past behind us."

She suddenly understood how Eve must have felt. She was tempted, her resolve so weakened by his voice. It was rich with the promise of the lover she had known last night.

"Henry will not allow the chancellor to interfere in our union, Bridget, you must trust me on that."

She pulled herself away from him, stumbling because of how fast she moved to avoid being held captive. Frustration showed in Curan's eyes, but it was edged with determination, and he was not alone in that desire.

"I will not be the cause of your downfall. We must think of any children we might have."

His eyes darkened. "There will be children. Be very sure that I will not allow you to sleep anywhere except by my side." His lips curved up. "And there will be no chemise worn in my bed, I promise you that, Bridget."

She believed him. Her cheeks colored, heating with a blush that told him how much she liked his declaration. He reached out and laid the back of his hand along the side of her face. It was such a simple touch, but she shivered in response.

"Swear to me, Bridget. I have no liking for this fight between us."

"If I give you that promise, I condemn you to whatever wrath the chancellor wishes to strike out with."

His eyes narrowed, and his hand fell away from her face. He hooked his fingers through his wide sword belt, gripping it so tightly his knuckles turned white.

"So be it." His voice was gruff with distaste. "You shall remain in this chamber unless you have my permission to leave it."

Bridget stiffened, but he was not finished.

"Without your dress."

"What?"

He offered her no mercy, only a hard expression. "I doubt that you will find it simple to slip across the yard without a dress, so you will disrobe and hand me your clothing. It will be stored elsewhere until you swear to me or I get a letter from your father ending this debate."

"That is barbaric."

"I consider it kinder than chaining you to the wall. Yet I would far rather have your word. The road is full of danger, Bridget; I will not have you risking yourself in some attempt to shelter me."

"Because I am a woman?"

"Because you are my wife."

She walked away from the bed, unable to quell her own longing for it. The man was unable to see reason when it was spoken plainly to him. She felt his eyes on her and turned to stare straight back at him. She watched a flicker of approval light his eyes, but it did nothing to soften his expression.

"Disrobe, Bridget. Do not make me handle you unkindly."

"I make you do nothing, my lord."

But she also recalled her first lesson from Marie, and the man had ordered her to disrobe . . .

Chapter Twelve

Raising her chin, Bridget stared into Curan's eyes. "I suppose there is little point in testing my strength against yours."

Surprise flickered across his eyes, but suspicion remained. Lifting one hand, Bridget reminded herself to move slowly. Her heart began beating faster, and her senses became keener. She heard a pop when she undid the hook that held her over-partlet closed. Thrusting a finger into the opening, she traced her own collarbone while drawing the wool garment aside to reveal her skin.

"Is this what you wanted, my lord?"

She drew the over-partlet off her shoulders completely and walked toward another table that was near the fireplace built into the wall near a huge set of windows.

"I would prefer your promise and the removal of your gown."

She offered him a raised eyebrow.

"You sound greedy. If I gave you my word, I would expect to keep my dress." She forced her words to pass her lips slowly. Curan seemed willing to wait for each one as well. His eyes followed her every motion, no matter how small. She gently unbuttoned one cuff and then separated the fabric before shifting her attention to the matching one.

"I believe you shall have to choose. My word . . ." She

trailed her finger along the newly exposed skin of her wrist. "Or my dress . . ."

He swallowed roughly.

The little response made her confidence swell. Heat began licking along her skin as she moved her hands to the hooks that held her bodice closed. The first gave way with a pop, and the next one, too.

"It's rather chilly . . ."

She turned her back but peeked over her shoulder at Curan. His lips were pressed into a hard line, but another little pop told him that a third hook had been released.

"The fire feels quite nice against my skin."

"You are toying with me."

Another pop, and the shoulders of her dress began to sag down her shoulders.

"Such a critical thing to say, especially considering my very perfect compliance with your demand, my lord."

She rolled the title and turned to display her half-open dress. Her corset was in plain sight, and his attention settled on the top of it, where her exposed breasts swelled up. Her fingers released the last two hooks, and she turned back to face the fire before allowing the dress to begin falling down her body. The garment caught on her hips, and she smoothed her hands down the length of her stays until she reached it.

"That courtesan taught you her tricks."

The dress slumped to the floor, and she stepped out of it. Turning back around, she toyed with the end of the lace that held her corset tightly closed.

"Is there something wrong with my actions? You did tell me to disrobe. Am I doing a poor job of it? Shall I try again?" She bent her knees and lowered her body so that she could grasp the pooled dress.

"Leave it." He blew out a stiff breath in response.

She straightened and pulled on the tie holding her corset closed. The cord gave way, and the weight of her breasts tugged the lace through the eyelets.

"You need not become cross, my lord. I am simply attempting to make certain that I understand your will."

"I find myself very pleased with your compliance, Bridget."

His fingers tightened on his belt but only for a moment. He grasped the end of the belt and tugged it so that the metal tongue that secured it loosened. With a practiced hand, he caught the entire belt and sword, lifting it up to place it on the table that was near the door. He reached up and unbuttoned the first few buttons that held his simple doublet closed. The sight of his shirt drew a memory of the previous night vividly to her mind. She cast her attention down as it planted ideas in her mind of how much she might enjoy being stripped again while he was with her.

He uttered her name in a husky tone that renewed her blush. His lips began to curve. "Dare I hope to be more pleased by your actions?"

She turned her back upon him instead. The lace holding her stays took only a few quick motions to pull loose. The garment instantly fell away from her body. A little sigh of relief rose from her throat as her chemise was allowed to float gently around her natural shape.

A pair of hands cupped her breasts in the next moment. Curan curled around her, leaning over her while his hands began massaging her breasts. Excitement twisted her belly, flooding her with hungry need.

"Perhaps a better question might be, may I hope to please you, sweet Bridget?"

Rapture flowed from his hands into her, the tender globes of her breasts rejoicing in their freedom and the soothing motions of his hands. He chuckled when she did nothing more than lean back to allow him to continue. Her body rejected any course of action that involved interrupting the delightful motion of his hands.

"I should have paid that courtesan, for she did me a favor in agreeing to instruct you."

He pressed a kiss against her neck and then released her. A whimper rose from her throat as she turned to see where he was. The expression on his face was fascinating to her. There had not been enough light last night to see him clearly. Now, the candles spread their yellow glow over him, giving her an unobstructed view of the hunger dancing in his eyes.

"For she taught you confidence, and that is something that should never be mistaken for a challenge to my authority. Too many fathers demand timidity from their daughters."

"I never expected a man to understand that."

"There are many things that you and I still have to learn about one another." His eyes traveled down her length, pausing on the junction of her thighs. "I have a few ideas on where to begin our study."

She was tempted to bend beneath the demand that was flickering in his eyes. Her fingers worried the fabric of her chemise, and feeling the fabric between her fingers offered her a path to regaining dominance.

Grasping the fabric, she drew it up her body, baring her knees and thighs, and farther up until the fabric slipped over her head.

"Perfectly done." His lips pressed into that hard line once again. "Perhaps too well done."

She lifted one shoulder. "What was that you just said about not caring for timidity?"

He scoffed at her, but amusement danced in his dark eyes.

"Touché, my sweet."

His hands moved to his britches. He made much faster work of opening the front of the garment, but she was no less captivated. It was a truth that she found his body pleasing to behold. His gaze remained on her the entire time, however, those dark eyes judging her response and possibly her nerve. His pants ended up being thrown away from him with no regard to where they landed.

The heat from the fire bathed her bare skin in warmth, but there was fire flickering in her belly. Knowing what his cock felt like deep inside her seemed to have removed all hesitation from her flesh. Passion sprang to life instantly and without any quibbling from her thoughts. Her nipples drew into hard points, and his gaze dropped down her body to linger on the two jewels. His face became a mask of hunger, and he pulled his shirt up and off with a motion that produced a soft tearing sound.

She did not get the chance to look at him. Curan closed the distance between them too quickly, his hands cupping her face before he claimed her mouth with a hard kiss. His lips demanded a response, and she did not deny him, could not deny him, for she was starving for his touch. Her mouth opened when his tongue teased her lower lip. The organ thrust deep into her mouth, tangling with her own in a dance that sent anticipation through her passage. Her hand reached for him, stroking over his hip and across his lean belly until she found his erect cock. Her fingers curled around the pole, delighting in the smooth skin.

He lifted his head but stood still while her hand stroked his length.

"You are more content in this marriage than you believe, Bridget."

He released her face and scooped her up in his arms. She gasped at the ease with which he took her complete weight. There was no hint of strain on his face, only a very clear look of victory.

"Passion for the flesh is not something to offer praise for."

"I disagree."

He walked to the bed and laid her in the center of it. Satisfaction flickered in his eyes.

"Passion is something that is too often faked by courtesans, and much too often lacking in noble marriage beds." He cupped one breast as his body stretched out beside hers. "And I intend to show you just how much hotter it may become."

He leaned down to capture one puckered nipple between his lips. His fingers curled around the soft mound of her breast, raising the nipple up in offering. His mouth eagerly feasted upon the delicate tip, sucking it deeper into his mouth. She had never dreamed that a man's mouth might be so hot. She twisted and arched while pleasure flowed down her body. His free hand smoothed over her chest and down across her belly until he touched the soft curls that crowned her mons.

"I believe it is time to show you how much I enjoyed your sweet lips around my cock last night."

His words didn't make sense, and her mind wasn't very interested in focusing in order to understand. Bridget was much more interested in his hand resting so softly just above her slit. Hidden between the folds of her sex, her clitoris begged for attention.

"By returning the favor."

Curan's voice dipped down until it was nothing but a dark promise. She shivered, her mind offering up an idea that was intoxicating with its imagery.

"Men do not do such things . . ."

One dark brow rose to mock her. "Why not, sweet wife? Because Marie did not mention it? I will tell you why she did not." He gently toyed with the curls his fingers were resting on, before his fingertips gently penetrated the moist folds of her sex.

"Men pay a courtesan and expect service for their coin, not to give service in return. You are my wife, and pleasuring you is a challenge that I do not intend to ignore."

"But men cannot—"

She drew a stiff breath as his fingers found her clitoris. Pleasure shot through her so fast she could not complete her thought. Her heart suddenly pumped harder, feeling as though it was going to bruise against her ribs.

"Cannot suck? I assure you they can, if they want to hear their wife moaning in pleasure." His finger rubbed over her clitoris, giving her no chance to form any retort. She was trapped by her own flesh's desire to give over completely to his touch, his command.

"And I do."

That dark promise returned to his voice. Her dropping eyelids opened wide to stare at his face. The promise was not just in his voice, it shimmered in the dark center of his eyes, sending a twist of anticipation through her.

"It must be wrong to . . . to . . ."

"Place my mouth on your slit while I tongue you?" He leaned down over her, trapping her on her back with his larger body. "The only thing wrong is the fact that we are talking when I should be letting action speak for me."

The breath froze in her chest, and she bit into her lower lip, suspended between shock and excitement. Curan took advantage of her shock, sliding quickly down the bed and pressing her thighs wide to allow for his shoulders to rest between them. His finger left her sex and helped to pull her folds wide.

"Curan, you cannot."

"I assure you I can."

Bridget felt his breath hitting the wet skin of her open sex, sending a ripple of need through her passage that was so intense her hands clawed at the bedding beneath her. She twisted, but he placed a hand on her belly, pinning her hips with ease.

His tongue gently touched her spread flesh, and she jerked; the feeling was too intense to endure.

"Curan, I cannot suffer this."

He didn't answer her or grant her any reprieve. His tongue lapped her from the opening to her passage to the top of her slit where her clitoris throbbed. Her spine arched, her head leaning back as her eyes closed. Too much sensation came from where he was gently flicking his tongue over her flesh, slowly, little laps that made her think insanity was soon to claim her. There was no possible way to endure such abundance of pleasure without her mind snapping.

"*Stop.* Or I fear I will go mad."

"Exactly what I hope for, Bridget. To hear you wailing in your pleasure-induced delirium."

He returned to her spread body, this time fashioning his lips around her clitoris. Pleasure burned up her passage to twist and pull at her insides. He sucked hard on the little nub, applying his tongue to it as well. The delight was too intense. Her mind stopped commanding her. Instead her body twisted and pulsed, her hips lifting up to press harder against his mouth while her cries bounced off the chamber walls. There was no fending off the explosion of pleasure that tore through her. It bit into her belly while she clawed at the sheeting and cried out.

She forgot to breathe and ended up grateful for the bed supporting her. Her chest rose and fell at an alarming rate while her heart felt as if it was intent on hammering a hole through her chest. But none of that truly made much impact on her, for her body was still shivering in the glow of delight. This feeling sent little waves along her limbs while satisfaction bathed her clitoris.

"Exactly what I was hoping to hear from you, *wife*."

Curan's voice was edged with hard need. Bridget opened her eyes to discover him looking at her from between her spread thighs. His eyes practically glowed with his need. He was gently smoothing his hand along the tender flesh of her inner thigh. It was the perfect companion to the satisfaction that was slowly receding in her belly, but he moved his hand to her sex and thrust one thick finger up into her passage, rekindling her passion in an instant. This hunger was deeper and harder. The touch of his mouth against her clitoris wouldn't satisfy the craving, and she knew that now. She hadn't realized the difference the night he invaded the wagon and fingered her. Tonight her passage eagerly tried to grasp that finger, begging to be filled. She wasn't completely satisfied and would remain unsatisfied until his hard cock consumed her once more.

Sitting up, she cupped the sides of his head and kissed him. Her own scent clung to his lips, but that did not deter her. She pressed a hungry kiss against his mouth, pushing him back onto his knees while she rose onto her own to keep their lips together. His hands reached for her hips, cupping each one in a strong grasp that pulled her up until the head of his erection brushed against her opening.

He lowered her onto his cock, the hard flesh easily penetrating her wetness. She was startled by the position and lifted her lips away from his.

"Did your tutor not tell you that there are many positions for lovemaking?"

She made a little sound of enjoyment as he pressed her all the way down. Her passage ached just a tiny amount as it was once again stretched by his hard flesh.

"I watched her ride like this."

"You watched them doing this?" He growled his question, jealousy evident in his eyes.

"It was the best way to learn since actually trying my own hand was not permitted."

"You are correct about that, madam. I would not have permitted another man to touch you."

His hands tightened on her hips, confirming his jealousy, but she found it tender. Clasping her thighs on either side of his hips, she lifted herself up, rising off his cock and then lowering herself back down until she felt the entire length lodged tight inside her again.

"I learned that the woman can ride, not simply wait."

He growled, but it was a sound rich with male enjoyment. "I begin to find my judgment softening."

She rose once again and then began a steady motion of up-and-down strokes that sent rekindled desire through her. "I rather enjoy you being rigid with me."

He chuckled through gritted teeth while his hands began to help lift her up and push her back down. "You have that effect upon me."

A soft blush colored her cheeks, and he made a low sound beneath his breath.

"Your blush is touching, Bridget. Does it surprise you to know that we might tease about intimacies?"

"It does."

Yet it was becoming much harder to concentrate on words. Her heart was racing again, and she wanted to move faster.

She pressed herself down with more force and heard him growl softly with appreciation. Her thighs clasped him tighter, and still she wanted to be closer.

"I am done with teasing and waiting. I want you beneath me, taking my seed."

He growled and pushed her back onto the bed without pulling out of her body. His chest pressed her down, but he clamped his hands on her wrists and pulled her arms above her head, stretching her body out while his hips began to pound against her.

The union was wild, and pleasure swiftly built under the hard strokes. The bed shook, but that only added to the fury of the emotions swirling deep inside her. She wanted to be thrown into the center of that storm, wanted to let it whip her flesh with its strength. Her hips rose to capture more of his hard flesh, her body straining against the hold he had on it as she tried to get closer to him.

She didn't need to; he came to her, riding her with lightning-fast thrusts that drove deep into her. Pleasure broke like a thunderstorm, the deluge drenching her in seconds. The flood rained down over every inch of her skin, and she laughed with delight, marveling at the amount of sensation her body could feel. Her lover pumped his hot seed deep inside her while his chest labored just as hard as hers. He lay on top of her for long moments, when the only thing that she could hear was the sound of his breathing and the beat of both their hearts.

Her body was limp and content with the glow of satisfaction, her eyelids drooping as sleep lulled her away. Curan rolled over and pulled her along his side. She nuzzled against his shoulder, wondering in her fuzzy mind just how she had ever slept alone without his warm body to cling to.

It was the most perfect moment of her life.

* * *

Curan slept deeply. But his hand remained curled around her hip, keeping her against him. Bridget moved slowly to avoid disturbing him. The bed was like a sanctuary, a place devoid of all of the worries that had plagued her. Here there was only the way that he held onto her, even while he slept. Tenderness filled her heart, and she did not resist its sweetness.

The fire crackled; the large log that had been burning when Curan brought her into the room split in half to expose the red-hot coals it had been reduced to. But one large chunk rolled too far over in the hearth for her liking. Fire was always a danger and one that must be given attention.

Easing herself out of the bed, she moved slowly to avoid waking Curan. The floor was cold, but there was a thick rug set down near the hearth. Sinking down onto her knees, she used a thick iron poker to push the glowing log back where its heat might be enjoyed but not cause worry.

The room was still very much a mystery to her. The hearth was large and had a good chimney that drew the smoke up and out of the room. Large glass-pane windows ran along one side of the room, and a long table with several chairs occupied one wall. Her trunks were pushed off to one corner, and Curan's own baggage was there as well. The more important items were stacked very precisely on the table. Things like his writing desk and his secretary's box. The candles had burned down and died while they slept, but her eyes were adjusted, and the ruby glow from the coals made it possible to see.

A stack of parchments was there, too, and it drew her attention. The parchments lacked any sort of wax seals or ornate ribbons that might have indicated their importance as papers a commander needed to carry. Parchments that would have confirmed Curan's authority with the king's seal or something of that nature.

Instead these were folded, and the small wax that had once sealed them long since fallen away. In the dim light it was difficult to identify the papers, but something drew her interest. She stepped closer and lifted a hand to her lips to smother a gasp when she recognized her own pen strokes on the outside of one.

They were her letters to Curan, the ones she had written once they took the blessing on their union. Once a month, without fail, she had penned a letter to him and sent them off when the chance permitted. Sometimes that meant that two or three months passed before someone stopped at their country estate who might carry letters to London so they might be sent on to France.

She looked at the stack, and every one was there. The folds along the edges were worn, showing that the paper had been opened and refolded many, many times. The very fact that the stack was placed with his desk and secretary's box was proof that he had held her letters in the highest regard. She was stunned down to her core. Never had she suspected that she meant so much to him. Suddenly, she saw all of his determination to see her brought to Amber Hill in a new light. Instead of possessive, she realized that he treasured her, *her* . . . not simply the union he had negotiated with her father. The letters would have meant little to him if his heart was not touched by them.

"Reading them kept me sane, when the campaign felt endless."

She gasped again and shook her head. "But there is nothing in those letters save the simple words of a girl."

Her husband merely lifted his eyebrow in response. "Each one was more valuable to me than gold."

He hadn't pulled anything from the bed to cover himself,

appearing perfectly at ease in nothing save his skin and the glow from the coals. He offered her a rare smile, but the look in his eyes was very serious.

"I cherished them. Every word, every sentence. Reading them took me to where you were and where I longed to be. You took me away from the war that was pinching out lives for nothing more than greed. It was my duty to be there, yet I needed your letters to keep me from deserting."

She reached for the stack, running her finger over frayed edges and even a few places where the parchment had cracked because it had been opened and closed so many times. They looked a decade old instead of merely three years. Her eyes filled with tears, for no man faked such longing. It was the sort of thing that words alone might never convey. Right there in the ragged edges was proof that his heart longed for her.

"I learned to love you through those letters, Bridget."

"But you rarely wrote me back . . . *Love* me? You cannot mean such a thing. We are still strangers . . . having spent little time in one another's company . . ."

He took the stack, and his face transformed into an expression of pure enjoyment, his fingers cradling the letters in a loving manner. This tenderness touched her because there were no words to describe it; only the sight was powerful enough to impart just how much he truly did value her letters.

"I marched my army into Scotland after you. That is my way of showing devotion." He sighed. "It is a truth that I feared you would find my attempts at wooing you lacking. I am a man of action, not rhyming couplets. Yet the thought of buying verse from some poet to send to you made me jealous. I wrote each letter with my own hand. That was the best I could do."

Many a noble knight paid for some other man to write his love letters. She realized instantly that she would far rather read the few, short ones he had sent her than any polished one bought like a beet in the market. The very fact that he had penned his letters himself sent tenderness through her. If she were naught but a mare to breed his children upon, he would have paid the poet and never considered the matter again.

"Action is not your only way of showing devotion." She reached out and stroked the top of the letter bundle. Her heart was suddenly filled with joy. It sent her lips up into a broad smile. Love . . . she had so feared it and yet she had discovered that it felt wonderful.

"You prove it in many other ways, Curan."

Too many wonderful ways to deny. The chamber suddenly became a place of comfort and solace. A place she did not want to leave no matter what judgment was cast onto her name.

"I promise that I will never willingly leave you again, husband."

His face became serious, his keen stare cutting into hers, but she stood steady, without flinching, for she had never been more sincere.

"I swear it, Curan."

He sat the bundle down and swept her off her feet a moment later, cradling her against his chest, his arms threatening to crush her with the amount of strength he used.

"I still want to keep you nude and locked in my chamber. But as a reward."

He settled her in the bed once more, and she pressed her lower lip out in a pout.

"You seem to not understand how to respond to the gift of my promise to you. Locking me up is not a reward, *my lord*."

He pressed her back, clamping his hands around her wrists and stretching her arms above her head while his body settled on top of hers.

"And you, sweet Bridget, seem to not understand that I intend to be locked in here with you. With nothing to do save show you how very devoted I can be."

"Ah . . ." She purred softly and gained a soft growl from him. "Now that is an altogether different proposal."

His eyebrow arched. "One that you are interested in entertaining, perhaps?"

"If you promise to be entertaining, I am definitely interested."

Someone pounded on the chamber door at dawn.

"Begone!"

Bridget smothered a giggle because her husband sounded gruff, but there was a sparkle of mischief in his eyes. He shot a glare at the door and pulled the bedding up around them to cover their bare bodies. His cock was hard against her thigh, and she raised her knee so that her leg brushed along it.

"I could become used to awakening at first light if you are in this bed with me, wife."

He nuzzled against her, his lips pressing a warm kiss against her throat. He captured one breast and gently thumbed the nipple until it hardened. The pounding began once more.

"I said, begone!" He roared loud enough to wake the stable grooms.

The door opened in spite of his order, and a male voice clearing his throat caused her husband's grip to flex against her breast. He muttered something against her neck before turning over to face his man. He yanked the bedding up to his shoulders so that she was covered.

"My apologies, my lord, yet I must speak with you."

"Nay, you do not." Curan rolled over, giving his back to Sinclair. He trapped her leg so that she could not toy with him any further, but his hand returned to cup her breast and toy with the nipple again. Little waves of enjoyment began to ripple down her body, and her face heated to know that Synclair knew what his lord was about.

"We are observing the French custom of a honeymoon. Tell someone to bring us some honey mead on your way out, and tell everyone to leave us behind a closed door for the rest of the month."

Synclair did not appear put off by his lord's gruffness. The knight boldly entered the chamber, his face a mask of fury.

"Forgive me, Lord Ryppon, but you are requested below."

Curan stroked her belly instead, his fingers sending little ripples of delight across her bare skin. She pushed at his hand, humiliation making her squirm.

"I am occupied, Synclair. I have given you the authority to act however you see fit. Use it to deal with whatever is below."

A soft sound came from the knight, and Bridget peeked over Curan's shoulder at him. Something flickered in Synclair's eyes that looked like triumph, but he canceled it quickly, his lips pressing back into a hard line. He drew in a deep breath.

"We have messengers from court arrived."

The hand teasing her belly froze, and she felt her husband's body tensing.

"You have been summoned to Whitehall along with Mistress Newbury."

Her husband rolled over and tucked the sheeting across her body in one swift motion. Synclair extended a parchment that Curan sat up and snatched from his hand. The bottom was fixed with a wax seal bearing the rampant lion of the king. But what sent ice through her veins was the clear ink spelling out her maiden name. The parchment crushed inside her husband's fist.

"Ready my men."

Curan spoke in a deadly whisper. His eyes glittered with outrage. Synclair did not hesitate but turned almost before his lord finished giving him his instructions. Her husband cupped her chin.

"I am sorry if you love your father, Bridget, for I believe I may have to kill him."

Curan meant his words. Bridget saw the rage burning in his eyes throughout the day. She did not get the chance to try to reason with him. His men were obedient, but it was clear that they did not care for the order to set out onto the road so soon again.

They did it nonetheless and with less argument than she might have expected. Reluctance tugged on her as well, the sight of her mare being led around to the front steps of Amber Hill making her frown. Several aches suddenly complained loudly, making her grit her teeth in order to gain the saddle. They took to the road without conversation, the expressions of the men around her grim.

Bridget felt the weight of judgment pressing down on her. She could not say that she had not been warned. Could not argue that she had not known fully what to expect if she celebrated her union with Curan.

Yet she would not have it undone.

That truth burned in her heart. She loved Curan and could not obey her father any longer. Childhood was past now, but that did not give her comfort. Along with her newfound maturity came the knowledge that she might have to protect the man she loved from ruining himself. Curan deserved that from her. Her thoughts remained dark as the road stretched out in front of them. Curan took no wagons this time, only his mounted men. They covered the distance much faster without the infantry and archers.

All that much faster to take her where she did not want to go. Curan's face reflected a similar sentiment, but he remained firm in the saddle, intent on answering the summons from his king. Witnessing how true he was to his honor only deepened her need to protect him. Love demanded no less.

Chapter Thirteen

The road to London was easier to travel since each day was warmer now. Yet it felt twice as long because she had no desire to go there. Instead, Bridget discovered herself looking back behind them throughout the two-day journey.

The night was the worst.

Her lover was missing. Curan lay next to her, but he did not touch her as he had before. He looped a hard arm around her that was more a mark of possession than tender affection. She awoke in a surly mood from kicking about most of the night. A soft grumble from her husband confirmed that his little amount of rest in the night equaled hers.

Nonetheless it was his lack of conversation that bothered her the most. His face remained in its stern mask again. Firm purpose etched into his features.

This was one nightmare she would have liked to quickly awaken from.

Instead, the road became increasingly crowded. Carts and wagons slowed their progress. They shared their path with heavy-laden vehicles that were carrying casks and barrels and sacks of grain into London from the surrounding villages. Curan's men rode in tight formation, their colors clearly displayed. Only border barons were allowed to approach the capital with so many mounted knights. Bridget felt the eyes of the curious on them as they headed toward Whitehall Palace.

The gate guards refused them entrance until a captain appeared. He slowly read the scroll that Curan offered him, before lifting his face to survey the mounted men. Around him, the royal guards were tense. The hair on the back of Bridget's neck stood up, and time felt frozen.

"You may enter, Lord Ryppon."

Curan nodded and led his men forward. Whitehall Palace was huge, covering more than two full city blocks. It was Henry Tudor's seat of government. The yard they entered was full of nobles and plainly clothed clerks alike. Horses were led away through gates that would take the animals and the smells that accompanied them away from the main halls.

The Thames ran along the back of the palace, allowing for barges to carry ambassadors to and from the great receiving hall. A mass of people hurried about. Groups of lavishly dressed courtiers climbed the steps that led up into one of the larger buildings, while their servants followed behind them. Men wearing wool and scholars' hats headed in another direction with their arms full of rolled parchments. Stable grooms threaded their way through the newly arrived, taking horses while attendants struggled to unstrap trunks from wagons.

Bridget had never seen so many people in one place. Dust rose from their travel-stained clothing, and she suddenly craved a bath just from smelling the mass of unwashed bodies.

Her husband did not hesitate once being admitted to the inner palace grounds. He dismounted and reached up to help her off her mare. His gaze was darting back and forth around them, never staying on any group too long. There was a tense look on his face that cautioned her to remain silent while surrounded by so many ears. He led her into one of the buildings and down what seemed like an endless series of corridors before one of his men fit a large iron key into a door and swung it open.

"Now let these men come and tell me to my face that they shall take the wife the church has blessed as mine."

The room they entered had a long table set with wide chairs. Off to the side was a cupboard, and large windows allowed the sunlight in. Curan's men opened the windows, allowing the early spring air into the room. A staircase in the back corner promised private sleeping chambers above them.

"You cannot say such things, my lord."

Her husband pulled his riding gauntlets off and tossed them down onto a table before answering her. Servants were scurrying to open shutters on the floor above, and their steps echoed in the room.

"I can and have. You are my wife, Bridget." He raised his hands. "Look about, madam, these are my private chambers, kept for my use by decree of the king. I will and shall protect our union."

Private accommodations at court were indeed a coveted thing and a mark of how much the king thought of him, but that did not wash her fears aside. Henry Tudor had married six times; the man was known to change his mind when it came to those he favored. More than one person had lost their head for forgetting that.

"A fact that you know I treasure, but that does not change the way the country works." She clasped her hands together tightly, forcing herself to face bitter reality. "We must prepare ourselves to be accommodating to the king's will."

A muscle along his jawline twitched. There was nothing else that gave away his true mood to those moving around them, but she felt it.

He blew out a hard sound. "Nor does it change the fact that I will never be content to have you shelter me. I will face down those who seek to wrong me, without hesitation. You are my wife and I shall shelter you, Bridget. No matter what it takes to impress that fact on those who seek to part us."

The man was as imposing and immovable as the moment that he had swept her away from her mother. There was part of her that could not even lament it because she loved everything about him. He was the embodiment of a noble knight— that fabled creature that so many talked about but few ever became.

Nevertheless, this love opened the door to fear. Its icy touch roamed over her, setting off all manner of horrible possibilities inside her mind. She began to notice every single sound, cringing when she heard anything that might be a knock upon the door. The chancellor's men might be on their way with an arrest warrant in hand to take Curan to the Tower. If the man was powerful enough to seek one for the queen, what hope did they have that there would be mercy?

Curan sighed. He closed the distance between them, cupping her chin in a gentle hand. In his eyes she witnessed the turmoil that his expression and words had masked.

"Be sure that I have not come to such confidence by being foolhardy, Bridget."

He pressed his thumb over her lips when she would have spoken. His gaze cut toward the servant lighting the candle on the table near them and then back to her eyes.

Of course . . .

She was foolishly naive. The servants might be paid to tell what they had heard. It had been one of the queen's friends who had been taken to the Tower to try to gain evidence against Catherine Parr. Here, within the palace, she must recall those words her mother had tried to instill in her. But it was Marie's words that came to mind.

"Stroke the ego of the man who thinks he owns you . . ."

Not Curan, but the men threatening to take her from him had large egos indeed. The king himself demanded complete obedience from his wife, and two of his past wives had lost their heads for forgetting that Henry Tudor did not share his power. The men serving in his court all followed the lead of their king. They divorced their wives and sent others into exile in the country, and there was no one to check their behavior. It was the reason her own mother had paid a courtesan to tutor her in things that no virgin should have seen. Because a woman had to know how to pretend and lull those watching her into thinking she was exactly what they wanted her to be—naught but a possession who was content in her place.

Maybe fate was trying to teach Henry Tudor a lesson by giving him two daughters and only one son. Clearly the man needed to be shown that women had more value than the ease they might offer while on their backs. She felt the eyes of the staff on her, evaluating her response to her husband's words. Never let it be said that she was a poor student or a fool. Only a child believed that throwing a tantrum was the only way to get what you desired.

She sank into a low curtsy, ducking her chin in a perfect show of obedience to her lord and master.

"As you instruct, my lord. Forgive me for doubting your ability. Clearly I am too newly wed but will pray for the wisdom to recall that you are my provider."

When she rose and looked back into his eyes she saw how frustrated he was with her meekness. But the grooms who were bringing in their trunks found her behavior very fitting. Approval shone from their smirks.

She detested the dishonesty but took comfort in the sight of disgust in Curan's eyes. He had no more liking for it than she even though the servants around them found it normal and expected. Seeing the way the servants watched them made

Bridget tighten her hands together as tension drew every muscle taut. There was nowhere to hide here, no privacy. Every word she spoke might be used against them, even in these private rooms.

So she must not allow her mind to wander. She looked at her husband and found his face set into the expressionless mask she had come to know so well.

She understood now. Her heart ached for him, yet admired him as well. His strength went so much deeper than she ever imagined. It was not simply the strength of his body; his mind was strong, too. Bridget hoped this combination was enough to defeat the men who were circling around the dying king.

If not, she would lose him, and she doubted she had the strength to survive such a blow.

Two more grooms entered the room with yokes across their shoulders.

"Excellent. My back is itching for a good scrubbing." Curan pointed at a slipper tub that was stored off to one side of the room.

"My wife will show you what I like my bath to be. She's quite good at tending to me."

The arrogant note in his voice irritated her, in spite of how much she understood its necessity. Such a deception should not be required, and yet it was.

The grooms looked to her, and she directed her attention at the tub. Moving it in front of the fire, she watched them begin filling it. Two more young grooms entered and added their buckets of water to the tub.

"Do not be too long with the hot water."

They ducked their chins in response, never breaking their stride. A maid brought soap and toweling to her that Bridget laid out neatly on a stool near the tub. She made the perfect picture of a wife, dutiful and meek. The grooms returned with buckets that had steam rising from them. They carefully poured them into the tub before leaving.

"Perfection."

Curan moved across the room and sat down in a chair to present one of his feet for her to help him remove his boot.

"I have pleasant memories of your skill at bathing me."

His eyes twinkled with amusement that she shared. It warmed her heart a bit, because not a single one of the maids moving about the chamber had any notion as to the true meaning of his words.

"I am pleased to hear you say such, my lord."

She rolled his title just a bit and watched his lips twitch at the corners. His boot pulled free, and she set it aside to grasp the other. He angled his toe up as she stood over his leg, the toes of his foot stroking across her inner thigh. Just a playful nudge and then he pointed his foot once more so that the boot slid free when she tugged on it.

Well, one good jest deserved an answering one.

She leaned farther over than necessary to remove the boot. Her breasts plumped upward, swelling above the edge of her dress. His dark gaze centered on her cleavage instantly, and his skin flushed.

He cleared his throat and rose from the chair. She watched him lift his hands to begin disrobing, but he stopped when she reached for his buttons herself. Her hands shook slightly, but not because she noticed the maids sneaking looks at them. No, her hands trembled in response to knowing just how much she liked what was hidden beneath the wool of his clothing.

Her hands were quick and efficient, too efficient for her poise. The creamy skin of his chest was too tempting. She wanted to run her fingers through the dark mat of hair that covered the hard ridges. Instead she unhooked the waistband of his pants and drew them down his legs.

His cock was hard . . .

She shivered and tried to avoid looking at it while disrobing him. There was nothing meek about her feelings, but the maids were still dressing the bed in the chamber next door; she could hear them moving around the huge bed even if she could not see them.

That didn't seem to quell the heat rising inside her, however. Passion was igniting with every garment she removed from her husband. She wanted to place a soft kiss against his collarbone and another against his neck, just as he had done to her the last moment that they lay entangled.

Bridget shook herself and turned her back on the temptation her husband's body presented. Taking a moment to shake out his pants, she folded them neatly and heard a splash behind her. She breathed a small sigh of relief and turned back around to begin bathing him.

It was going to be pure torture to have her hands upon him.

Picking up the soap, she walked over to the tub. Curan was struggling to maintain his expectant demeanor as well. She noticed his gaze returning to her in spite of him directing it away. The flush remained on his face, and when she leaned over to begin washing his feet, his dark gaze was full of heat. She felt her face turn scarlet, but it was not in shame, instead fueled by the growing need to have him to herself. She never looked at his feet, but washed them with her attention centered on his eyes.

"Remove your dress."

"What?" Her voice was breathless and husky, betraying the passion licking along her insides.

One dark eyebrow lifted mockingly. "I told you to remove your dress, wife. It covers too much of you for my taste."

Her gaze cut to the bedchamber and the maids taking far too long to dress the bed. Clearly the maids were intent on spying, but to order them to leave was to suggest that she and Curan had something to hide.

"Come now, wife. You should be used to my desire for your sweet flesh by now. I have demonstrated how much passion you evoke often enough."

Curan raised his voice just enough to ensure that it carried into the next room, proving that he agreed with her thinking. Bridget bit into her lower lip to keep her thoughts unspoken. She moved up to his shoulders, rubbing the soap and cloth across the wide expanse of his back.

"That isn't very kind." She whispered her words near his ear, appearing as though she was intent on her task.

"Neither is the idea some members of this court have of trying to take you from me. If Wriothesley wants to hear what we are doing, I plan to make sure the tale is not a dull one."

He turned his head so that their faces were a breath apart. His voice was low and edged with need. A shudder shook her, touching off a throbbing in her clitoris.

"I will also make sure those same villains hear how much you are truly my wife now."

He reached up and grasped her, his hand cupping the back of her head and holding it still for a hard kiss. His kiss was demanding, but she met it because it was impossible to resist something she craved so much. Heat swirled through her belly, quickly and white-hot as his mouth demanded a deep taste from hers.

He chuckled a moment later, pulling his head away from hers just enough so that their eyes met.

"Out!"

His roar gained instant response; the maids scurried out of the bedchamber clearly having been listening. They inclined their heads on their way toward the door.

"Are you more pleased now, wife?"

Mischief sparkled in the dark orbs. He suddenly rose up and looped a wet arm around her body. She shrieked in surprise as he pulled her right into the tub. Water splashed up in a torrent. She sank down until her knees hit the bottom of the tub on either side of his hips. Her dress got caught on the surface of the water, slowly wicking it up before the wet fabric sank.

"Ah, exactly what I was craving, your thighs wrapped around me."

He settled her on top of him, and she felt the unmistakable bulge of his cock between her open legs. Her stockings ended at her knees, leaving her bare thighs to connect with his. It was a true torment to feel him between her thighs. Need clawed at her, and he gripped her hips, increasing it because she recalled exactly how it felt to have his hands holding her hips while he rode her. The walls of her passage suddenly felt empty, too empty to worry about anyone who might be listening. The man was her husband, wasn't he?

"Curan . . . they are no doubt standing outside the doors listening."

She battled the urge to raise her voice.

"I do enjoy my name on your lips."

His voice was deep now and sincere. But his hands lifted her up until his cock sprang up, no longer pressed against his belly by her.

"You cannot mean to—not while they are here." It was a truth that most nobles did not care if servants were about.

They did as they pleased, when they pleased. Most wedding consummations were witnessed as an added precaution against annulment. Gossip spread so quickly at court because nobles didn't take the time to notice the staff.

"I assure you I do, and they can see nothing." He lowered her down, the head of his cock easily slipping into the entrance of her body. Her own thoughts had prepared her for his entry; her passage was moist and welcomed the hard thrust of his flesh.

She shivered, caught between mortification and excitement. The maids couldn't see anything, but they knew that she was seated on his cock. The act was darkly erotic, and the look of possession in his eyes doubled her excitement. She bit back a soft exclamation of delight as he filled her. Curan pressed a kiss against her lips, gently coaxing her lips to part.

"I want him to hear how you whimper while I'm inside you. I want to know that they will tell him that you enjoy being my wife." He braced his feet on the bottom of the tub and gripped her hips tighter. His eyes glowed with need, and it was more than physical. Love shimmered in his eyes, a love that would not let modesty prevent him from doing what he thought best in order to keep her.

"Your dress covers you, Bridget, and the door is shut. That is the most privacy anyone has at court."

He whispered against her neck, and she lost the will to deny him. She angled her head and bit him gently on the side of his throat.

"Ride me, wife." Curan raised his voice so that it filled the chamber. "Hold on tight or I shall throw you!"

Her heart was already accelerating, sending her blood surging through her veins. Curan did not wait but lifted her off his length and thrust back up into her almost in the same motion. The water swished back and forth, getting closer to the rim of the tub, but that did not stop him. His next thrust was hard and faster. A whimper rose from her throat as delight filled her. His cock was sliding along her clitoris and producing too much pleasure to ignore. Her hips curled toward his next penetration, and there was nothing her thoughts might do to prevent it. She was responding out of instinct. Need fueling her actions while pleasure took command of her.

Curan pulled her close, so that she was pressed tightly against his chest. The position increased the amount of friction each thrust applied to her clitoris, drawing another cry from her lips. She shivered violently, taking control of raising herself up and pushing her body back down as well.

"That's it, my sweet."

The water was sloshing onto the floor, and she did not care. The wool of her dress was wet and scratchy against her skin, but his body was warm and smooth between her thighs. She clasped him tighter, rising and falling faster. His hands gripped her firmly, and she heard his breathing growing husky. His cock felt harder and larger with each downward plunge.

"Look at me, Bridget."

His voice was raspy and low. She raised her eyes to stare into his, instantly hypnotized by the burning desire she witnessed there.

"You are mine."

He surged up into her with his words, pushing harder while his hands tightened. His motions became frantic, but he clenched his jaw, holding back his own release while watching her face.

She couldn't hold back the pleasure any longer; a harsh cry hit the ceiling as joy ripped through her. Curan continued to thrust in short, hard motions until she felt his seed erupting inside her. It was hot and touched off another little explosion of pleasure deep inside her belly. Her thighs clamped harder around his hips in an effort to keep his offering deep inside her. It was pure instinct, like the impulse to curl her hips toward him when he was thrusting into her. Little things that she had never known she craved until Curan touched her.

He clasped her tightly against him, his hands smoothing over her back while the water became placid once more. Bridget wasn't interested in moving; she felt more content than ever with his scent filling her senses and his warm skin against her cheek.

In the next instant movement caught her attention, and her husband jerked as the two maids appeared and dropped a curtsy before departing.

"That should reach the chancellor's ears before you finish stripping off your wet clothing."

"Curan."

She slapped at his chest but misjudged where the water level was and ended up hitting its surface. Water splashed up into his face, earning her a mocking grin.

"I admit that I enjoyed that part of making my case quite a bit."

She gasped and tried to climb off him. Her wet dress made it nearly impossible to rise, the water-soaked fabric weighing quite a bit more than she was accustomed to. "You speak shamefully. It will serve you right if a bishop arrives to have you taken to the stocks for an hour of shame."

He hooked her beneath her arms and lifted her out of the tub. Water rained down on the stone floor tiles, filling the chamber with the sound of rain when there was none.

"I speak the hard truth needed to end this dishonorable business."

He reached for the toweling and began drying himself. "It is time I sought out your father. There are words we need to have with each other."

"I agree."

His hands froze, and he looked up to meet her eyes. Tenderness was shining in his eyes, by far the most beautiful sight she had ever beheld. He reached out and curled an arm around her waist. She wasn't sure if he moved to her or if he pulled her against his body. Truly she did not care. All that mattered was the kiss he pressed against her lips. Soft and full of tender emotions, the caress was sweet, too sweet for words.

"You do not know how much I enjoy hearing such words from your lips, Bridget. I feel as though I have longed for them for two lifetimes."

The approach of the chancellor was heard before a hand pounded on the door. Curan's body tensed, and in a flash Bridget was behind him. The men escorting Wriothesley did not wait for permission to open the door. A quick pounding preceded both doors being yanked open so fast the iron hinges groaned.

"Unhand her at once, Lord Ryppon."

Chancellor Wriothesley strode forward without hesitation. Another man strode close on his heels, who could be no other but Lord Oswald. The chancellor was richly dressed with a large coat sewn with a wide fur collar. His chain of office was tied carefully in place at each shoulder so that the medallion with St. George slaying the dragon hung directly over his heart. The man aimed a narrow-eyed look at Curan, raking over him and even stopping at his cock for a moment.

Curan didn't flinch. He stood tall and straight, refusing to be intimidated.

"Good afternoon, my Lord Chancellor. You will have to pardon my lack of clothing. We are very newly arrived and newly wed. You must be Lord Oswald."

"I shall not pardon it. The girl is not yours."

It was Lord Oswald who fired the accusation at Curan, but the chancellor sent his hand cutting through the air to silence the man. He shut his mouth instantly, sickening her. What a dog. He was everything Curan was not. A sniveling coward who waited for scraps to be tossed to him by his master. The man sported a soft, round belly that further confirmed just how much he liked to pamper himself.

"Not mine? Bridget is very much mine, sir. We took the church's blessing three years ago. Henry was there."

Curan sounded mocking and arrogant. More than one of the guards' lips twitched in response. The guards held their position, yet it was clear that they did not respect the men they were escorting. Curan reached behind him and patted Bridget's bottom. She gasped at the boldness of the action.

"Had you arrived a few moments earlier, you would have witnessed exactly how much she is mine." Curan stepped over to where his pants were and pulled them on, still without any outward sign that he was embarrassed to be seen nude. "But your informants had yet to leave, hadn't they? I believe they remained until we finished, so I will trust that they told you that Bridget is, in fact, very much my wife." Curan aimed a look at the two maids who were now lingering behind Lord Oswald.

Lord Oswald turned red. He pressed his lips together and sputtered. "You had no right to touch her."

Curan shrugged into his shirt. "I could not disagree more, gentlemen. I had the blessing of the church and the seal from her father's ring to confirm that I had every right to plant my seed in her belly."

Bridget gasped again, the blunt comments shocking her. Curan turned and offered her only a softened look before he pointed to the bedchamber.

"Perhaps you should see if those maids know how to do anything save carry information." He shrugged, clearly uncaring. "At least change your dress, wife. It is wet."

Bridget lowered herself before quitting the room. She discovered that her legs were shaking by the time she made it to the bedchamber. There was a snap from her husband's fingers, and she heard the maids following her. For all of Curan's valor, the chancellor was a powerful man.

"Make way for the king!"

More footfalls echoed around the outer chamber. Bridget peeked out of the open door and felt her eyes go wide. Henry Tudor arrived wearing a coat that was far richer than the chancellor's. He was a large man who limped a little. Everyone lowered themselves, and his escort placed a chair behind him when he stopped.

"My leg pains me these days." He sounded gruff and frustrated by the toll age was extracting on his body, but sank down into the chair, stretching his leg out with a soft intake of breath to betray how painful it was.

"Hurry, miss, they will be calling for you shortly."

The two maids pulled her away from the door, reaching for her wet dress with quick hands.

Calling for me . . .

That was exactly what she dreaded. Tension twisted through her, but she was not afraid. Suddenly, she felt determination rising up inside her so strongly she understood why her husband was willing to behave so lowly and fondle her bottom in front of others. The reason was, when dealing with men of low quality, you had to make your argument in a fashion they would understand. Chancellor Wriothesley was a man driven by his own greed for power. He would never hear any argument that pitted honor against gaining what he desired.

Which was her. The chancellor would give her to his dog like a scrap of meat, happily doing so because he had taken the scrap from someone else and need not give his hound anything of his own.

It sickened her.

Lord Oswald began sputtering in the outer room, and the maids increased their speed.

"You'd best hurry, mistress. Lord Oswald does not like to be kept waiting, and he is sure to be cross with you for having known another man before him."

"He'll likely strike you, but better keep your chin steady if you want to earn his forgiveness."

"He won't want me now."

The maids both froze, but it was the look of pity in their eyes that convinced her that they knew of what they spoke.

"He will, and he will punish you for not coming to him a virgin."

The maids kept their voices low, to be heard only in the bedchamber. Their familiarity with Lord Oswald's expectations set Bridget's spine straight.

There would be no simpering to that hound, and maybe she needed to follow her husband's example and fight the man in the manner that he would understand. She cast a glance behind her at the door that was still slightly open. Just a finger width, yet 'twas enough for her needs.

"Ah! You clumsy fool! You pinched me. Awhhh . . ."

Bridget raised her voice just enough so that it would filter past the door.

"Look at my skin! It is pink! And it hurts! You must be the worst maids in all of Whitehall Palace!"

She added a few more wails that gained her wide-eyed looks from the maids. But she felt no pity for them.

"Pardon, mistress."

"Mistress? You dare to call me mistress? I am a lady! Are you so simple that you do not know who your betters are?" Bridget made sure that her voice was whiny and irritating. She reached for a silver pitcher that was sitting on the side table and threw it against the wall with every bit of strength she might muster. It hit with an explosive sound, the water in it splattering across the wall before it fell to the floor with another loud clang.

"I am a lady. *A lady!* Do you hear me? You had better make sure every stupid maid that you call friend here knows not to forget who I am. I am set to be Lord Oswald's wife. His wife. He is the very best friend of Chancellor Wriothesley who is a member of the king's privy council. By tonight I will have a much better set of chambers, with a grand bed and the finest sheets. By tomorrow I will be a lady of the queen's privy chamber, I tell you! And I deserve it . . . ."

She stomped her feet and blew out large huffing sounds beneath her breath.

"Now get me dressed this moment. If you even know how to serve someone of my station, that is. Did you get promoted from the fields this very morning?"

"No, my lady."

"I do wonder. You are so slow and clumsy . . . Completely lacking in any skill worthy of nobility . . . Your mothers must have cleaned privies to earn their bread . . . ."

Curan lost his focus.

He gritted his teeth with frustration, for only Bridget could steal his attention so easily and completely. Her words drifted through the closed door with just enough volume to be understandable. He wanted to chuckle at how contrary she was behaving to her true nature.

Yet part of him was furious that she was not allowing him to fight for her. He turned his attention back to the men in front of him and watched Lord Oswald turning pale.

"You said she was country raised and meek."

Something hit the wall, filling the room with noise. Chancellor Wriothesley looked disgusted.

"I read most of her letters when they passed through on their way to France. The girl seemed sweet enough. There was no hint of greed in her words."

"You read my letters?" Curan growled through his teeth, his temper nearly proving too much to control. His hands itched to wrap around the chancellor's throat and choke the life out of him.

"I find that a most interesting bit of information myself." Henry Tudor eyed his chancellor with growing unhappiness.

Chancellor Wriothesley laid a hand over his chest and stared at his monarch. "I read every dispatch that went on to Your Majesty. It was a precaution against spies passing false information to your Grace."

Bridget was still having her fit, berating the maids and wailing behind the door. Lord Oswald was turning redder, and the man looked as though he had forgotten how to draw breath. When she began to use his name to berate the servants, his eyes bugged from his head.

"I'll not have that brat for my wife. Absolutely not. I will select someone else." He offered a wide reverence to the king before turning a swirl of his richly decorated coat, and departed, a few of the guards following behind him.

The chancellor lifted one hand that was sporting several large gold rings and began stroking his beard while he stared at Curan. "Interesting. I never perceived the girl to be anything but sweet tempered from her writings."

For all his pompous dressing, Chancellor Wriothesley was no fool. His mind was sharp, and he did not like losing.

The king suddenly cleared his throat. "The nature of a woman is not easy for a man to judge. I have learned that lesson."

"Yes, Your Majesty."

Henry shared a glance with Wriothesley that was very serious. "Perhaps you should take Lord Oswald over to York Place. I hear there are some newly arrived faces there. Ones I have not even seen myself."

The chancellor reverenced his king, lowering his head in submission, but when he resumed standing there was a look of satisfaction on his face.

"Thank you, Your Majesty. Your concern for your humble servant is most treasured indeed."

"As I treasured your sure hand directing my affairs while I was away in France."

Chancellor Wriothesley's lips rose into the smallest of smiles before he departed, taking more of the guards away. The ones who remained were the personal escort of the king.

"He has a keen wit and runs the country better than anyone else I have given the authority to." The king slid a glance over to Curan. "Removing him would not be my first choice. Edward is too young to rule."

This utterance was the closest the king had ever come to admitting his time was growing short. But the signs were there. The pallor of his skin was more yellow than Curan recalled, and his eyes bore dark circles beneath them.

"It is not my choice, either, sire. Since it appears that my bride has managed to send them both looking for another, I suppose I shall have to be content with the outcome, if not the means."

Henry smiled. "You don't care for that, do you, Curan?"

"No, I do not. She is mine to shelter."

The King tilted his head to one side. "I would normally agree with you, but there is something about that fit she just threw that makes me believe you may have discovered your match in female form. That girl has fire in her belly and a sharp wit. It would have been messy sorting out your claim against Wriothesley. The man will remain once I am gone. Your bride is wiser than you to realize that it is better he thinks her a spoilt brat and nothing he can make use of."

"I still don't like it, sire."

"Neither would I, except for the outcome, of course."

Curan growled, low and deep, and gained a chuckle from the king he had ridden with for years.

Henry Tudor cast a look at the bedchamber door. "I believe I would have a closer look at your bride, Lord Ryppon."

Lord Oswald's words came clearly through the door. Bridget froze in mid-wail when she heard the man rejecting her.

Rejection had never, ever been so sweet. She would cherish it for the rest of her life.

She blew out a long sigh but froze when she noticed the maids staring at her. Their eyes narrowed, but the elder of the two pointed a finger at the younger and lifted another finger to her lips. She moved closer to Bridget and plucked at her sleeve, mimicking the actions of dressing.

"We'll keep your secret, miss. I'll see to Agnes there. No one is hated more than Lord Oswald, but we all do his bidding else suffer for it."

"Thank you."

"Your husband is a fine man and right easy on the eyes. If I had one half as good to take care of me, I'd leave this palace in the flutter of my eyelashes. But the good ones want a girl with a dowry because they've a mind for setting up a good future and all."

Bridget heard the lament in the girl's voice. She met the maid's eyes and recognized that they were very much the same, only fate had been kinder to Bridget in giving her a man that she loved to fight for.

"Spying for the chancellor is the only way to keep our positions, and without them, we shall never earn enough silver to marry. We're both on our own."

Bridget suddenly recalled the money her mother had given her to bribe Curan's men. Moving over to her trunk, she lifted the lid and dug it out of the shoe that she had stuffed it into.

"If you will keep your word to me, I shall give you what you desire so that you may leave this place."

Bridget held out two gold angels. The women's eyes widened because each one of the coins represented over a year's wages.

"Do you mean it, lady? A gold angel for naught but our word on the matter?"

"I do. No one should suffer this life without the chance to love." Bridget pressed the money into each of their hands. "Go and make sure you choose a man for his values, not his handsome face."

"You truly do not belong here, Lady Ryppon. You're a fine, decent soul. A true lady, not like the others who demand respect they do not earn."

Bridget could not agree more. For all the finery that surrounded her, all she could see was the plotting and scheming. Amber Hill beckoned to her like a clean-flowing river that was not fouled by too many people living near its shores. The door pushed inward, and Curan looked at the two maids.

"Leave us."

His gaze was hard and leveled straight at her. Bridget returned it while the maids offered them curtsies and fled the room.

Curan closed the distance between them, his footfalls silent. He reached out to tap her chin with a single finger of reprimand. She saw his thoughts turning in his eyes, but he shook his head.

"The king awaits you."

Her eyes widened. "The king is still here?"

"Henry Tudor heard every word, my sweet Bridget."

Bridget felt herself go pale. Her mother would be shamed, her father humiliated. Her brothers would never be able to show their faces at court again.

She was still not sorry. Not if it meant she might go back to Amber Hill with her husband.

"I will not keep him waiting."

She walked into the outer chamber that still had the tub and water lying in puddles on the floor. The length of toweling was lying trampled among it all, and there sat the king of England. His royal guards stood at attention around him, while his head turned to her the moment she appeared. He lifted one hand that was crowded with large rings.

"Come here, Lady Ryppon."

Curan squeezed one side of her bottom from behind the door where the king could not see his actions. She jumped forward, certain her cheeks would blister from the blush heating them.

"Your Majesty." She sunk into a low reverence before completing the journey to stand in front of him.

"Straighten up, I would have a good look at you." Henry Tudor might be sitting down, but the man sounded as though he was mounted on a horse in command of an army. There was no weakness in his tone, no hint of him thinking that his will might be refused.

"Yes, Your Majesty."

Bridget stood up and stared back at him with the same courage that had prompted her to behave so shamefully. The king's stare was brilliant, almost cutting into her, but she refused to duck her chin. For some reason, she needed to hold her chin steady, to prove that she was worthy of being called Lady Ryppon.

"Strength is always best matched with strength, Curan." Henry Tudor nodded. "I believe she has enough to give you the family you long for and not bore you to death throughout the seasons."

"Thank you, Your Grace."

There was the sound of hurried steps on the hallway, and the guards watching over the king tightened their hands on their long pikes. A hand knocked on the door, pounding on it without stopping.

"Open up! I must speak with you immediately, Lord Ryppon!" Even muffled through the heavy planks of the door, Bridget knew her father's voice.

"Father? My father knows I am here already?"

"Gossip moves far too quickly through these corridors, Lady Ryppon. Personally, I find it disgusting."

The king flicked his hand at the door, and one of his men opened it instantly. Bridget gasped when her father was revealed, but Curan made a low sound under his breath and grasped her wrist possessively. The strength he used startled her because he had always handled her with control. This was an iron hold, one that betrayed just how unhappy her husband was to see her father.

"Bridget? I could not believe it when I heard you were

here." Her father began speaking without looking at who else was in the room, his attention focused on her. He pegged Curan with a hard glare that she recalled very well from her childhood. It was the look that declared her father's extreme displeasure.

"Lord Ryppon, I thought you were taking my daughter to the border land. I disagree with her being anywhere near court and its games. I believed that we had an agreement, else I would never have given my blessing to the match with you."

"I believe Curan did indeed take your daughter to the border, Lord Connolly."

Her father jumped, his coat jerking around as his gaze took in the king. But he didn't perform any lavish reverence. Instead of sinking into some exaggeration of a respectful lowering of his head before his monarch, her father offered his king a dignified dipping of his head before straightening.

His hair was more silver than she recalled, and his face bore more lines from worry. Unlike Oswald and Wriothesley, her father wore good English wool. His half coat was cut in the same fashion and set with a rolled-back collar that served to keep the wind from chilling him instead of displaying costly and rare fur. There was nothing presumptuous about her sire, only neatness and order. Hanging over his shoulders was his knight's chain, every link shiny and free of tarnish. On his left hand was a single ring, his signet ring, the mark of his nobility.

"Forgive me, Your Majesty, but your court is not the place I wanted my daughter."

It was a bold thing to say to the king, many would say foolish, for Henry was rumored to enjoy his entertainments. Her father didn't make excuses for his words; he simply finished speaking and remained silent while his king considered him.

"My court is full of schemes and vultures waiting for me to die." Henry sighed and looked at her for a long moment. "I value your father's straightforwardness a great deal, and for that I apologize because it has kept him from his family."

Her father merely lifted his own gray eyebrows in the face of his king's bluntness. "Or it is possible they are waiting for me to die, sire. All the more reason for me to be alarmed to know my daughter is here. Forgive me, but she is my only daughter and I would have her live a wholesome life. Far away from this nest of gossip and insinuation. Your Majesty's own daughters bear that burden, and it makes my heart ache to see their faces marked with worry so young in life."

"They do wear the yoke of gossip, yet Catherine is determined to see me learn who my daughters are." Henry Tudor rose, gritting his teeth as he did so. But his expression remained unchanged, the pain held behind a stern exterior. "I believe my wife is correct. The Princesses Mary and Elizabeth should know more of their father, and there is little enough time for that."

The king looked at her father. "Which is why I need you to remain and offer me clear counsel when the schemes begin to swirl around them both."

"As you wish, Your Majesty."

The king turned to look at her and Curan. His gaze lowered to the grip Curan maintained on her wrist, pausing there for a long moment while something flickered in his eyes, like a ghost of a love long past. He looked younger for a moment, more alive, but it was fleeting and vanished before Henry Tudor raised his attention back to their faces.

"You have my leave yet again, Curan, and my thanks for your service at my side. I treasure the memory of you riding beside me. Tell your sons about it someday. I have told mine. Edward enjoys my tales full well."

"The honor was mine, Your Grace."

The king paused in front of her, a hint of a sparkle in his eye. "And you have tickled my envy. If I were a younger man, I might have to challenge Curan for you."

Henry Tudor actually winked at her before making his way down the hallway. His guards followed him, and the grooms that had brought the chair in took it up and fell into step behind the king. She heard him limping and winced for the glimmer that she had witnessed in his eyes.

Her father only waited until the king was halfway down the corridor before turning around to peg Curan with a hard glare once more.

"Why did you bring my daughter here?"

With the king gone, her father's tone returned to being sharp. Outrage edged his words, and despite the clear advantage Curan had in size over him, her father boldly faced him without flinching.

Her husband was clearly fighting for control because he spoke through his clenched teeth. "Why did you send for her to attend you at court and wed another if you did not want her here?"

Curan pushed her behind him and stood nose to nose with her father.

"I did nothing of the sort. This is the last place that I wanted Bridget. The men here have become villains when it comes to virgins."

Bridget pushed her way between them, which was no easy task considering how intent each man was on making the other see his way. It was her father who stepped back to allow her to separate them.

"A letter arrived from you, Father, instructing Mother to send me to you here at court because . . ."

Her words failed her because having so recently escaped his hold, the very name Oswald felt dirty on her tongue.

Curan suffered no such difficulty; his voice cracked like a whip.

"To send her to court to wed Lord Oswald." Rage edged each word, but her father looked angrier after hearing them, if such a thing were possible. Rage drew him up straighter, and he shook with it.

"What manner of trickery is this?" He pointed at Curan. "I keep my word, sir. Never once have I been a man of deception, even if I serve at this court. The match was sealed and blessed. I do not break such promises, and I am stunned to discover you think that I might do so without the application of the rack to force me into false words."

Curan shook his head. "I arrived to discover her trunks packed and your wife telling me that I would have to seek you in London because you had arranged another match for your daughter."

"I never wrote such a letter, would not have written such a letter." Her father remained steadfast in his position. The difficulty was that Curan was just as determined. Tension was twisting tighter and tighter, promising to snap at any moment. They were the two men she loved the most in her life; she had to discover a solution. There had to be an explanation.

"The letter had your seal upon it, Father." Bridget wanted both of them to be right, but that was not possible. "I watched Mother break it with my own eyes."

Her father reached up and clamped his hands around the turned-back front of his half coat. His fingers dug into the wool while he appeared to contemplate the situation. His face suddenly became sad, as though he had just heard that a friend had died unexpectedly.

"There is only one man who might have written that letter and convinced my captain to have it delivered unto my wife." He drew in a deep breath and let it go. "Even so, it is my fault. I shall not deny the blame, Lord Ryppon, for my family is my first duty. There is no excuse for such a lapse. Thank the Lord God for his intercession in this matter."

Curan lost his condemning expression. He hooked his hands into his belt and studied Lord Connolly. The muscle that had been twitching along the side of his jaw eased.

"You suspect your secretary?"

"There can be no other culprit. He is the only man who might ever dispatch my captain onto the road. He is also the only man I have ever given my signet ring to while I bathed." Her father shook his head, more sadness entering his eyes. But he drew himself up stiffly. "I owe you a great deal, Lord Ryppon, and am glad to see you are every inch of the man I thought you to be when I selected your offer for my daughter."

Her father reached out and stroked her cheek, a smile brightening his features. Bridget felt herself returning it because no one made her heart warm as her sire did.

Except Curan.

"I know that there is a great fascination with sons, yet I will tell you that I cherish my daughter. God only blessed me with one, but he has graciously allowed me to watch her grow into womanhood. It is a gift that I thank him for each day."

Her father looked back at Curan.

"I would never allow her here at court, even when she asked me to bring her when she was too young to know what she was saying. This place steals the sparkle from the eyes of the innocent and true of heart. Wriothesley knows that and hoped that I might not suspect that any rumors of her arrival were true." He faltered, his voice becoming hard and angry once more. "That I would not have investigated those rumors until it was too late. I am happy to say that the chancellor does not know me as well as he believes."

"Your daughter sent him off with a fit that will likely be legend before supper is served."

"She did?"

Her father looked at her with new respect.

"Why, Bridget, that is perfect. Wriothesley can save face and you may depart without worry that he will bother you ever again. How brilliant you are, my girl, and how unselfish to sacrifice your own reputation."

"I threw a fit, Father. Your daughter will be known as a brat. I shamed you and Mother. "

"But you will be away from here with no one's ego offended. That is no easy task, my girl. I battle such every day. It was brilliant, I say—brilliant."

She couldn't help but smile; her father's praise meant too much to her. It always had.

Lord Connolly drew himself up. "Now do as you promised me, Lord Ryppon, and take my daughter north."

"Yes, sir."

It was by far the most docile tone of voice Bridget had ever heard pass her husband's lips. Curan offered her father a reverence that he truly meant. She witnessed the respect shining in his dark eyes.

"Good-bye, Father. You must come to Amber Hill and see me."

"I shall come soon, Daughter." Her father shared a look with Curan.

"Too soon and yet not soon enough. Now please excuse me, I must attend to a difficult matter."

Lord Connolly turned and left, his posture stiff, but he

rubbed his signet ring and took to the distance in front of him with a determined speed.

"I am relieved." Her husband reached out and curled his hand around her, pulling her close with a sigh. "Greatly so. For I like your father."

"I love him."

One dark eyebrow rose. It was subtle and yet so very telling, coming from such a strong man. Bridget placed her hands on his chest and smoothed them up and over the hard ridges that delighted her so.

"As I love you, my lord."

He frowned at her.

"Do not be cross with me, Curan. I would gladly suffer more humiliation to remain your wife."

"I will shelter you, Bridget."

"I am looking forward to it. Yet why is it that you believe a woman should not have to stand up for her husband? It was but one fit that maintained the ego of the man who was set to give me to his hound. One temper tantrum to keep you from having to risk everything you have earned."

"I would have risked it and more to keep you by my side." Her husband suddenly lost his stern expression and grinned. "It was quite a fit, sweet Bridget."

"I love you and care not what others say about me. Let them gossip."

"You may not love me so greatly when I confess that I cannot stomach the idea of passing the night beneath this roof. I would rather sleep on the road, in stinking mud."

Relief washed through her, sweeping away the tension and fear that seemed to have been her constant companions. A smile lifted the side of her lips, and she lowered her hands until she might grasp one of his.

"I'll race you down the hallway . . ."

He laughed. Full volume that drew curious looks from those they passed. Bridget led the way, but only until they reached the yard. Curan surged past her then, showing her the way to the portion of the stable where their horses were kept. If anyone thought their departure in the late afternoon was odd, they both gave them no time to voice such thoughts. Curan's men were eager for the road, too, saddling their mounts in quick motions before swinging up into the saddle.

Bridget watched her husband, proud of the way he sat so confidently in command. The crowd lingering in the yard parted when they headed for the gate. Bridget dug her heels into her mare, sending the animal up beside her husband so that they passed out of the curtain wall together.

May they remain so forever.

"Stop it, Curan. I told you, not tonight. I am freezing."

Her husband grumbled but nuzzled against her neck again. "And I am trying to warm you, wife."

They lay on the ground, beneath the limbs of an old oak tree. A tarp was tossed across the limbs to provide them shelter, but it did little to cut the chill of the night. Curan suddenly pulled her tighter against his body, inhaling deeply next to her skin.

"I fear to sleep, fear that I will open my eyes to discover that you have never told me you love me."

His voice was husky and low, as though the darkness gave him the opportunity to say such words, words that no commander might say while his men watched.

"I will tell you again at sunrise and every hour after, if you will look at me with love in your eyes while I declare myself and my love unto you, Curan."

His warm hand slipped along the side of her cheek as he

rose up above her. In spite of the darkness, she saw the faint glitter in his eyes that she had come to cherish so dearly.

"You have my solemn promise, Bridget, along with the promise that I will march an army after you every time I must for I will not live without you. You hold my heart, and I must have it near." He lowered his head until she felt his breath against her lips. "Have you near, my love."

He pressed a soft kiss against her mouth, but it traveled straight to her heart, sealing them together. The night was suddenly much warmer, the heat coming from within.

From her heart.

If you liked this book,
try Donna Kauffman's OFF KILTER,
available now from Brava!

"**M**an up, for God's sake, and drop the damn thing."

"We're not sending in nude shots," Roan replied with an even smile, as the chants and taunts escalated. "So I don't understand the need to take things to such an extreme—"

"The contest rules state, very clearly, that they're looking for provocative," Tessa responded, sounding every bit like a person who'd also been forced into a task she'd rather not have taken on—which she had been.

Sadly, that fact had not brought them closer.

She shifted to another camera she'd mounted on another tripod, he supposed so the angle of the sun was more to her liking. "Okay, lean back against the stone wall, prop one leg, rest that . . . sword thing of yours—"

" 'Tis a claymore. Belonged to the McAuleys for four centuries. Victorious in battle, 'tis an icon of our clan." And heavy as all hell to hoist about.

"Lovely. Prop your icon in front of you, then. I'm fairly certain it will hide what needs hiding."

His eyebrows lifted at that, but rather than take offense, he merely grinned. "I wouldnae be so certain of it, lassie. We're a clan known for the size of our . . . swords."

"Yippee," she shot back, clearly unimpressed. "So, drop the plaid, position your . . . sword, and let's get on with it. It's the illusion of baring it all we're going for here. I'll make sure to preserve your fragile modesty."

She was no fun. No fun 'tall.

"The other guys did it," she added, resting folded hands on top of the camera. "In fact," she went on, without even the merest hint of a smile or dry amusement, "they seemed quite happy to accommodate me."

He couldn't imagine any man wanting to bare his privates for Miss Vandergriff's pleasure. Not if he wanted to keep them intact, at any rate.

He was a bit thrown off by his complete inability to charm her. He charmed everyone. It was what he did. He admittedly enjoyed, quite unabashedly, being one of the clan favorites because of his affable, jovial nature. As far as he was concerned, the world would be a much better place if folks could get in touch with their happy parts, and stay there.

He didn't know much about her, but from what little time they'd spent together that afternoon, he didn't think Tessa Vandergriff had any happy parts. However, the reason behind her being rather happiness-challenged wasn't his mystery to solve. She'd been on the island for less than a week. Her stay on Kinloch was as a guest, and therefore temporary. Thank the Lord.

The island faced its fair share of ongoing trials and tribulations, and had the constant challenge of sustaining a fragile economic resource. Despite that, he'd always considered both the McAuley and MacLeod clans as being cheerful, welcoming hosts. But they had enough to deal with without adopting a surly recalcitrant into their midst.

"Well," he said, smiling broadly the more her scowl deepened. " 'Tis true, the single men of this island have little enough to choose from." The crowd took a collective breath at that, but his attention was fully on her. Gripping the claymore in one fist, he leaned against the stacked stone wall, well aware of the tableau created by the twin peaks that framed the MacLeod fortress, each of them towering behind him. He braced his legs, folded his arms across his bare chest, sword blade aloft . . . and looked her straight in the eye as he let a slow, knowing grin slide across his face. "Me, I'm no' so desperate as all that."

That got a collective gasp from the crowd. But rather than elicit so much as a snarl from Miss Vandergriff, or perhaps goading her so far as to pack up and walk away—which he'd have admittedly deserved—his words had a rather shocking effect. She smiled. Fully. He hadn't thought her face capable of arranging itself in such a manner. And so broadly, with such stunning gleam. He was further damned to discover it did things to his own happy parts that she had no business affecting.

"No worries," she stated, further captivating him with the transformative brilliance of her knowing smile. She gave him a sizzling once-over before easily meeting his eyes again. "You're not my type."

That was not how those things usually went for him. He felt . . . frisked. "Then I'm certain you can be objective enough to find an angle that shows off all my best parts without requiring a blatant, uninspired pose. I understand from Kira that you're considered to be quite good with that equipment."

The chanting of the crowd shifted to a few whistles as the tension between photographer and subject grew to encompass even them.

"Given your reluctance to play show-and-tell, I'd hazard to guess I'm better with mine than you are with yours," she replied easily, but the spark remained in her eyes.

Goading him.

"Why don't you be the judge?" Holding her gaze in exclusive focus, the crowd long since forgotten, he pushed away from the wall and, with sword in one hand, slowly unwrapped his kilt with the other.

He took far more pleasure than was absolutely necessary from watching her throat work as he unashamedly revealed thighs and ass. He wasn't particularly vain or egotistical, but he was well aware that a lifetime spent climbing all over the island had done its duty where his physical shape was concerned, as it had for most of the islanders. They were a hardy lot.

The crowd gasped as he held the fistful of unwrapped plaid in front of him, dangling precariously from one hand, just on the verge of—

"That's it!" Tessa all but leapt behind the camera, and an instant later, the shutter started whirring. Less than thirty seconds later, she straightened and pushed her wayward curls out of her face, her no-nonsense business face back. "Got it. Good! We're all done here." She started dismantling her equipment. "You can go ahead and get dressed," she said dismissively, not even looking at him.

He held on to the plaid—and his pride—and tried not to look as annoyed as he felt. The shoot was blessedly over. That was all that mattered. No point in being irritated that he'd just been played by a pro.

She glanced up, the smile gone as she dismantled her second tripod with the casual grace of someone so used to the routine and rhythm of it, she didn't have to think about it. "I'll let you know when I get the shots developed."

He supposed he should be thankful she hadn't publicly gloated over her smooth manipulation of him. Except he wasn't feeling particularly gracious at the moment.

Here's a sneak peek at Maggie Robinson's
MISTRESS BY MIDNIGHT,
in stores now . . .

London, 1820

Laurette knew precisely what she must do. Again. Had known even before her baby brother had fallen so firmly into the Marquess of Conover's clutches.

To be fair, perhaps Charlie had not so much fallen as thrown himself headfirst into Con's way. Charlie had been as heedless as she herself had been more than a decade ago. She was not immune even now to Con's inconvenient presence. She had shown him her back on more than one occasion, but could feel the heat of his piercing black gaze straight through to her tattered stays.

But tonight she would allow him to look his fill. She had gone so far as having visited Madame Demarche this afternoon to purchase some of her naughtiest underpinnings. Laurette would have one less thing for which to feel shame.

Bought with credit, of course. One more bill to join the mountain of debt. Insurmountable as a Himalayan peak and just as chilling. Nearly as cold as Conover's heart.

She raised the lion's-head knocker and let it fall, once, composing herself to face Con's servant.

Desmond Ryland, Marquess of Conover, opened the door himself.

"You!"

"Did you think I would allow you to be seen here at such an hour?" he asked, his face betraying no emotion. "You must indeed think me a veritable devil. I've sent Aram to bed. Come into my study."

He *was* a devil, suggesting this absurd time. Midnight, as though they were two foreign spies about to exchange vital information in utmost secrecy. Laurette followed him down the shadowy hall, the black-and-white tile a chessboard beneath her feet. She felt much like a pawn, but would soon need to become the White Queen. Con must not know just how desperate she was.

Though surely he must suspect.

He opened a door and stepped aside as she crossed the threshold. The room, she knew, was his sanctuary, filled with objects he'd collected in the years he'd been absent from Town and her life. Absent from his own life, as well. The marquessate had been shockingly abandoned for too long.

She had been summoned here once before, in daylight, a year ago. She was better prepared tonight. She let her filmy shawl slip from one shoulder but refused Con's offer of a chair.

"Suit yourself," he shrugged, sitting behind his desk. He placed a hand on a decanter of brandy. "Will you join me? We can toast to old times."

Laurette shook her head. She'd need every shred of her wits to get through what was ahead. "No thank you, my lord."

She could feel the thread of attraction between them, frayed yet stubborn. She should be too old and wise now to view anything that was to come as more than a business arrangement. As soon as she had seen the bold strokes of his note, she had accepted its implication. She was nearly thirty, almost half her life away from when Conover first beguiled her. Or perhaps when she had beguiled him. He had left her long ago, if not quite soon enough.

A pop from the fire startled her, and she turned to watch sparks fly onto the marble tiles. The room was uncomfortably warm for this time of year, but it was said that the Marquess of Conover had learned to love the heat of the exotic East on his travels.

"I appeal to your goodness," Laurette said, nearly choking on the improbable phrase.

"I find good men dead boring, my dear. Good women, too." Con abandoned his desk and strode across the floor, where she was rooted by feet that suddenly felt too heavy to lift. He smiled, looking almost boyish, and fingered the single loose golden curl teasing the ivory slope of her shoulder. She recalled that her hair had always dazzled him and had imagined just this touch when she tugged the strand down.

She had hoped to appear winsome despite the passage of time, but her plan was working far too well for current comfort. She pushed him away with more force than she felt. "What would you know about good men, my lord?" She scraped the offending hair back with trembling fingers and secured it under the prison of its hairpin. It wouldn't do to tempt him further. Or herself. What had she been thinking to come here?

"I've known my share. But I am uncertain if your brother fits the category. A good, earnest young fellow, on occasion. A divinity student, is he not? But then—I fear his present vices make him ill-suited for his chosen profession. Among other things, he is so dishonorable he sends his sister in his stead. Your letter was quite affecting. You've gone to a great deal of trouble on his account, but I hardly see why I should forgive his debt." He folded his arms and leaned forward. "Convince me."

Damn him. He intended her to beg. They both knew how it would end.

"He does not know I'm here. He knows nothing," Laurette said quickly, and stepped back.

He was upon her again, his warm brandied breath sending shivers down her spine. She fell backward onto a leather chair. A small mercy. At least she wouldn't fall foolishly at his feet. She closed her eyes, remembering herself in such a pose, Con's head thrown back, his fingers entwined in the tangle of her hair. A lifetime ago.

She looked up. His cheek was creased in amusement at her clumsiness. "He will not thank you for your interference."

"I'm not interfering! My brother is much too young to fall prey to your evil machinations."

Con raised a black winged brow. "Such melodramatic vocabulary. He's not that young, you know. Much older than you were when you were so very sure of yourself. And by calling me evil you defeat your purpose, Laurette. Why, I might take offense and not cooperate. Perhaps I *am* a very good man to discourage him from gambling he can ill afford. But I *will* be repaid. " He leaned over, placing his hands on the arms of Laurette's chair. His eyes were dark, obsidian, but his intentions clear.

Laurette felt her blush rise and leaned back against her seat. She willed herself to stay calm. He would not crowd her and make her cower beneath him. She raised her chin a fraction. "He cannot—that is to say, our funds are tied up at present. Our guardian . . ." She trailed off, never much able to lie well. But she was expert at keeping secrets.

Con left her abruptly to return to his desk. She watched as he poured himself another brandy into the crystal tumbler, but let it sit untouched. "What do you propose, Laurette?" he asked, his voice a velvet burr. "That I tear up your brother's vowels and give him the cut direct next time we meet?"

"Yes," Laurette said boldly. "The sum he owes must be a mere trifle to you. And his company a bore. If you hurt his feelings now, it will only be to his ultimate benefit. One day he will see that." She glanced around the room, which was appointed with elegance and treasure. Brass fittings gleamed in the candlelight. A thick Persian carpet lay under her scuffed kid slippers. Lord Conover's study was the lair of a man of exquisite taste and a far cry from Charlie's disreputable lodging. She twisted her fingers, awaiting his next words.

There was the faintest trace of a smile. "You give me far too much credit. I am neither a good man, nor, despite what you see here, so rich man a man I can ignore a debt this size. We all need blunt to keep up appearances. And settle obligations."

Laurette knew exactly what his obligation to her cost him and held her tongue.

Con leaned back in his chair, the picture of confidence. "If I cannot have coin, some substitution must be made. I think you know what will please me."

Laurette nodded. It would please her too, God forgive her. Her voice didn't waver. "When, Con?"

He picked up his glass and drained it. "Tonight. I confess I cannot wait to have you in my bed again."

Laurette searched her memory. There had been very few beds involved in their brief affair. Making love to Con in one would be a luxurious novelty. She was not prepared, however; the vial of sponges was still secreted away in her small trunk at her brother's rooms. She had not allowed herself to think the evening would end in quite this way. But she had just finished her courses. Surely she was safe.

"Very well." She rose from the haven of her chair.

His face showed the surprise he surely felt. Good. It was time she unsettled *him*.

"You seem to be taking your fate rather calmly, Laurette."

"Did you arrange it? That it would come to this?" she asked softly.

"Did I engage your brother in a high-stakes game he had no hope of winning? I declare, that avenue had not occurred to me," Con said smoothly. "How you must despise me to even ask." He motioned her to him. After a few awkward moments, Laurette walked toward him and allowed him to pull her down into his lap. He was undeniably hard, fully aroused. She let herself feel a brief surge of triumph.

Con placed a broad hand across her abdomen and settled her even closer. "How is the child?"

Was this an unconscious gesture? Con had never felt her daughter where his hand now lay, had never seen her, held her. She fought the urge to slap his hand away and willed herself to melt into the contours of his hard body. It would go quicker if she just gave in and let him think he'd won. "Very well, my lord. How is yours?"

"Fast asleep in his dormitory, I hope, surrounded by other scruffy little villains. I should like you to meet him one day."

She did not tell him that his son was already known to her, as his wife had once been, improbably, her friend. "I don't believe that would be wise, my lord."

"Why not? If you recall, I offered you the position as his step-mama a year ago. It is past time you become acquainted with my son, and I with your daughter." His busy fingers had begun removing hairpins.

Laurette said nothing, lulling in his arms as his lips skimmed her throat, his hands stroking every exposed inch. In dressing tonight, she'd bared as much of her flesh as she dared in order to tempt him. She wondered how she could so deceive herself. Nothing had changed. Nothing would ever change. And that was the problem.

Laurette pressed a gloved finger to his lips. "We do not need to discuss the past, my lord. We have tonight."

"If you think," he growled, "that I will be satisfied with only one night with you, you're as deluded as ever."

An insult. Lucky that, for she suddenly retrieved her primness and relative virtue. She straightened up. "That is all I am willing to offer."

He stood in anger, dumping her unceremoniously into his chair. "My dear Miss Vincent, if you wish me to forgive your brother's debts—all of them—I require a bit more effort on your part."

"A-all? What do you mean?"

"I see the young fool didn't tell you." Con pulled open a drawer, fisting a raft of crumpled paper. "Here. Read them and then tell me one paltry night with you is worth ten thousand pounds. Even you cannot have such a high opinion of yourself."

Laurette felt her tongue thicken and her lips go numb. "It cannot be," she whispered.

"I've spent the past month buying up his notes all over town." Con's smile, feral and harsh, withered her even further. He now followed in his father-in-law's footsteps.

"You did this."

"You may think what you wish. I hold the mortgage to Vincent Lodge as well. You've denied me long enough, Laurie."

Her home, ramshackle as it was. Beatrix's home, if only on brief holidays away from her foster family. Laurette had forgotten just how stubborn and high-handed Conover could be. She looked at him, hoping to appear as haughty as the queen she most certainly was not.

"What kind of man are you?"

Keep an eye out for Sylvia Day's
PRIDE AND PLEASURE,
coming next month from Brava!

"And what is it you hope to produce by procuring a suitor?"

"I am not in want of stud service, sir. Only a depraved mind would leap to that conclusion."

"Stud service . . ."

"Is that not what you are thinking?"

A wicked smile came to his lips. Eliza was certain her heart skipped a beat at the sight of it. "It wasn't, no."

Wanting to conclude this meeting as swiftly as possible, she rushed forward. "Do you have someone who can assist me or not?"

Bond snorted softly, but the derisive sound seemed to be directed inward and not at her. "From the top, if you would please, Miss Martin. Why do you need protection?"

"I have recently found myself to be a repeated victim of various unfortunate—and suspicious—events."

Eliza expected him to laugh or perhaps give her a doubtful look. He did neither. Instead, she watched a transformation sweep over him. As fiercely focused as he'd been since his arrival, he became more so when presented with the problem. She found herself appreciating him for more than his good looks.

He leaned slightly forward. "What manner of events?"

"I was pushed into the Serpentine. My saddle was tampered with. A snake was loosed in my bedroom—."

"I understand it was a Runner who referred you to Mr. Lynd, who in turn referred you to me."

"Yes. I hired a Runner for a month, but Mr. Bell discovered nothing. No attacks occurred while he was engaged."

"Who would want to injure you, and why?"

She offered him a slight smile, a small show of gratitude for the gravity he was displaying. Anthony Bell had come highly recommended, but he'd never taken her seriously. In fact, he had been amused by her tales, and she'd never felt he was dedicated to the task of discovery. "Truthfully, I am not certain whether they truly intend bodily harm, or if they simply want to goad me into marriage as a way to establish some permanent security. I see no reason to any of it."

"Are you wealthy, Miss Martin? Or certain to be?"

"Yes. Which is why I doubt they sincerely aim to cause me grievous injury—I am worth more alive. But there are some who believe it isn't safe for me in my uncle's household. They claim he is an insufficient guardian, that he is touched, and ready for Bedlam. As if any individual capable of compassion would put a stray dog in such a place, let alone a beloved relative."

"Poppycock," the earl scoffed. "I am fit as a fiddle, in mind and body."

"You are, my lord," Eliza agreed, smiling fondly at him. "I have made it clear to all and sundry that Lord Melville will likely live to be one hundred years of age."

"And you hope that adding me to your stable of suitors will accomplish what, precisely?" Bond asked. "Deter the culprit?"

"I hope that by adding *one of your associates,*" she corrected, "I can avoid further incidents over the next six weeks

of the Season. In addition, if my new suitor is perceived to be
a threat, perhaps the scoundrel will turn his malicious attentions toward him. Then, perhaps, we can catch the fiend.
Truly, I should like to know by what methods of deduction he
formulated this plan and what he hoped to gain by it."

Bond settled back into his seat and appeared deep in thought.

"I would never suggest such a hazardous role for someone
untrained," she said quickly. "But a thief-taker, a man accustomed to associating with criminals and other unfortunates . . . I
should think those who engage in your profession would be
more than a match for a nefarious fortune hunter."

"I see."

Beside her, her uncle murmured to himself, working out
puzzles and equations in his mind. Like herself, he was most
comfortable with events and reactions that could be quanti-
fied or predicted with some surety. Dealing with issues defying reason was too taxing.

"What type of individual would you consider ideal to play
this role of suitor, protector, and investigator?" Bond asked finally.

"He should be quiet, even-tempered, and a proficient dancer."

Scowling, he queried, "How do dullness and the ability to
dance signify in catching a possible murderer?"

"I did not say 'dull,' Mr. Bond. Kindly do not attribute
words to me that I have not spoken. In order to be acknowl-
edged as a true rival for my attentions, he should be someone
whom everyone will believe I would be attracted to."

"You are not attracted to handsome men?"

"Mr. Bond, I dislike being rude. However, you leave me no
recourse. The fact is, you clearly are not the sort of man whose
temperament is compatible with matrimony."

"I am quite relieved to hear a female recognize that," he
drawled.

"How could anyone doubt it?" She made a sweeping gesture with her hand. "I can more easily picture you in a sword-
fight or fisticuffs than I can see you enjoying an afternoon of
croquet, after-dinner chess, or a quiet evening at home with
family and friends. I am an intellectual, sir. And while I don't
mean to imply a lack of mental acuity, you are obviously built
for more physically strenuous pursuits."

"I see."

"Why, one had only to look at you to ascertain you aren't
like the others at all! It would be evident straightaway that I
would never consider a man such as you with even remote se-
riousness. It is quite obvious you and I do not suit in the most
fundamental of ways, and everyone knows I am too observant
to fail to see that. Quite frankly, sir, your are not my type of
male."

The look he gave her was wry but without the smugness
that would have made it irritating. He conveyed solid self-
confidence free of conceit. She was dismayed to find herself
strongly attracted to the quality.

He would be troublesome. Eliza did not like trouble over-
much.

He glanced at the earl. "Please forgive me, my lord, but I
must speak bluntly in regard to this subject. Most especially
because this is a matter concerning Miss Martin's physical
well-being."

"Quite right," Melville agreed. "Straight to the point, I always say. Time is too precious to waste on inanities."

"Agreed." Bond's gaze returned to Eliza and he smiled.
"Miss Martin, forgive me, but I must point out that your inexperience is limiting your understanding of the situation."

"Inexperience with what?"

"Men. More precisely, fortune-hunting men."

"I would have you know," she retorted, "that over the course of six Seasons I have had more than enough experience with gentlemen in want of funds."

"Then why," he drawled, "are you unaware that they are successful for reasons far removed from social suitability?"

Eliza blinked. "I beg your pardon?"

"Women do not marry fortune hunters because they can dance and sit quietly. They marry them for their appearance and physical prowess—two attributes you have already established I have."

"I do not see—"

"Evidently, you do not, so I shall explain." His smile continued to grow. "Fortune hunters who flourish do not strive to satisfy a woman's intellectual needs. Those can be met through friends and acquaintances. They do not seek to provide the type of companionship one enjoys in social settings or with a game table between them. Again, there are others who can do so."

"Mr. Bond—"

"No, they strive to satisfy in the only position that is theirs alone, a position some men make no effort to excel in. So rare is this particular skill, that many a woman will disregard other considerations in favor of it."

"Please, say no—"

"Fornication," his lordship muttered, before returning to his conversation with himself.

Eliza shot to her feet. "My lord!"

As courtesy dictated, both her uncle and Mr. Bond rose along with her.

"I prefer to call it 'seduction,' " Bond said, his eyes laughing.

"I call it ridiculous," she rejoined, hands on her hips. "In the grand scheme of life, do you collect how little time a person spends abed when compared to other activities?"

His gaze dropped to her hips. The smile became a full-blown grin. "That truly depends on who else is occupying said bed."

"Dear heavens." Eliza shivered at the look Jasper Bond was giving her. It was . . . expectant. By some unknown, godforsaken means she had managed to prod the man's damnable masculine pride into action.

"Give me a sennight," he suggested. "One week to prove both my point and my competency. If, at the end, you are not swayed by one or the other, I will accept no payment for services rendered."

"Excellent proposition," his lordship said. "No possibility of loss."

"Not true," Eliza contended. "How will I explain Mr. Bond's speedy departure?"

"Let us make it a fortnight, then," Bond amended.

"You fail to understand the problem. I am not an actor, sir. It will be evident to one and all that I am far from 'seduced.' "

The tone of his grin changed, aided by a hot flicker in his dark eyes. "Leave that aspect of the plan to me. After all, that's what I am being paid for."

"And if you fail? Once you resign, not only will I be forced to make excuses for you, I will have to bring in another thief-taker to act in your stead. The whole affair will be entirely too suspicious."

"Have you had the same pool of suitors for six years, Miss Martin?"

"That isn't—"

"Did you not just state that many reasons why you feel I am not an appropriate suitor for you? Can you not simply reiterate those points in response to any inquiries regarding my departure?"

"You are overly persistent, Mr. Bond."

"Quite," he nodded, "which is why I will discover who is responsible for the unfortunate events besetting you and what they'd hoped to gain."

She crossed her arms. "I am not convinced."

"Trust me. It is fortuitous, indeed, that Mr. Lynd brought us together. If I do not apprehend the culprit, I daresay he cannot be caught." His hand fisted around the top of his cane. "Client satisfaction is a point of pride, Miss Martin. By the time I am done, I guarantee you will be eminently gratified by my performance."